DYRE:
BY MOON'S LIGHT

by

Rachel E. Bailey

2016

DYRE: BY MOON'S LIGHT

ISBN 13: 978-1-62639-662-3

This Trade Paperback Original Is Published By
Bold Strokes Books, Inc.
P.O. Box 249
Valley Falls, NY 12185

First Edition: January 2016

CREDITS
EDITOR: JERRY L. WHEELER
PRODUCTION DESIGN: SUSAN RAMUNDO
COVER DESIGN BY JEANINE HENNING

Acknowledgments

To my first and best creative writing teacher, Laurence Carr, for telling me to just *write it*. To my mother, Irene Bailey, for telling me how *creepy* the first chapter was, and thus making my day. To Alice Knudsen, a stellar writer in her own right, whose awesomeness I tried my best to translate to the page. Ruby's only a tenth as cool as the real thing, Veebs. To Thom Oldford, fellow writer and unsung hero, who's rescued me from my own stupidity, writing-wise, more times than I can count. To Jennifer "Kron-Bomb" Kronowitz for inspiring so many of Des's good traits. To Tabaqui and my LiveJournal Friends-list, whom I will never forget even if I become the next Edgar Allen Poe. To Dina Peone and her writing group (Margaret Norway, Angelina Peone, Andrew Gebert, and Donald Kenly III) for their epic amounts of great advice and unending support... chapter by chapter, guys. To all my friends who supported me and gave me feedback—especially Alice Knudsen, Jared Zwiefel, Donnis Kempley, Desiree Hossack, and Sara Troeller: fantastic cheerleaders and epic wordsmiths. To Adam Duff, Erik Hrycun, Selena Jones, and Sara Eckel for moral, professional, and financial support when it was most desperately needed. To Betsy Reville, for being unbelievably sweet, and driving me to my monthly writers' group. To Uncle Roy for *being* "Uncle Roy," and all that comes with that esteemed title. To everyone in my DBT group for dinners bought, earrings and scarves given, seminars paid for, and friendships maintained. To Brett Perry, up-and-coming director and generous friend, who helped me get peace of mind. To Mrs. Edward and Ms. Peers, for drilling into my head that I have the power and for giving me her own copy of *The Fellowship of the Ring* to read (sorry I never gave it back!), respectively. To everyone who read and supported my year-long short story project/website. To *People Who Get It* for helping to keep me (relatively) sane. To Denise Sherman, Catherine Lala, Rafael Perez, and Fred Harris for the same. To my editor extraordinaire, Jerry Wheeler. And to you, Reader, for trusting that I'll lead you into the woods and back out again, and make the journey a memorable one.

Rachel E. Bailey
Hudson Valley, N.Y.
2015

Dedication

For my grandmother, Elaine Phillips.
I was lucky to have you, even if it was only for a little while.
I will never, ever forget you. Rest in peace.

PROLOGUE

"Women!" he muttered. "Can't live with 'em,
can't escape even by killing 'em."
—NAOMI KRAMER

"There wasn't supposed to be no girl, just the old man...
but whatever," Ron Early grunted, bloodshot eyes ping-ponging
back and forth between the old man and the black girl shielding
his head and torso. She was sobbing and keening: "Oh, *George,
no!*"

This is very much a fuck-my-life *moment in a life that's
been full of 'em*, Ron decided.

"Shh. Don't cry...don't cry," he said almost kindly, aiming
the heavy, unwieldy pistol at her head. At this range and her
not moving, it'd be the easiest kill shot he'd ever had. Easier,
anyway, than the target, who'd taken three to the chest and still
had enough fight left in him to stagger toward Ron.

But another two to the chest had taken care of *that*.

Sort of, anyway. Because the old man was not only still
breathing, but trying to *talk*.

And that's just another fucked up aspect of this job, Ron
admitted to himself as he reloaded. *First the creepy, hairy, dog-
faced sonuvabitch that gave me the job; then the weird orders
on how to go about the job; then the designer, high-tech pistol*

and soft-core hollow points they ordered *me to use—oh, no, the job was too good for my own Beretta and rounds, but at least they let me use a silencer—then the old bastard does his best impersonation of the Terminator! And now, this crying, fucking* girl *sobbing her heart out like she lost her best friend.*

It was nearly enough to break the heart Ron didn't even *have.* Mostly, it made him want to get this job over and done with, get his money, and get the hell out of Lenape Landing.

"Sorry, it's nothing personal...just business," he told the girl, grinning nervously without realizing he was. And she looked up at him with wide, wet dark eyes, accusing and innocent. This was the moment that had always bothered him, the silencing of an accidental witness. If he'd had a conscience, it would've been scolding him. Instead, he had an accountant.

It's like doing a whole different job for free, the accountant whined. *And that really puts sand up my crack!*

What did he tell that voice to shut it up?

"Wasn't supposed to be no girl." He aimed, squinted, and put pressure on the trigger.

PART I:
BLOOD-OATHS AND BULLETS

"There are nights when the wolves are silent
and only the moon howls."

—GEORGE CARLIN

CHAPTER ONE

Des arguably had a better nose than any Loup in the Pack, but she didn't need it to tell her there was trouble.

All she needed was the muffled chuffs of a gun with a silencer coming from the direction of George's apartment to tell her that the shit was finally going *down*, and it was going down *without her*. George was in danger and she, his *Geas*-Protector, a genuine, old school, blood-oath bodyguard, was definitely not doing her job.

"Ah, fuck." She rolled out of bed and felt around on the floor for her clothes.

"Well, that's what I thought." The pretty brunette Hume in Des's bed leaned up on one elbow watching Des dress, her dark eyes confused and annoyed. "What the *hell*, man? Where're you goin'?"

Pulling on her jeans, worn sweater, and oversized army coat—heavy with silver daggers, silver bullets, and silver throwing stars stashed in well-hidden inner pockets—Des stepped into her beat-up combat boots and stretched till every joint in her five foot, two inch frame cracked loudly enough to make the brunette under the covers wince. "I have business . . . sorry, *chica*."

"But—"

Des squatted and felt under the bed till she found the stock of her shotgun. When Des stood up, grim-faced, the brunette's eyes widened and she cringed away from Des, squinching her eyes shut. She covered her mouth, unable to prevent a tiny, nasally whimper from escaping.

Des almost said something intended to comfort this woman whose name she'd already forgotten, but she wasn't good at remembering names or giving comfort. So, she locked and loaded instead. "Please be gone when I get back. And don't take anything you didn't come here with, *comprende*?"

The brunette nodded quickly, eyes still shut, hands clutched prayerfully together between pale, perfect breasts. She smelled of cheap perfume, sweat, sex, and fear. The Loup within Des reared its furry head, wanting to pin her and finish what they'd started. Taste her skin and fear and blood.

But Des quashed the Loup easily—something that'd taken far too long to learn—then she strode to the door of her one room apartment. When the door shut behind her, she stretched again, letting the molten heat of The Change run along muscle and bone for a moment. Every hair on her body stood on end. They bristled in preparation for battle, and the Loup within was suddenly not so *in* anymore, fighting desperately to get *out*. It bared her teeth in a feral, futile snarl. Growling low and guttural in her throat, Des stalked toward the staircase.

❖

Des reached George's landing and crept up to his door, her ears pricking and nostrils flaring. She heard George's labored breathing and a woman's soft, horrified sobs. She also smelled three Scents, two familiar and one decidedly not.

George's pungent, musky Scent, like iron, blood, Loup, and pine needles.

The soft, sweet Scent of cinnamon, vellum, Hume, and *woman*, familiar only because Des had scented it the few times she'd visited George's apartment on Council business.

And the unfamiliar Scent of the interloper, old blood-tears-Hume-gunpowder residue, and the slighter but more dangerous scent of liquid silver nitrate.

Des's hackles rose straight up and she saw...*red*.

Felt *it*, the *red*, in her *bones*, wanting to *Change* her. The Loup always wanted out, always wanted to fight, fuck, and feast, in that order. It smelled the opportunity for at least two of the three waiting in the Dyre's den.

Back in your cage, cabrón, she told it quickly, giving it her solemn word that she'd let it out soon. *Later. Now isn't the time.*

With a sullen, impatient growl, it subsided. But its *want* still throbbed within Des like a second heartbeat. The Loup had tasted Hume flesh, and it'd never lost that taste.

Fight, fuck, and feast.

Those three things were enough to drive even a sane Loup absolutely rabid.

Fucking Humes always have to get tangled up in Loup matters, Des thought bitterly, but not without a strange feeling of anticipation.

She kicked in the door with one blow and stalked into George's formerly cozy apartment. The furniture had been upset, and blood spatters were everywhere. In the center of this chaos was a tableau that might make Des want to give voice to the Loup. To let it howl until the Moon set, and she woke up from this nightmare of abject *failure* on her part.

Of the three people in George's apartment, only one was still standing. Only one wasn't covered in blood. The other two, one of whom was George, were laying on the floor. Shielding George's body with her own, was a sobbing, horrified girl, staring up into the face—or gun—of the man who would shortly be her killer.

Now not being a time for subtlety or self-reflection, Des strode over to the one other person who was still standing, the Hume who smelled of old blood, tears, gunpowder residue, and silver nitrate, and reversed the shotgun in one smooth motion. The killer barely began to turn and see what form his death had taken before Des was swinging the shotgun like a bat.

When the stock hit the assassin square in the temple, he went down without a sound: a limp puddle of long, greasy blond hair and dark polyester blends. The assassin's bullet that'd been meant for the sobbing girl on the floor next to George's body, this . . . *woman-Scent*, buried itself in the exposed brick wall behind her.

Des loomed over his body, panting. The Loup wanted to tear and rend and, so help her, if the interloper wasn't already dead, she'd be more than happy to finish him off. To go back to that awful place where Changing meant fighting and fighting meant killing and killing meant *devouring*—

Suddenly the weeping girl tore the silence in the apartment to pieces with a pained shriek and Des shook her head once, snapping herself back to the present. In a split second, she had the shotgun business-side forward once more, centered on the head of the previously sobbing woman-Scent, who was now *screaming*.

And who *wouldn't* scream with someone's teeth buried to the gums in their neck? Who wouldn't be in utter agony as their flesh was rent by some horrible *thing* out of legend?

While Des had been wool-gathering and staring at the assassin's corpse, deciding whether or not to eat it, George had bitten the girl who'd tried to save his life—was gnawing and worrying the bite like a dog with a bone. He'd clamped his huge, bloody hands down like manacles around the screaming woman-Scent's upper arms. Even as Des looked on, George's mortally wounded body attempted to Change: long, unassuming features elongating further, hands warping and sprouting coarse gray-blond fur. But thanks to his injuries, he was caught mid-change, neither fully Human in appearance, nor fully Loup.

He opened his eyes, a wild, dangerous yellow, and he growled low in his throat. Des bared her own throat in unhesitating submission and took a step back. He shut his eyes once more.

The Hume-woman's screams tapered off into coughs and gasps as George worried at but didn't rip out the junction where her neck met her shoulder. Finally, her eyes rolled back into her head and she went limp, sagging in George's arms. Her body twitched and ticked, then finally went grave-still.

But she was *not* dead, Des knew. Later, maybe. If she didn't survive the Fever or the first Change. But for now, she was alive, and George was letting go of her. He gently laid her on the blood-stained carpet with a tenderness Des had rarely seen him display. Then he himself was flopping to the floor with little grace. His eyes, no longer that baleful yellow, lit on Des and he nodded once, in unconcealed agony. His barrel of a chest was a map of ragged, smoking holes that smelled of singed silver nitrate and charred meat.

Des was more than familiar with the type of shell the assassin had used. As a Protector and a killer herself, she'd carried it on her person for the express purpose of putting dangerous and enemy Loups in their graves. What made these shells so lethal was once they pierced flesh, the outer casing broke apart, and the silver nitrate leaked out into the Loup's system like a river of poison. Even if she had the tools to remove the bullet fragments, Des could never get all the silver out of George's system. George was dying. And fast.

Des stepped closer and knelt next to him, putting down the shotgun and taking his cold hand. He smiled, the woman-Scent's blood and flesh in his teeth. His *fangs*. He *definitely* didn't look full-Hume anymore. Instead, he looked like what he *was*, the distilled essence of the *Loup-Garoul*, large, long-faced, raw-boned, and fierce.

Only Des had never seen that fierceness leavened by such pain and shock.

This is all on me. I did this. It's my fault. My failure. My leader, my charge is lying here, gasping out the last of his life in a puddle of blood and I did nothing to protect him when he needed me most. Oh, Moon Above.

"I failed you, DyreFather," Des began, hoarse-voiced and tight-jawed, tears scalding her eyes. Unbidden, one escaped to roll down her cheek and she hastily brushed it away. Crouched and whining in a very small corner of Des's being, the Loup was howling its grief and despair. The Change had never been as far from Des as it was in that moment.

George, meanwhile, laughed a little, blood foaming between his gray-red lips.

"My life—my *reign* has run its course." He coughed again and turned his head to look at the Hume-woman lying unconscious next to him, his face regaining some of its figurative humanity, his pale blue eyes warming. "*Her* reign, however, is just beginning."

Des, somewhat horrified herself, miles below the lowering storm of grief, looked over at the unconscious, erstwhile Hume-woman.

She was nothing special to look at first glance: above average height, slightly more than average weight, dressed in frumpy, muted mismatched clothing that bagged on her healthy frame and dulled her rather lovely, unlined café-au-lait complexion. Her wavy, brown hair was scraped back from a clear brow in a severe ponytail that looked ridiculous, considering her soft, round features. No, nothing special to look at, but when had that ever mattered? Especially when she'd done more to protect George than Des had.

"What...do you suppose the Pack Alphas...will have to say about their new Queen? A Packless, fresh-turned Loup... whose only connection to the *Loup-Garoul*...is the charitable act of reading to a weak-eyed old man?" George coughed up more blood trying to laugh and talk. "Ahhh...those who cursed me in life...yet jockeyed to be next to me as I neared death...I wonder what they'll make of *her*."

Not much, Des thought bitterly, shaking her head and sighing. It was not her place to judge the person George, that most Dyre of Loups, Alpha of Alphas, Leader of all the Packs, had thought fit to pass his lineage and power on to. But she couldn't be less than honest with her leader, either. Not after all that'd happened. "They'll probably kill her."

"Not...with you to be her teacher and guardian, Daughter."

Des's mouth dropped open, and George actually grinned. "But—I can't—I mean, I *didn't*..." *protect* you. *What makes you think I could protect* her?

"You failed in your *Geas*...it's true." More blood bubbled from between George's lips. "So you must redeem yourself." George's smile turned steely and unforgiving. "In blood...if necessary."

Des shook her head again, brow furrowed in shame and consternation. She'd spilled enough blood, Hume and Loup, to know no redemption was in it. "I don't understa—"

But George was taking her hand with mortal effort, his breathing becoming even more forced. With his other hand he reached feebly for the woman-Scent's hand. Thinking she'd guessed his intent, Des placed it in George's. Or tried to. He refused to take it, and instead placed Des's other hand on the Hume-woman's warm, lax one.

"Jennifer Desiderio...with my last breaths...I charge you with the care and protection of Ruby Knudsen...Dyre-apparent...ah...to keep her and teach her...until such time as she wins true Dyrehood...through contest or compromise. To die in service of her...if so called." George took a deep, shaking breath, but he pinned Des with his eyes just as surely as if he'd picked her up and slammed her against a wall. "Do you accept this *Geas*, child? And with it your chance at redemption?"

Des swallowed and glanced at the already closing, but still gruesome wound on the Hume-woman, then back at George. His eyes were keen and clear despite his deteriorating state, and they seemed to see right through Des, to every wrong and terrible thing she'd done that might need redeeming. And there was definitely a lot to see: all the mayhem and trouble she'd caused for the Packs. All the people, Loup and Hume, that had ended their lives in Des's jaws. All the *people*.

Swallowing again, Des nodded and squared her shoulders. She'd never hesitated to accept her responsibilities, and she didn't plan to start now. "I accept the *Geas* with a heavy heart, but a willing one, DyreFather."

"Ahhh," George exhaled, smiling in obvious relief. "That's good."

His smile didn't fade even as his eyes glazed over. He exhaled one last time and then didn't take another breath. With a sigh that came out as a brief, muffled whine, Des reached out and closed his eyes. His skin was already cooling.

"Run with the Moon." Des bowed her head.

George Carnahan, the *DyreFather,* was dead. This strongest, canniest, most cunning of Loups was dead; the large, ever-present force of the spirit that had once animated his strong, tall form was utterly gone. The Dyre, Wolf of all Wolfs had gone on to join his forefathers and mothers.

The towering, charismatic leader who had once spared Des's miserable life despite the entirely just death sentence passed on her by the Tribunal was no more. The man who'd welcomed Des as his protector after all the terrible things she'd done, the *oaths* she'd broken, and who'd always treated her more as a beloved niece than a hired goon, had gone to a place where she couldn't yet follow.

Des couldn't seem to think beyond that single, incredulous thought:

The DyreFather is dead.

"Long live the DyreMother," Des whispered to the unconscious Hume-woman, scooping her up and standing with her as if she weighed nothing. The Hume-woman, *Ruby,* moaned and twitched, her eyes fluttering open. She licked her full, dry lips and tried to speak.

"George..." she said, with obvious effort. Des hesitated then shook her head *no.*

Ruby moaned again, her eyes shutting briefly before opening once more. "He bit...me." Her hand flopped feebly up to her shoulder to feel at the wound. With her weak fingers, she traced a raw, vicious-looking scar that would soon fade to practically nothing.

"It's already healing," Des murmured. "The rest is up to you. Surviving and shit."

Ruby wrapped her shaking arms around Des's neck and attempted to hold on tight. Ruby's gaze never wavered from Des's. It was pained, confused, and begging for answers. "Surviving what?"

Chewing her lower lip, Des averted her eyes for a moment then met Ruby's gaze again. "The Fever. The Change. The Packs. The goddamn *politics*. Being the *Dyre*."

Ruby shook her head a little. "*Dire*? I don't understand."

"No, *Dyre*. The *Queen*," Des spat out, straight to the point. She felt like she'd done more talking in the past ten minutes than she had in all her twenty-three years. At any rate, they had to get out of there before more trouble showed up. So longer, less traumatizing explanations would have to wait. "Of the *Loup-Garou*. The *Werewolves*," she added quickly, before Ruby could ask.

After a moment, Ruby turned her face away. "You're awful. This whole dream is awful."

She sagged in Des's arms again and this time she really was out for the count. The Fever was taking her fast. Ruby wasn't going to be any help in saving her own life. Which meant it was entirely up to Des to get them both somewhere hidden and defensible until Ruby woke up. Or didn't.

"With all my strength and power, I will protect you," Des promised, hugging close her only chance at redemption. She already felt the heat baking Ruby. "With all my craft and cunning, I will save you. To my last breath, Ruby."

One last glance at George's body, and she exited the apartment with Ruby in her arms. They needed to go underground and stay there until the next Full-Moon Waxing. Till Ruby was strong enough to fight for the Dyrehood and *win*. And Des could only think of one defensible, completely unexpected place they could hide, but she'd almost rather chew off her own foot than go back there.

Almost.

Chapter Two

The steps leading downstairs to Des's basement apartment normally groaned like an elderly person getting out of bed. They barely made a sound as she descended. When she arrived at her apartment, the door was wide open, and the brunette was gone, though her scent lingered heavily.

Kicking the door shut behind her, Des carried Ruby across the room to the bed and reluctantly laid her down. No time for niceties such as changing the sheets. And anyway, it wasn't as if they'd be staying for any longer than it took Des to get her stuff.

Des grabbed her emergency duffel out of her cramped closet and tossed it on the futon next to Ruby. Then she pried up the loose floorboard on which the duffle had sat. She got a few splinters for her haste: tiny, but bright flashes of pain gone as quickly as they came, the splinters themselves plinking to the floor as her body rejected the intruders.

Swearing to herself in Spanish, Des extracted the seven thick, neat rubber-banded wads of cash from their hiding place. She knew how much was in each wad down to the exact dollar, not to mention just how far away from Lenape Landing such a pile of accumulated cash could get them.

Pretty goddamn far, Des thought, briefly remembering the months spent wandering the wide world post-rabidity, but pre-

Geas and George. The only responsibility she'd had in those stark, hard, empty, drifting days had been keeping her own temper and desires in check. Surprisingly not hard to do since all her formerly endless rage and hunger had seemed to finally be quenched with the passing of her rabidity. Not that said quenching had made living with all she'd done any easier.

Not that Des deserved to have it easy after—

"Time and place, Jennifer. Time and place," Des muttered to herself, getting to her feet and shutting her closet door with a final click.

A moment later, she stuffed the money inside the duffel under her shirts, except for one wad of twenties, which she put in an inner pocket of her jacket. Des took a quick look around the Spartan, one-room apartment, but she didn't feel any loss or nostalgia, just the vague sense she'd forgotten something, but that seemed to attend every leave-taking she'd ever had. However, just in case the feeling was right, for once, Des divided the room into quadrants and scanned it carefully.

Closet and bathroom? Nothing there she couldn't do without for the next day or so. And anyway, the point was for the apartment to look as if it was still lived in, despite the fact that it wasn't.

Kitchenette? Barely any food in it anyway, and nothing worth carrying except for the small microwave Des had invested in a year ago. But she was definitely *not* going on the run with a microwave.

The small desk-and-bookshelf that'd been there when she moved in? Nothing on it but an ancient thesaurus, which had also come with the apartment, and Des's old, bulky but powerful laptop. A gift from Jake, built by Jake. Three years old, and it still consistently outperformed the other laptops Des occasionally looked into buying. Not to mention that whatever alloy the case was made of was tougher than nails, having survived several falls from high places, falls in which it stood up not only to impact, but to Des landing on top of it.

It'd be a shame to leave it behind, but she barely had room for the cash in the duffle, and anyway, she could *buy* another easily—

"Fuck it." Des carefully shut down, disentangled, and unplugged the laptop. It'd been all over the world with her, a constant companion. Sometimes, it'd been like having Jake with her, and the Moon Above knew that for some months, months she'd spent living in places she'd only ever read about, it had been her only contact with the world she'd known.

Grim-faced, Des turned to the final quadrant with the bed and the woman lying in it.

Moaning and *shivering* in it, like someone who'd eaten fruit from the Fever Tree.

"It sucks, now, but it gets better," Des found herself saying as she pounded the stuff in her duffle into submission, then jammed the laptop down lengthways, between her jeans and leather jacket. "I promise. Maybe at first, for the first few months, it's gonna be rough. But if you can survive them, well, it ain't gonna be a cake-walk, but it'll be okay. It'll be okay."

The only response Des got was another moan, followed by a soft, desperate sob.

"Your lack of faith in me is justified. But trust me on this. I know whereof I speak." She swung the duffle on her back then stood looking down at Ruby, arms akimbo. In the forgiving light of the Hunter-Moon, Ruby looked as if she was merely sleeping, not nearly comatose with a fever that would in all likelihood kill her.

She looked as if a kiss could wake her from her slumber and save her, all in one press of lips against lips. A police siren wailing in the distance snapped Des out of her reverie and, red about the face, she got her arms under Ruby's legs and around her waist, and hefted her up.

Neither woman nor duffle was heavy for Des.

Stalking out of her apartment for the second time that night, Des gave no thought to the groaning of the stairs this time. Within seconds, she was stepping out into the windy, moonlit night, eyes always searching-searching-searching for the ever-present danger. In her arms, Ruby started to shake almost immediately, unconsciously huddling in Des's arms, as helpless as she'd ever be.

❖

On such a patchily overcast, gloomy night, it was easy enough to keep to the many shadows Lenape Landing offered. What wasn't so easy was getting out of the city without using public transportation or a cab.

From her vantage point of a stinking, dark alley, Des watched yet another L.L.P.D. cruiser go by. The police presence seemed heavier to Des tonight. Not an hour into her flight with Ruby, and she'd already evaded twelve cruisers. No telling how many more were out on the streets of the rest of the city. It was enough to make Des wonder why the extra bacon. Why tonight? What or who could possibly have the Commissioner so spooked that he put so many units out on patrol. And why tonight? Looking down at the moaning woman in her arms, Des felt a cold, prickling sensation that ice-danced its way down her suddenly rigid spine.

They're looking for us, she thought with a start. *They may not know who we are, or at least who* Ruby *is, but they definitely know who I am, because I am*—was—*George's Geas-Protector.*

If they find us, it won't be hard for them to figure out who Ruby is. Or, if they have a Loup in their midst, she or he will smell *it on her.*

And on the heels of this surely unbelievable premise: *Holy shit, how deep does this rabbit hole* go?

Des had a feeling she didn't want to know.

Not that what she wanted had anything to do with what she was obligated to do, and she was quickly realizing the *Geas* placed on her to protect George, and now Ruby, was more than just a night job as a bouncer at a club. It was a life-and-death duty that included her gathering information as needed to keep her Dyre safe. She was not just a hired gun. She was a soldier, a spy, and a nursemaid, all rolled into one. Maybe more, as time went on. Looking down into Ruby's soft, innocent, troubled face, Des for the first time wondered if she was up to the challenge. Another cruiser went by, and Des moved deeper into the alley.

Just then, it started to rain. Hard. The clouds that had been sporadically hiding the waning Gibbous-Moon released a torrent that immediately soaked Des and her charge.

Sighing, Des hefted Ruby. When she was sure the cruiser had turned a corner, she scurried out of the alley and headed east. It wasn't the fastest or safest way out of the city, but it was mostly abandoned, and only occasionally patrolled by the cops. Maybe less occasionally tonight, but still, their presence wouldn't be as heavy as it was here in the Northside, or in the more commercial Downtown.

And from the Eastside, they could make their way out of the city proper through the brief, iffy eastern suburbs, then they could circle around north to safety. It was a plan. And it had the added benefit of leading any pursuers of the Loup persuasion on a merry chase, what with all the backtracking Des'd have to do just to find their way.

And that was assuming Des wouldn't have to fight for their lives.

That may be a lot to assume, Des thought and stopped, standing stock-still and letting her shoulders slump for a few moments.

Then she was shaking off her despair and sniffing the humid, slightly reeking air. After a moment of hesitation, she turned east toward their only chance at safety.

❖

An hour later, she was skulking among old warehouses and factories, grimly weathering the rain and hoping Ruby was doing the same. She was still moaning weakly, still shivering. But she was barely radiating any heat Des could feel. That worried her, but another hour, two, at most, should find them at their destination.

All Ruby has to do is not die for that long. No, not die for long enough for us to get a Loup doctor to look her over, Des corrected herself with stern pragmatism. *She's in a bad way. I don't know anything short of a miracle that could save her if I can't get her to Nathan's place in time.*

Her ears and nose pricked up, assaulted by a sound and scents she did *not* like: gun oil, silver nitrate, evil intent, and *Loup*, approaching fast, no attempt at stealth.

Shit-shit-shit, Des thought, picking up her pace to a light jog that jostled Ruby enough to make her moan. It was as worrying as it was heartening that she was still alive enough to feel discomfort.

Des dodged right, around the corner of two old condemned warehouses that looked like they were ready to fall down. On going deeper into the alley, she found a section of the warehouse on the left *had* fallen down, blocking the egress on the other end of the alley. The clouds diffused the overcast light of the Waning Gibbous, but Des still couldn't see a safe way up that pile of boards, nails, and concrete. Which left Des in the unenviable position of having to backtrack, only that scent of gun oil, silver nitrate, and Loup had been slowly filling the alley even as Des had jogged to the blocked exit.

Climbing that rubble was *not* an option while carrying Ruby.

So Des scrambled carefully up the rubble as far as she dared, not wanting to leave Ruby vulnerable on the ground, and placed her on a relatively flat spot that didn't seem to have any nails or splinters waiting to impale the unwary. She settled Ruby's head on the solid duffle and covered her with the army jacket.

She wouldn't need knives for this fight.

Ruby opened her eyes briefly, wide and staring, blind in the milky, faint light of the Waning Gibbous. But they nonetheless seemed to lock on Des's.

"I got this," Des promised, leaning down to kiss Ruby's cool, damp cheek. "Don't go anywhere, gorgeous. I'll only be a minute."

Ruby moaned again and closed her eyes once more.

Des turned and leapt off the heap of rubble and began removing her clothes. *Now?* the Loup growled from just under the surface of her psyche, and Des smiled. But it was more of a snarl.

Now, she told it as she kicked off her soaked jeans, boots, and socks. They lay where they fell, next to her sodden shirt.

Lightning struck through the heavens and through Des, like the brightest flash of pain, like a full-body cramp that split her in two. She dropped to her hands and knees, keening. As her bones began to crack and break and reshape themselves, her pale, drenched skin rippled with the suggestion, then the reality of a coarse black pelt. As every bone in her face re-formed, her human keening slowly became an animalistic growl.

Then a howl.

A howl that was answered from the mouth of the alley.

❖

Anka Patsono was old-fashioned, even though she was a relatively young sixty years old.

When supplied with the silver nitrate bullets and the gun, she'd initially sneered at their clunky, new-fangled impersonality. At the lack of honor they represented. What about the Old Ways? What about the honorable fight? The Right of Challenge?

And when her erstwhile employer had assured Anka that in a fair fight between herself and this half-blood mongrel, Anka would lose, well Anka had nearly turned down the job right then and there, almost too insulted to even continue the meeting, let alone accept it.

But she'd been intrigued by the supposed challenge presented by this mongrel pup, this youngest bastard of a Pack full of the same. So she'd taken the job and the gun, even though its very touch seemed to soil her hands, and she waited to follow her orders.

Then everything had gone straight to Hell when the Human assassin had partially failed in his duty, getting himself killed before Anka could kill him. Which wasn't necessarily a disaster as far as Anka's job went, but the mongrel pup had gotten away with the heir-apparent to the North American Dyrehood, and Anka had nearly lost their trail in the downpour that'd started earlier in the evening and hadn't let up.

But Anka had eventually found their trail. Had tracked them for two hours, always staying just out of scenting range until the mongrel pup had gotten to the abandoned edges of Lenape Landing.

Tactically, she'd dug hers and the Dyre-Apparent's graves. Anka couldn't have been more pleased. Now, as she stood at the mouth of the alley, scenting the pup's Change, all ideas of following the orders to use the gun and silver bullets on any *Loup* who got in her way flew out the figurative window.

Rolling her shoulders, Anka tossed the gun back the way she'd come and began shrugging off her clothes, letting the sweet agony of the Change flow through the muscle and bone and marrow of her body.

In the dim moonlight, she could only barely see the pup shifting and Changing with little yips of pain and the usual cracking of bones and tearing of muscles. Coarse black hair sprouted up all over her small frame, and she focused her dark, dark eyes on Anka with keen, cold intelligence.

Anka laughed, and it came out as a mocking growl. Perhaps her employer had been right, after all. In any event, after years of easy kills, Anka welcomed a challenge. Even one it was likely she would win.

Change completed, the pup threw back her head and howled in response: both defiance and challenge. There was no fear in it. Not a single note.

Snarling her anticipation, Anka stepped forward.

❖

The smaller Loup trotted warily forward, a lean black shadow in a sea of the same, obsidian-dark eyes shining like marbles, hooded and cold. Her teeth were bared, white and long.

The larger Loup, mouth also open in the Loup-ine equivalent of a smile, loped forward confidently, reddish-brown fur a-bristle, nonetheless.

Turn around now, or I'll kill you, the pup said emotionlessly. That surprised Anka, as most pups tended to be hotheads. This one was as cold as ice, with deadly unconcern in her scent and death in her eyes.

For a moment, Anka felt actual fear, then she shook her head, muzzle twitching as she side-stepped her way closer, heartened when the pup took a step back. *It's you who'll die tonight, little mongrel. It's you who should be—*

But Anka didn't get to finish, because the mongrel pup was leaping for her, all red rage and sudden fury.

Anka faked to the left then dodged to the right, but the pup seemed to have anticipated her, landing on Anka like a hundred-pound weight. Solid despite her lack of size, she bowled Anka onto her back. She immediately sought Anka's throat with her muzzle. Anka tried to shake the pup off, but couldn't. She was like Velcro, her claws embedded in Anka's flesh.

Wondering when this fight had gone so wrong, had gotten so far out of her control, Anka did some throat-seeking of her own, expecting the pup to waste time trying to evade her. But the pup didn't. She was as fearless as she was diminutive, her eyes burning, red, and rabid.

Anka's employer hadn't mentioned that part.

Suddenly the discarded gun seemed like not such a bad idea.

That bolt of fear came back with a vengeance, and Anka struggled even harder not to be bitten in any way by the rabid mongrel on top of her, growling and dripping poisonous slather all over Anka's face. Anka dared not let that slather drip into her mouth. At even the suggestion of rabidity, the Patsono Pack would kill her, assuming some other Pack didn't take care of her first.

This *is the Loup they let guard their leader? This half-cocked gun? This mad little* thing *with poison in its veins and murder in its heart? What were they thinking, these upstart American* Garoul? *What were they—*

Then bitter, murder-salty, madness-coppery saliva dripped into Anka's nose, and she yelped in horror, more of it dripping into her mouth. Horror mounted upon horror, made her toss her head away and to the side. It was in her, now. And no Pack or Clan would be able to hide her or overlook the growing scent of madness that would overlay her once the rabidity really got its claws into her blood. No one would help her. She would find no forgiveness here in the New World or back in the Old Country. Unlike the *Loup* of the rumors, rumors that had made their way back to Romania, of the mad wolf who was supposedly allowed to run rabid because its father was an Alpha, there'd be no reprieve for—

And oh, it all made sense too late: who this mongrel pup was and why the American Council of Alphas had spared her. They'd taken a vicious, remorseless, lunatic of a Hell-hound, and turned her into a guard dog. The Council's pragmatism and refusal to see any opportunity pass without exploiting it had let them consider and do the unthinkable.

It was practical and so perfectly *American* an idea.

And the renewal of that initial horror proved to be Anka's undoing, for the jaws from which that evil, poisonous saliva fell descended upon her. Upon her throat, and through it, till those purposeful teeth were gripping her spinal column and yanking upward. Outward.

The pain isn't as bad as I thought. Why, it barely hurts at—

Then a flash of silver-white light, so bright it obliterated even as it exalted, burned even as it soothed, took Anka with it. This light ran and without even a sense of transition or disorientation, Anka was running with it.

❖

Des's Loup paced around the fallen body of its enemy, snarling and growling.

Hungry.

No, Des told her Loup calmly, a small, easily ignored voice from within. Her Loup laughed its snickering, mad, growling laugh and stopped pacing, lowering its muzzle to the pool of blood spreading around their enemy's cooling body. It was thirsty, too. Hungry, thirsty, and—

From behind Des and her Loup came a soft cry that seemed to bring with it the gentle scent of woman-vellum-lilies-innocence. Of power and potential.

Power and potential the Loup wanted to take into itself.

Enemy forgotten, the Loup trotted toward the source of that scent.

As it trotted, that scent became stronger, purer, irresistible. It began to mean everything Des's Loup wanted and no longer had. It slunk up the rubble, jaws wide and dripping, till it was crouched over the sleeping form from which all things emanated.

Wide eyes opened again, still blank and unseeing, once again, however, seeming to land on Des's Loup. To *command* it, and that command found an anchor in the Loup's rabid, buzzing-mad blood and brain. In its empty, barren heart.

And something began to bloom in that arid space. Something that hadn't touched Des or her Loup in so long, they'd forgotten that feeling even existed. It was both lead and helium, this feeling, heavy as earth and light as air. As frightening as Des's rabid Loup, itself—more so. And it was also quite beautiful . . . so much so, neither Des nor the Loup could look directly at it for long, for fear that they might be obliterated entirely. Made hollow and refilled with this feeling, and once that happened, where would they be?

Taken aback, Des's Loup found itself sitting on its haunches and leaning down to touch its nose to the soft, cool cheek of the Hume-seeming *Loup* that lay both fevered and freezing on rubble and duffle. Nothing could have startled Des's Loup more than when a gentle hand settled on its head like a benediction, scratching and ruffling the fur at the scruff of the Loup's neck before falling away.

Des's Loup sat up, only to find those wide, unseeing eyes falling shut again.

It howled plaintively, wanting them to open once more. To feel that benediction, that sense of belonging and welcome again.

But it didn't.

The Loup finally hung its head . . . and after a minute's stillness was able to find that blooming sensation welling up within, watering dried, cavernous hollows, bringing life to the lifeless and joy to the joyless.

Elated and humbled, it tentatively touched this feeling. . . .

It was pure Moon's Light. It burned and soothed. It was still as a pond, deep as a river, and it *ran*.

It washed clean, and Des's Loup—*Des*, belonged to it. Was of it and made for it.

Des and her Loup, as close to being one as they'd ever been, bathed in it, and let themselves be immersed, until their whole world was Moon's Light.

❖

Nearly half an hour later, Jennifer Desiderio stood up shivering, arms crossed over her breasts, knees knocking as they tried to support her in a way of standing that barely seemed to make sense after what seemed like an eternity spent in *Loup*-form.

At her feet lay Ruby Knudsen, still shaking, still moaning, but now once more radiating that alarming heat, which showed up as a deep flush under her café-au-lait complexion. For minutes Des could only stare dumbly at her and feel something so big and alien, it defied explanation and forbade observation.

Thunder rumbled in the distance, shattering this reverie and startling Des into taking a step backward onto nothing. She pinwheeled her arms, but nonetheless fell back down the pile of rubble, scraping and bruising every scrapeable and bruiseable part of her. She landed spine first on her own boots and grunted, the wind knocked out of her. It was several moments before she sat up and reached for her drenched clothes.

It was time to play Human again.

❖

By cloudy, drizzling midnight, Des was exhausted from carrying Ruby around and keeping to the shadows and alleyways of Lenape Landing. From the fight with that murderous bitch. From Changing to full *Loup* form and back in less than an hour.

She and Ruby were both drenched. At least that would muddy their scents in case someone else came sniffing after them, but Ruby had acquired a racking cough Des didn't like one bit.

Keeping that thought firmly in mind, Des stepped up to the huge wrought-iron gate and glanced at the CCD camera mounted atop it like a watchful raven. She knew she must have looked like a drowned rat, carrying a corpse for company.

Des was, yet again, not remotely in a position of power. But there was nothing to be done about it. She'd barely reached out for the intercom buzzer before the gate swung silently open like something out of a gothic novel.

Any second thoughts she had about entering were quashed by the suddenly increasing downpour, and Ruby's soft, pitiful moans and weak shivers. Des trotted down the gravel driveway, past the gatehouse and whichever goon was playing guard that night, to the brooding front door of the estate house. She wouldn't bother reaching for the knocker. He obviously already knew she was there. Indeed, the front door was already open by the time she climbed the shallow front steps.

A somber man of middling height waited in a rectangle of soft yellow light that did nothing to soften his features. Unreadable dark eyes flicked from Des, to Ruby, then back to Des. He flared his nostrils disdainfully and sighed as one greatly put upon.

"Good evening, Jennifer," Nathan Coulter murmured in his smooth, eternally unruffled tenor. He was the only person who called her Jennifer. *The only person left who has a right to*, she supposed tiredly. But it still pissed her off.

"Good evening, sir," Des mumbled, then gritted her teeth and firmly reminded herself that beggars couldn't be choosers. "Father."

Nathan smiled his thin, amused smile and that also pissed Des off, as did his regal, languid gesture to enter. But for the moment, Ruby Knudsen was safe. That was all that mattered.

So, Des checked her ego at the door and stepped inside.

CHAPTER THREE

Des scurried down the front hall, Nathan gliding along ahead of her. The manor hadn't changed one bit. It was quite manly, baroque, and richly appointed. Wine-red carpeting ate the sounds of footsteps and voices alike. Wood-paneling and exposed brick infused the air with their own peculiar scents. Dim lighting, barely adequate for Human eyes, made the atmosphere seem both intimate and abyssal all at once. High, vaulted ceilings and entryways hinted at more rooms than Des had ever bothered to count, certainly more than she'd ever been in during her four year tenure here.

Des could remember the first time she saw the manor house from the outside, at the ripe, old age of fifteen. She'd thought nothing could be more intimidating than the tall, wide, fortress-like pile. Then she'd seen the inside. The house, as well as its owner, seemed to frown down on her from an unimaginable height, the weight of ages looming over her and finding her wanting.

She shook her head to clear the tired fog from it, and followed Nathan up the wide front staircase, Ruby moaning in her arms. She didn't look good at all. Her eyes were already sunken into shadowed hollows, her light-brown face visibly flushed from the fever. Her waving hair was dripping wet and coming out of its scraped-back bun, and her clothing was sodden.

Not that Des looked too much better.

At the landing to the second floor, Des began to feel mildly awkward. It'd always been this way from the day she came to live at the manor. Her mother's death was still a fresh, sharp ache in her chest. And Nathan always waiting for her to speak, holding his peace like he was a judge and she was some self-incriminating low-life.

Despite her discomfort, Des followed Nathan down a familiar stretch of corridor, holding her own peace as they trailed silently through the east wing. Before long, Nathan stopped at a door Des also remembered well.

"Your room is as you left it...but noticeably cleaner," Nathan said, opening the door for her with a quiet sigh. One quick look was enough to see that was true, from the funky braided rugs, to the posters of bands she'd now disavow having ever liked.

Not that it mattered much to Des that her room had been kept as if waiting for her return.

"Uh, thanks." She bit her lip and sighed, too. "Look, Nathan—"

"I take it George is dead?" Nathan cut her off, looking at Ruby. He frowned, looking vaguely perturbed for the first time in the eight years Des had known him. "You reek of his blood and of silver nitrate. And this one smells of his Death-right."

Des hung her head for a moment then met Nathan's eyes, straightening her posture and bearing up under his scrutiny and, no doubt, judgment. Nathan had been part of the Tribunal that had decided to entrust her with George's life. He'd been one of the *yea* votes that had talked down the *nay*s. At the time, that had floored Des, and even two-plus years later, still did.

"Yes. Whoever it was, sent a Hume assassin with a nitrate gun after him. Before he died, George swore me to her."

"Another *Geas*." Nathan nodded, then he snapped his dark eyes back to Des. "That would be his way. Did he say why he chose this particular Hume to be his heir-apparent?"

I think it may have been his idea of a joke, Des thought, but didn't say. After all, Nathan hadn't asked for her opinion. "He said she came to read to him, sometimes. And I've smelled her scent in his apartment more than once over the past year or so." Shrugging, Des turned and entered her old room, not stopping till she was laying Ruby in her bed, on top of the patchwork coverlet Phil had made for her way back when.

After a few moments of not knowing what to do next, Des tugged the coverlet out from under Ruby, who'd curled into a fetal position, and threw it over her. Des would've tucked her in, too, if she'd known how. It was one of those things Des's own mother had done for her, once upon a childhood. But unfortunately she'd never taught Des the how of it before she'd died. Of that and a great many other things.

She sensed Nathan lingering in the doorway behind her.

"There are those on the Council who'll want your throat for this," he said finally, and for once, he didn't sound offhanded. He sounded grave. "George's *Geas* tying you to this Human probably saved your life. For as long as *she* lives, anyway," he added.

Looking at the moaning, limp, fevered girl in her bed, Des sighed again. "Fan-damn-tastic."

"Did the assassin say who sent him before you dispatched him?"

Gritting her teeth, Des glanced at Nathan, catching a strange look on his saturnine face. As usual, she couldn't read it. "It was either kill him or let him kill the girl. So he didn't get to say a damn thing. Something else the Council can crucify me for."

"Mm. I'll have Angus lead a cleaning crew to George's apartment and yours."

"And to the alley between the warehouses on Van Allen and 40th Avenues. There's another assassin there. This one was a Loup." Des paused. "I'm pretty sure she was sent as back-up in case the first assassin fucked up."

Nathan *hmm*ed. "Whoever sent them really went all out to end George's line."

Des nodded, and silence fell between them again, but it was loud. That silence *tsk*ed and took Des to task in Nathan's off-hand tones.

His gaze was, as always, impenetrable—obsidian upon which to break oneself.

He looked at Ruby again with what Des could have sworn was genuine curiosity. He approached the bed.

"The other Alphas will be distressed, to say the least. Several of them had hopes of replacing George as Dyre." He reached out to touch the already fading scar at the junction of Ruby's neck and her left shoulder. Without thinking, Des interposed herself between them, slapping his hand away and growling low in her throat.

Nathan smiled his thin smile again and made no further attempt to examine Ruby's scar.

"Very well," he said simply, his voice rich with what was probably suppressed laughter. Of course, he was amused. After over a century of living and killing when the need arose, Des probably posed no real threat to him. In a contest between the two of them, despite her own prowess in a fight, Des knew she would likely die.

And it had nearly come to that, not so long ago. Sometimes, Des thought it might have been better if Nathan *hadn't* spared her life that awful night. He looked at her. "Will this new *Geas* of yours allow Philomena to treat and monitor her through the Fever, or will you be assuming nursing duty as well as guard duty?"

Des blinked and rolled her shoulders to release the tension in them. It didn't work. "Phil's in town?"

Nathan cleared his throat and looked chagrined for a moment. "She is. She's staying at the manor."

"She's staying here? Why? Are you or Jake sick, or something?" Rolling her stiff shoulders again and taking a covert whiff of Nathan, Des's eyes suddenly widened.

Nathan didn't smell of sickness. No, he smelled of flowers, bitter herbs, and something indefinably feminine, as well as his own musky scent, like iron and freshly-turned earth. He smelled of Phil, and of...*sex*.

Des crooked a disbelieving eyebrow, and Nathan smugly crooked it right back at her.

Ew, Des thought, shuddering. Then she put it aside for the moment. She had more pressing things to think about than Nathan's sex life. And, if nothing else, it was a relief to know that of all the problems that plagued the Coulter family, physical illness was still not one of them.

"Yeah," she said finally, forcing away mental pictures of her father and her surrogate mother rolling around like a couple of wild animals. "Phil can check her out. She's...uh, she doesn't look like she's doing too well."

"Mm," Nathan agreed absently, frowning at Ruby once more. "The Council will have to be notified and convene before Full-Moon Waxing."

Des groaned. "There's gonna be a Contest, isn't there?"

"Several, I should imagine." Nathan looked at her. "*Will* you be ready to champion her by the Full?"

Des skinned her lips back from her teeth and clenched her fists. "I'm ready now."

Nathan snorted, running a hand over his silvering dark hair. Des rarely saw him do that. He was probably worried about the Council having to convene. "Ready to *fall* down if you don't *sit* down, child. *Sit*," he commanded. Des immediately obeyed, perching on the edge of the bed, near Ruby's right foot. Then, off Nathan's indulgent, triumphant smile, she started to stand up again, but Nathan held out a hand, effectively halting her.

"Now, stay. Good girl," he added when Des remained poised between sitting and standing. Then he crossed his arms and rocked back on his heels as if surveying his handiwork. Finally he turned and strode out of Des's room, every inch the master of his den.

"Bite me, *Nathan!*" Des called childishly after him. That was all she *could* do besides sit. And stay.

On the bed behind her, Ruby began to toss a little, and mutter. After a few minutes of puzzling it out, Des finally began to make sense of them.

"Please, George...make it stop..."

Des furrowed her brow in concern and took Ruby's clammy right hand, muttering to herself, "C'mon, Phil, hurry up."

❖

"It lives."

Des started out of a half sleep she hadn't even realized she was in, snorting and shaking her head. Then she winced at the ache of her tense shoulders and neck. That ache was making its way across her skull with no signs of stopping. "It wishes it didn't. How's it goin', Phi—whoa! Is there something you wanna tell me?"

Philomena Simms stood leaning against the door post to Des's room, smiling and barefoot...and pregnant. The prominent bulge of her belly was easily visible in the simple white nightgown she wore. Between the gown and the bright smile, she seemed to literally glow.

"Well," she said, stepping into Des's bedroom, fluffing her mid-length afro. "I let my hair grow out. Do you like?"

"You're beautiful," Des yawned, though she meant it. "You and Nathan? Seriously? How long's this been going on?"

Phil shrugged, settling one hand on her stomach. "Almost two years, hon. Which you'd know if you bothered to keep in contact with the people who care about you." She arched her graceful ebony brows and Des looked down at her hand. She still held Ruby's.

"I've e-mailed you guys a couple of times," she said guiltily, nostrils flaring as she scented Phil: bitter herbs, flowers, sex, and Nathan. And the primal, tidal, indefinable smell of pregnancy. "You could've told me."

"Would you have wanted to find out about your father and I, not to mention your little brother and sister, via e-mail?"

"Well, no." Des shrugged uncomfortably. "I guess not. You're having *twins*?"

"Nothing gets by you, does it?"

Des shook her head. "This is so weird. I can't even process it on top of everything else. Maybe an e-mail wouldn't have been so bad."

Making an exasperated little moue, Phil huffed. "I don't believe in disclosing important personal information the same way robots try to sell me cheap Viagra and live porn. And since you absolutely refuse to get a cellphone—"

Des shook her head once, implacably. "Those things cause brain cancer."

Phil rolled her eyes and crossed the room, suddenly brisk as business. "You need a brain to get brain cancer, dear. Now budge over and let me get a look at our new queen."

Chastened, Des let go of Ruby's hand and scooted down to the very foot of the bed. Phil gingerly lowered herself to the bed with a small sigh, then took the hand Des had been holding. Her other hand she held over Ruby's mouth, then placed it gently on Ruby's head.

Ruby moaned, but otherwise was still.

Phil sat like that for maybe a minute before withdrawing her hands and standing up. "The first thing that needs to happen is getting her out of these wet clothes and into something dry and warm," she said with a brisk air that didn't quite hide the worry in her voice and scent. She threw back the coverlet, and Ruby began to shiver immediately.

"Right." Des stood up, only then realizing she hadn't taken off her duffel. She placed it in the room's only chair and shrugged off her jacket. Phil was already removing Ruby's soaked sneakers and socks. Des bit her lip and pitched in.

"How long since she was bitten?"

"Um, maybe four hours?" Des sat on the bed and half-propped Ruby up, tugging on the shapeless black sweater she wore. A few seconds later it landed across the room with a sodden splat. A plain gray wife-beater soon followed it, leaving Ruby in a white cotton bra that hooked in the front. Des hesitated. "Uh—"

"That, too," Phil said absently as she went to work on Ruby's black corduroys, skinning them down Ruby's legs. "She'll be lucky if she's not fighting off pneumonia as well as the Fever."

Feeling another twinge of guilt, Des unhooked Ruby's bra and tried to peel it off without looking over much. "It's raining like a bitch out there, Phil. And I had to backtrack all over Creation just to confuse our scent-trail. And more cops were out tonight than usual, so I spent a lot of time crouching in alley-puddles with her, waiting for them to disappear."

Phil hummed and made short work of Ruby's blue granny panties by simply ripping them off her. "Nathan's turned the heat up in this wing, so that should help her. I've also got my Feverfew tea brewing."

"Yuck." Des made a face. One of the few things she remembered from her own Fever was Phil's cool, gentle hand on her head and the taste of Feverfew tea, like rancid mulch steeped in week-old rainwater. The former had been lovely, the latter vile.

From the looks of Ruby, however, she had a lot more on her plate than some nasty-tasting tea. Her breathing was labored and fast, her chest rising and falling noticeably as she shivered and shook. Beneath those frumpy clothes, Ruby was all dramatic curves: ample, rounded hips, full breasts, and solid, well-shaped limbs. Then Phil was whipping the coverlet back over Ruby and tucking her in tight. When she looked at Des, Des blushed, knowing she'd been caught staring.

"Des, honey, are you two...?" Phil lifted her eyebrows again, and her nostrils flared. She was scenting Des, who probably still smelled like the pretty brunette from earlier, as well as the million unsavory scents of Lenape Landing's secret ways.

"What? No!" Des blushed even harder, scratching her arm just above the bend of her elbow. "I've barely even spoken to her. She was George's friend. She used to come to read to him. She was just at the wrong place at the wrong time when the shit went down."

Phil's keen, regal face softened as she looked at Ruby again. "Poor thing. She has no idea what's in store for her. It's a good thing she has you for a guardian," she added quietly.

Des sighed, shaking her head again. "Yeah, because that worked out so well for George."

"You did your best. And sometimes even our best isn't enough. Some things are just fated."

"Fated? You wanna know what I was doing when that assassin shot George? I was doing some Hume-chick I didn't even know." Des turned away from the bed and shoved her hands in her pockets, balling her fists till her nails bit into her palms. "I was getting laid while George was getting killed."

This admission was greeted with silence. "You let the mission slip," Phil said after a few beats. "It happens. But if you're going to be any good to the new Dyre, you'll need to stop blaming yourself and wallowing in pointless guilt. For the next few months at least, it's got to be all about *her*."

Des clenched her fists even harder, till skin broke and blood began to leak around her nails. The pain was negligible. It was nothing compared to the pain that George had felt, or the pain Ruby would be going through for the next few days, so why shouldn't Des bleed? It wasn't atonement, but it was as close as she'd likely ever—

"Stop that, Jennifer Desiderio," Phil commanded. "Stop whatever it is that you're thinking and doing that's making you smell like blood and despair."

Des loosened her fists and took her hands out of her pockets so she wasn't tempted to clench them again. Her palms were indeed covered in half-moon punctures that began to close even as she watched, till no evidence of them remained but the drying blood on her palms and under her nails.

Disturbed for some reason she couldn't quite put her finger on, Des crossed her arms over her chest, hiding her bloody palms, and hung her head. "George's death is on me. Another life ended because of something I did."

Phil sighed again. "Sweetheart, there was no malice in you toward him, was there? You weren't hoping he'd end up dead as a result of your actions, right?"

Des let tears well up behind her eyes, but she trapped them before they fell. "Intent doesn't matter. What matters is the result. I caused his death just the same as if I'd shot him myself."

Another weighty silence.

"Well," Phil said softly. "Now that you've managed to take the weight of the entire Loup history of politics and murder on your shoulders, do you feel better? Do you feel more able to do your job as the blood-protector of the new Dyre? Because if you do, I'll agree with you till the cows come home. But if you don't, might I suggest you stop blaming yourself and start shouldering your new responsibility?"

Des closed her eyes and forced back more tears. She hadn't cried when her mother died ten years ago. Crying wouldn't have solved anything then, and it wouldn't solve anything now. Neither would feeling sorry for herself. She'd been focusing on her own needs when she took home that pretty brunette at the cost of George's life.

Thinking of Ruby—of the sobbing girl, the woman-Scent who'd tried to shield George with her own body, who'd done more to protect him when he'd needed it most than Des ever had—Des's resolve hardened. She accepted her own culpability, shame, and guilt. Swallowed them whole and buried them deep down. Further down than her Loup, further down than the Incident. Buried it in the deepest, darkest well of her heart.

"You're right," she murmured, standing a little straighter. "Of course, you're right."

Phil settled her warm hands on Des's shoulders, kneading and squeezing. "But before you can make it about her, it has to be about you forgiving yourself and letting it go. You made your mistake. Now *learn* from it. Don't let yourself be distracted like that again. At least not while she's still so vulnerable."

"Yeah." Des nodded tersely then shrugged Phil's hands off her shoulders. Forgiveness wasn't what she needed at the moment, and it was more than she could bear. More than she'd ever been able to bear.

"Look, I put some leftovers to warm in the oven for you. Why don't you take a quick shower, get into some dry clothes, and get something to eat," Phil said kindly. Des shook her head *no*, facing Phil again. She caught Phil's look of concern and smiled wanly.

"Thanks, but I shouldn't leave her."

Phil rolled her eyes and made her sternest face, but it still didn't hide the concern. "This is the safest place for her to be, right now. And in the fifteen minutes it'll take for you to shower, dress, and bring a plate back up here, I promise you nothing bad will happen to her."

"But—"

"You have *my* oath on it, Des." Phil was already herding Des toward the door. "Trust me. You're going to need to keep up your strength to defend her. Nathan's already contacting the other Alphas so the Council can convene. He expects there to be no fewer than seven Contests."

"*Seven*?!" Des sputtered and froze, and Phil took that opportunity to shove her out the door and close it. The lock engaged.

Holy fuck! He said several, *not* seven*! The odds of me surviving not one, not two, not even three, but seven fights with seven Alphas or their champions are...fuck, astronomical!*

She turned and was about to start pounding on the door, when it opened again and Phil shoved a pair of her old navy blue sweats into her hands.

"Oh, and by the time you're done showering, the Feverfew should be ready, so be a love and bring up the kettle and a teacup. Thanks." Then Phil closed the door and locked it again, leaving Des to lean against it and sag in complete exhaustion and something very like hopelessness.

At least for a few seconds, anyway. But hopelessness was a luxury Des couldn't afford with Ruby's life in the balance, not to mention her own.

Rolling her still tense shoulders again, Des turned left down the hallway, toward her bathroom.

❖

Wiping the condensation off the bathroom mirror with her arm, Des took a good look at herself. Long, deceptively mild dark eyes watched her tiredly from a rather gamin face, fine-featured and square. Normally spiky blue-black hair clung damply to a high, clear brow and cheekbones that could cut glass.

It was the *Coulter* face, all angles and not-unattractive sharpness. In fact, but for her pale olive complexion and diminutive build, she saw a feminized version of Nathan Coulter in the mirror, complete with the poker face and obsidian eyes.

Des never had trouble meeting those eyes, even on her worst day, which this was definitely in the running for. She had no one and nothing to blame this death on but her own inattention. It couldn't be explained away by the sly, slow sneak of rabidity— no two ways to look at the cause of George's death.

Des's reflection looked suddenly grim and as forgiving as stone.

You can't make it right unless you know a trick for bringing Loups back from the dead. But you can get it right. There's a new Dyre tossing and turning her way toward a life that she likely doesn't want and can't handle yet. It's your job to guide her through and protect her till she comes into her own, the reflection whispered.

"But what if she doesn't? What if she never does?" Des asked it. Her reflection didn't respond, merely watched her with those long, unreadable eyes. It was too much like being stared down by Nathan, so Des finally looked away.

"If she doesn't, then…well, I guess that means a lifetime of job security for me," Des muttered wryly, a little nonplussed at the sense of freedom that accompanied the thought. The next few months of her life were going to be nothing but sleepless nights, days spent in training, and fighting for Ruby's life and her own. Assuming she survived the Contests, the rest of her life would be spent guarding and protecting, fighting and killing.

Fighting and *winning*, for nothing less would do, the Loup within growled. Des let it growl, let it come forward in their shared body and headspace and grin. It had no qualms about a life spent fighting and killing. And if it could do it for a cause that would allow its Hume-half to live with herself, so much the better.

So they, Des and the Loup within, returned the wild, vulpine grin in the mirror.

"It's not like I was planning on doing anything with the rest of my life, anyway," Des said, and she whistled as she toweled herself dry.

❖

On her way back to her room, piled-high plate in one hand, teapot and teacup in the other, Des stopped at Nathan's office. The door was ajar, but she knocked with the teapot anyway. "It's me."

"Come in, Jennifer," was the immediate, rankling response. And she did, biting her tongue against any less than diplomatic words. She nudged the heavy door a bit wider with her bare toes and slipped in.

Whatever she intended to say died on her lips as she realized the man sitting with his feet up on Nathan's baroque, antique desk wasn't Nathan Coulter at all. This man was much too tall, his wavy, russet-brown hair was much too long, and he was wearing a Hawaiian shirt and cargo shorts. On his feet were a pair of black socks and broken-in sandals. In fact, the only thing he had in common with Nathan Coulter was the same low, oiled-smoke voice and slightly scratchy timbre.

"Well, fucking *shit*," Des breathed, grinning and nearly dropping plate and tea implements, other worries forgotten as her heart leapt in her chest. All she could do for several moments was stand and stare.

"Hmm, I've been called worse. But usually not by my own sister," Jacob Coulter said amiably, swinging his feet down from Nathan's desk and standing. He looked Des over for a moment, then that mischievous grin turned into a warm, slightly daffy smile. "Long time, no see, Jenny-Benny."

Des was agog. How many years had it been since she'd seen Jake in person? Three, at least. Jake stepped around the desk and crossed the room to take plate and tea things away from her. She almost let him, then remembered Ruby and smiled apologetically, holding them away from him. "No, I can't stay, I've got—"

"Yeah, Pop told me," Jake said, the mirth in his light hazel eyes dimming. "I'm sorry, Des."

"Not as sorry as I am." Des's own smile slipped away. "But hey, I get a second chance to screw it all up. Nathan told you that part, right?"

Jake's plain, every-man face fell. "Yeah. He told me you're sworn to the new Dyre. That George passed his Death-right to a Hume."

"Correct and correct, *hermano*!"

"Shit. Triple shit." Jake pinched the bridge of his nose and tipped his head back, as if trying to prevent a nosebleed. "God, how're you gonna handle this?"

Des shrugged irritably. "The same way I handle everything. Go in with guns a-blazin'. Kill 'em all and let 'em run with the Moon."

Jake rolled his eyes. "I meant how're you gonna handle giving our new Dyre the Talk?"

Des shrugged again. "I'll just tell her. And if she doesn't believe me, I'll *show* her." She flashed a bit of fang to Jake who rolled his eyes once more.

"Subtlety is not your strong-suit, Li'l Sis," he said, chuckling. "Has it even occurred to you that going Loup right in front of her so soon might make matters worse? Okay, I can see that it hasn't," he added dryly when Des blinked blankly up at him. He stooped a bit, put an arm around her shoulders and led her to the door.

"Lemme tell you what I'd do and *have done* in your position..." he began sagely.

This time, Des was the one to roll her eyes. But Jake caught her at it and tugged on her still-damp hair. She elbowed him hard, and he let it slide till they got to the staircase. Then, with truly impressive speed, barely breaking the flow of his words, he gave her a wet-willy.

Des squawked and nearly dropped plate, pot, and cup, and Jake laughed, darting ahead of her, taking the stairs three at a time.

"I will *murder* you in your sleep, Jacob Callum Coulter!" she called after him, suppressed laughter in her own voice as he disappeared around the turn that would take him to the east wing. "Bloody murder!"

"Good thing I sleep with both eyes open, Jenny-Benny!"

For those few moments, anyway, it was good to be home.

❖

By the time Des got back to her room with a pork chop smothered in apple sauce hanging out of her mouth, Jake and Phil were already deep in conversation.

"...never seen the Fever come on so fast," Phil was saying, shaking her head. She was sitting at Ruby's side, holding her hand the way Des had. Biting down on the chop hard enough that the bone splintered and apple sauce ran down her chin, Des ignored her Loup's quiet, possessive growl and kicked the door gently shut behind her. The room was noticeably warmer than she'd left it.

"...was one of the most powerful Dyres we've ever had in recorded history. Maybe that's got something to do with it." Jake's changeable face was now worried and unhappy. He leaned forward in the room's only chair, large hands dangling helplessly between his knobby, hairy knees. "And if she was sick or compromised *before* he bit her..."

"I'd thought of that, but from what I can tell, she was healthy when George bit her," Phil said, seeming just as helpless. With a glance at Jake, Des crossed the room and placed the teapot and cup on her night table, then folded into a full lotus at Phil's feet with her plate. "Her breathing is so congested, though, on top of the Fever," Phil said. "Maybe she's asthmatic."

"Won't be, after the Fever," Des noted around her mouthful of sweet and salty goodness. She put the pork chop down and licked her fingers clean before going for the T-bone steak next to it. After a moment's thought, she swished it in the applesauce covering the pork chop and worried a big piece off the bone, making hungry, happy little growls.

It was only when she noticed the silence had dragged on for most of a minute that she looked up at her brother and stepmother. They were both watching her with mixtures of exasperation, sympathy, and fondness. "What?" she asked, licking the applesauce and meat-juice off her chin with one long swipe of her tongue.

Jake smiled wryly. "Your table manners used to be much better."

"Get me a table, and I'll show you some manners." Des grinned widely, knowing bits of meat were caught in her teeth. Jake mock shuddered and leaned back in the chair, crossing one long, lean leg over the other.

"Des, sweetie," Phil began slowly as if trying to find the right words. "There's a substantial chance she won't survive the Fever. Whether or not she has asthma, the Fever itself is hitting her like a wrecking ball. Not only is it escalating quickly, it's a *higher* Fever than any I've ever dealt with."

"She'll survive," Des said confidently, without stopping to think about the strength of her conviction. She didn't need to think about it. If George had thought Ruby fit to be Dyre, strong enough and tough enough to lead the Packs, then she was strong enough to come through the Fever. And Des told Phil and Jake as much.

The two of them exchanged a look then focused on Des again.

"We know she must be tough stuff if George picked her, kiddo, but that has nothing to do with how she handles the

Fever. It hits each Hume and Loup differently." Jake held out those huge hands of his as if to forestall any protests. "The Fever isn't *just* a fever, Des. It's a Human body being changed on a cellular level, one cell at a time." He glanced at Phil, who nodded, then went on. "As all the old cells are consumed by the new, the Human in question suffers immensely. Sometimes the stress of that can kill them. Sometimes their hearts just give out under the strain."

Des snorted, and nearly hocked meat up into her sinuses as a result. "It's not *that* bad, right? I came through mine fine. If I can do it, she can do it, right? Right?" Des looked from Jake to Phil, then back again.

Phil reached down to run her fingers through Des's hair. "But that's different, hon. You were born a Loup. Getting the Fever for the *Garoul*-born is a consequence of puberty. It's about as deadly as the Chicken Pox, with proper care. It's different for a *Hume* who's been bitten. They're generally adults, for one thing, and not as resilient as adolescents. And, like Jake said, these changes are happening on a cellular level. For the *Garoul*-born, their bodies are bred to handle that change as an eventuality. For Humes, their bodies are bred to *fight* the change every step of the way. So in a sense, the stronger the Hume, the less likely they are to survive the changes wrought by the Fever. Their bodies will fight it and fight it till they're all used up."

Des dropped the T-bone, which was literally just a bone, now, clean of meat and gristle, back on the plate, appetite forgotten for the moment, and frowned. "So you're saying that if Ruby was some scrawny, sickly weakling—"

"—she'd be more likely to survive this." Jake nodded solemnly. "Though the risk of death is still pretty high. If the Hume is sickly enough, the Fever'll kill them, anyway. It's a fine line, one that most Humes who get bitten don't walk."

Closing her eyes tight, Des stretched as Phil scritched and scratched her scalp comfortingly. "What kinda odds are we looking at, Phil? Straight-deal me."

Phil sighed. "I'd say there's a less than one in five chance that she'll make it through the next twenty-four hours, let alone the next two days."

"Fuck."

"*Triple* fuck," Jake agreed, leaning forward again, peering deeply into one of Des's psychedelic throw rugs as if it had answers or reassurances.

For a moment, Des felt a spiraling sense of despair she wasn't about to give in to. She shook her head and gritted her teeth. She was *not* about to lose another Dyre. Dislodging Phil's fingers, Des looked up at the older woman, steeling herself against the compassion in those perceptive eyes. "She'll survive."

"Honey—"

"*She'll survive,*" Des said again, putting her unfinished dinner aside. The heavy curtains at each window were drawn, but she could feel moonset in her bones and knew false dawn wasn't far off. "Just tell me what I have to do to make that happen, and it'll get done."

Chapter Four

She just wasn't herself these days. Or, at least, what seemed to pass as days.

It didn't help that every time was crazy-time in this purgatory, this non-place in which she'd been stashed. There were no stopwatches or clocks, and if there were, they'd look like something Salvador Dali had been at with a paintbrush.

Millennia passed in mere hours, while seconds oozed by like unhurried eternities. She was a being of the senses, trapped in a place of the mind, and she was surrounded in all ways, at all times, constantly under attack.

By what she wasn't sure, only that they were hungry, disorganized, and legion. They threw themselves at her, threw themselves into invading her with no more plan and design than a flu virus. They slobbered and gibbered, cavorted and howled, gleeful even as she repelled them or simply let them dash themselves silly against her defenses, only to shake it off and hurl themselves at her again and again.

By the end of the first eternity, she was pretty sure there was a pattern, but she couldn't see it. She couldn't see anything. She had only a fuzzy-at-best sense of who she was, what she was, and where she should've been.

But she knew that she should have had light and warmth and laughter.

Fortunately for her sanity, she did not remember exactly what any of those things were. She simply knew they were missing and missed. Absent from the Non-Place, where it was always crazy o'clock.

And so she stood alone, an impregnable tower with an eroding sense of self. She was eternally under siege with no memory of why it must be this way, only that this was the way it was.

Always would be.

❖

She couldn't imagine why the things that attacked her wanted in so badly, when all she wanted was out.

The scraps of logic she had been left with cautioned her against anything so rash as letting them in. But the larger part of her that still had hope of an end, of rest, of going back to The Good Place, where light-warmth-laughter lived, had little use for logic.

She poked and pried, till she poked a chink, then a dent, then a small hole in the battlements of her logic and reason. She peered out and was nearly blinded by a stark silver shine, after so long in soothing velvet darkness.

This, at last, was light. But it wasn't warm and full of laughter and love. It was hard and cold and somehow feral. And, in a contest of wills, she'd be dashed to pieces upon it. Like tarnished moonlight, this light seemed to defy the very things that had come to define "light" for her.

She hastened to seal the wall, seal herself off. Surely an eternity of eternities walled up alone would be better than the primal lunacy that awaited beyond—but then she hesitated . . . there was... Something..

Ah, *the Something sighed, and one of her other senses was returned. No, a sense was given to her. A* sixth *one, and it came bearing rough translations. The slobbering and gibbering that had been her air, her music, her only companion, became a ravenous chorus of the Untamed.*

They moved through the cold, silvery, shivering light, beings made of brittle bits of the same illumination. They were all eyes and all teeth. What they saw, they wanted to consume.

They saw *her. They always had. And now, she saw them.*

The erosion of her self had now spread to the walls that protected her. As fast as she could close the breach, another opened, and another, and another, till she was finally laid bare, shrinking and cringing from beings that had no concept of mercy and light that had no concept of warmth.

Voiceless, she screamed, bodiless she turned, directionless, she fled, relentlessly pursued by the Untamed. As she fled, at her heels flew the Something, The Ah. *It did not attack but watched her with something akin to amusement, yet closer still to respect.*

Stop. Wait.

This was neither a question nor a command, but the mellow rumble of a curious predator. And she stopped. Waited. Though the Untamed clamored at her, tried to consume her, she stopped. Though bits of her were washing away like a sand castle at high tide and splintered away by jagged silver claws, she waited.

Look, *the Something urged, from in front of her now. It was not blocking her way, but blocking* them *out. It easily captured and held her formerly divided attention. And how could it not? In this place of mad, silver, bright, howling light, this thing was the maddest, the most silver, the brightest. Its howl was the din of a thousand-thousand wolves, loud beyond the point of loudness, a perfect white noise that soothed and reassured. Here was the* heart *of the Untamed, the Midnight Sun around which lesser satellites merely orbited.*

It was ancient and solitary, wild and beautiful.

It didn't want to consume *her, but rather* become a part of her.

Close your eyes and listen, *the* Something *hummed.*

She closed her eyes, and she listened.

And was seduced.

And was rebuilt.

The eroded edges of her self were shored up, and the fractured bits were gathered and laced together with silver stitchery. The chorus of the Untamed became a part of her, a glue that held her together. The stitching made her both weaker and stronger than she ever had been. What had once been a whirlwind of mad satellites tugging at her with their primeval gravity was now a shield, a spear, an ally and an alloy inextricably bound to her forever.

She opened her eyes and that light, once too-bright and annoyingly alive *with the slinking movement and shifting awareness of* them, *was no longer too intense to be borne. In fact, the light seemed to be emanating from* her, *from the depths and dark crevices of her self, like phosphorescence expelled from a quasar. Her universe was a combination of stark silver light and sumptuous, restful darkness. It was an* inner-verse, *not a Purgatory. A way station between what she once was, and what she was on the verge of becoming. The choice she was on the verge of making.*

No, the choice she had already made.

Let there be Light? *The Something yawned from within her, quiescent and content, for the moment, its words laced with the exact amount of self-conscious irony needed for such a question.*

Irony, yeah. I remember that, *she thought, with what felt like way too many bared teeth to be a grin.*

She had a lot to re-learn and remember, a lot to assimilate and actuate.

But she wouldn't be doing it alone. Ancient and canny, clever and mercenary, the Something that had become a part of her would be with her every step of the way, guiding her and informing her. Could easily overwhelm *her, if it so chose.*

Without one of the Tame People, I would be the Untamed Heart set loose in a world that has forgotten the Dark Forest, and the time when we all lived there. I would be the spirit of the Hunter at large in a world of prey, with no mercy to leaven me.

That time, the time of the Predator-King has passed, and the time of the Philosopher-King is at hand. Your place will be to serve the Great Balance between Human and *Garoul* that exists in yourself and in your people.

And with that, the Something subsided, curious but confident as to what her response would be.

That's Philosopher-Queen, *she reminded it after an infinity of weighing and thought. And though she had never had a lust for power, only a desire for* order—*for the righting of wrongs, where possible, and the fixing of what had been broken. The pushing back against chaos that separated Humans from beasts. This offer was greatly tempting.* And you're asking an awful lot of me, aren't you? Who says I'm even fit to be the diplomat to your despot? I'm just a nobody cubicle-jockey. I've never led anything or anyone in my life!

That stark light wrapped itself around her. It still wasn't warm, but it was illuminating, for suddenly, she could see how it could be done. Oh, it wouldn't be easy. Mistakes would be made—were already being made—and not just by her, but it could be done.

More importantly, it needed *to be done, if the* Garoul *were to survive in the long run. Strange days were coming, stranger than the ones that had ever gone before. And despite the pretense of democracy among the Packs, the intensely feudal system in place hindered both progress and evolution.*

The last Dyre had tried but, being a product of that system himself, had been unable to change it, merely lighten its grip on the Packs.

What was called for was a revolution. A new order.

A diplomat, not a despot was needed to guide the North American Garoul, *not to mention the spirit of the Untamed, which now resided in a nobody cubicle-jockey, into the new era.*

Choosing to live meant choosing to live for *the* Garoul *and* as *the* Garoul.

But there was so much work *to be done. So much struggle and strife.*

Not that that had ever scared her away from what needed to be done, before. And at least with the Garoul, *as the* Garoul, *her life would have meaning once more. A purpose.*

And you'll never, ever be bored, *an amused voice added. It was different, somehow, from the Something, from the Untamed Heart. Her own heart supplied a name for that voice, one that shook it to its very depths.*

George.

You've already decided, child, *George went on.* Now speak the words and awaken.

The words? *she thought, confused. Then laughed as she realized she knew exactly what words. She suddenly felt freer and more empowered than she ever had in her short, penned-in life.* Sure, why not?

Still laughing, she took a deep breath and steeled her entire self for the ride.

"LET THERE BE LIGHT!"

For one eternal moment, the silver light of the Untamed Heart intensified within her and around her. It grew so bright there was, momentarily, just a smidgen of warmth...then the light, all of it, was gone. She was by herself in the dark.

But only for a moment. Then space seemed to rush past her, like flying. Like falling, but that didn't matter. Nothing mattered, but the sudden stop was an entire world rushing up to meet her and landing squarely on her shoulders. It was the weight of a body, and memories that were suddenly cumbersome after so long without them. It was itching and burning like the heat of a thousand suns, and how had she ever, ever felt that she was cold?

It was agony.

Almost too weak to take her first breath in what felt like forever, she surfaced—

—to bright white light. To her body convulsing and screaming, as if every single cell of her was on fire. She screamed and thrashed and flailed but something stronger than herself held her down.

It hurt.

Everything hurt: the shrill, banshee-sound of her own scream, the feel of someone's calloused hands clamped on her arms; the scents in the air, so distinct she could have damn near tasted each one separately. And the light. After so long in silver-stitched darkness, the light was the worst of all. She felt it battering her eyelids and burning her skin, eating at her in a way the Untamed never had.

She flailed once more, *hard*, and threw off whatever was on her, only to find herself scrambling for purchase in something with slippery sides. It was only then she noticed that water, icy and stinging, was pelting her from above.

"FUCK!" a voice roared, pained and angry. Then new agony blossomed on her face, like a flower opening to disclose sweet, blissful darkness.

❖

They found Des panting over Ruby's unconscious body in her bathtub, soaking wet and bleeding from a nasty gash on the back of her head. Ruby lay in a sodden heap in one corner of the shower. Blood leaked slowly from her now slightly crooked nose, which straightened and healed even as they watched.

"Bitch is *strong*," Des mumbled, stepping out of the tub, dazed and nearly slipping in a puddle of water. Nathan darted forward and grabbed her by one arm. She steadied herself and shook him off.

"What the *fuck*, Des?" Jake asked into the stunned silence.

"So say we all, Jacob," Nathan sighed, his eyes ticking between Des and Ruby.

Des looked them over: father and brother and, a few seconds later, her stepmother, breathing hard with one hand on her rounded stomach. Then Des reached up and gingerly touched her lip, bitten while trying to keep Ruby from braining herself in the bathtub. The blood on her fingers was a red, red spot in Des's white, white bathroom. The brightest thing in it, aside from the sluggish trickle of red still coming from Ruby's nose.

Des grinned at her family. "Told you she'd survive," she said jaggedly. Then: "Ow, *fuck*."

Des's own pain and exhaustion hit her like a freight train. After three-plus days without sleep, spent stepping and fetching for Phil, she could barely keep herself conscious. In fact, she was drifting sideways into a soft, gray place, her cares and worries gone as Nathan hoisted her up in his strong arms. His somehow comforting scent surrounded her.

"Ruby's Fever has broken," she heard Phil say from the vicinity of the bathtub, in a surprised, relieved voice. "Moon Above, I think she's gonna make it."

Of course she is, Des said, or tried to say. Just then, the world was swallowed by silver-speckled darkness. Then, just darkness.

PART II:
THE DYRE FATHER IS DEAD. . . .

"Life is like a steering wheel, it only takes one small
move to change your entire direction."

—KELLIE ELMORE

CHAPTER FIVE

When Des opened her eyes a full day later, she was lying alone in her own bed, dim sunlight spearing her eyes and making her blink until they teared up. Suddenly, someone moved into the light and blocked it. Des squinted, then blinked some more.

"They tell me I gave you a concussion," Ruby said slowly, her smoky voice solemn but uninflected. She looked wraithlike and queerly Victorian in what had to be one of Phil's diaphanous, floor-length nightgowns. Her thick hair was unbound and curling tightly around her shoulders, framing a tired, rather woebegone dark face in which her round, brown eyes seemed huge.

She licked her lips and began again. "While I was sick, they say I was tossing and turning, and threw you off me when you tried to hold me down in the shower. And you hit your head. Hard." She licked her lips once more. "I apologize."

"Uh, no problemo," Des said, though she honestly couldn't remember much about what had happened after carrying a half-dead Ruby into her bathroom. It was mostly a haze of white light, red splotches, and darkness. Shaking her head, she sat up carefully but didn't experience the dizziness or weakness she half-expected. In fact, she felt better than she had in a very long time.

Des threw back the covers and swung her legs over the side of the bed without thinking about whether or not she was clothed. Ruby blushed but Des noted with relief she was wearing a t-shirt and boxers. The same ones from before everything went dark and fuzzy.

"Maybe you should take it slow," Ruby ventured, reaching out to take Des's arm as she stood. Des huffed at this reversal of positions, Ruby worrying over *her*. "You've been out for a long time."

"Not as long as you were."

Frowning, Ruby looked away. "And how long would you say that was?"

Des opened her mouth to answer, then did some frowning of her own. "What have you been told?"

Ruby took a breath and looked back at Des. Tears stood in her eyes, threatening to spill over. She swiped them away impatiently before they could, but they eventually overflowed.

"Nothing!" she exclaimed, her voice cracking. "No one tells me anything, except that I've been sick, but that I'm well now, and among friends." She snorted, rolling her eyes. "Among friends who won't tell me how or why I'm here, or where *here* is, or who any of you *are!*"

Des groaned and ran a hand through her hair. It was still standing up in spikes in the front, but flat in the back. "I see. Other than that, have they been treating you okay?"

Ruby sniffled and wiped her face. "Yeah. I get free run of the wing and meals whenever I want, whatever I want." She sat down on the bed and Des sat next to her after a moment. "I've been all over the wing trying to find out something—*anything*—about where I am, but the only clue I've got is *you*." Now she looked at Des almost accusingly. "I had this awful dream, and you were in it. You said some pretty weird things, and the next thing I know, I'm waking up in this room, in a bed that's not mine, with you wrapped around me, snoring in my ear."

Des blushed again and cleared her throat. "Ah."

Ruby rolled her wet eyes and laughed shakily. "*Ah*? Is that all you have to say?" She stood up again and paced to the window, twitching aside the curtains so she could look out. "Are you a prisoner, too, or one of my jailors?"

"Neither," Des said softly. "And you're not being jailed here, I promise. You're being kept here for your own good, till we can explain what's happened to you, and what's *going* to happen to you."

Ruby glanced back at Des defiantly. "Don't *I* get a say in what happens to me?"

Des looked away from that fierce, tear-shiny gaze. "To a certain extent. But the decisions you make don't just affect you anymore. They need to be informed."

"About *what*?"

"I think you know what, subconsciously. Maybe a little consciously, too," Des murmured.

"I don't know what you're talking about!" she said, her voice full of anger and frustration. "None of you people make any sense! Just *tell me* why you're holding me here!" She crossed the room again, stopping a few feet shy of Des, who still wouldn't meet her eyes. "*Please*, I'm *begging* you. Tell me what's going on!"

Des sighed again but nodded. This was probably not the best idea, but she couldn't stand the helpless, fearful, frustrated look in Ruby's eyes. No Loup, let alone the *Dyre*, should look like that. "I'll do better than that, Ruby, I'll *show* you. But you have to promise me that no matter what you see, you won't freak out."

Ruby shook her head. "I can't promise that. But I'll try. Just, please don't show me anything *too* weird."

Des smiled sadly. "Sweetheart, it's gonna get pretty weird. And kinda scary. And gross. But I promise you won't be hurt."

Ruby stared at Des hard for a few seconds, then nodded, wiping at her eyes again. "Okay. Show me—no, wait! What's your name?" Ruby almost smiled. "It's just—I mean, you know my name, but I don't know yours."

Pleased for some reason she couldn't name, Des answered, "Jennifer Desiderio. But everyone calls me Des."

"Des." Ruby took a deep breath, let it out, and smoothed her hands across the front of the nightgown. "Okay. Show me whatever you need to show me, Des."

Standing up, Des stretched again till her joints cracked. Then she gripped the hem of her t-shirt and quickly shucked it. Ruby blushed, but didn't look away as Des hooked her thumbs in the waistband of her boxers and shoved them down.

Taking a deep breath of her own, Des closed her eyes and called to the Loup within. As always, she never had to call loud or long. It was right there, seemingly just under her skin, waiting to break free.

Alright, cabrónito. Time to come out and play again. But this time, be nice, she added. The reply she got was a sly, snickering growl.

And then, the Change began.

❖

As Ruby watched, Des seemed to blur, then sharpen, as if the universe had applied CGI special effects to her. Her face seemed to cave in a little, and Ruby heard the sounds of cracking bones.

The breaking and snapping seemed to be coming from all over Des as she shuddered and crashed to the floor on all fours, moaning in a pain-distorted voice. Her fingers clenched and unclenched in the carpet pile. Instinctively, Ruby stepped forward to help her, but Des threw one shaking hand up, head still hanging. "Don't! Stay back!"

"But there's something wrong with you. I should get help." Ruby turned toward the door, suddenly scared that this person—the only one who'd even begun to answer Ruby's many questions, the one who had been vulnerable in Ruby's presence and thus was at least somewhat sympathetic—was about to keel over and die in agony.

She was turning the doorknob when she felt a hand on her shoulder. She jumped and glanced back to see some misshapen *thing* that bore a passing resemblance to Des. Ruby could see the bones of its face warping as she watched, and she could hear that awful, unmistakable sound of bones cracking and grinding together.

The thing opened its mouth and tried to speak.

"Wait," it struggled to say, its voice a low, rumbling growl emitted from a maw absolutely crowded with teeth. With *fangs.* "Wait, Ruuuu . . . wait."

Ruby was the one to shudder this time. Only her father had ever called her "Ru," and as for the *wait,* that, too, struck a familiar chord. She let go of the knob and turned to face the creature just as it fell to the floor again, whining and coughing. As Ruby watched, its skin began to writhe and sprout patches of thick, bristling black fur.

Ruby stared at the dark eyes in its unnaturally elongated face, filled with wariness and pain and hunger. And hadn't Ruby seen something very similar to this in a thousand B-movies? A person, turning into some sort of monster? Yes, she had. The only question was what monster lurked inside of Jennifer Desiderio?

Ruby didn't want to know.

So she wasn't waiting around to find out.

❖

She ran.

With a frightened little scream, Ruby turned to the door, yanked it open, and *ran*.

This was not exactly unexpected by either the Loup or Des. And when the Change was over, Des prodded her Loup impatiently.

Well? What are we waiting for? she demanded. *Let's get after her before she does something stupid!*

The Loup didn't need to be told, as it was already loping out of the room, fast on the fear-scent left in Ruby's wake. To the Loup, it smelled entrancing—a perfect mix of female-purity-sweet-sweat-musk. The idea of letting that scent get away was patently ridiculous as far as the Loup was concerned. Especially when all it wanted to do was make that scent its own: to roll around in it and drown in it. To be immersed in this olfactory version of Moon's Light.

The Loup took them around to the back hall, and found the owner of that scent, shaking and sobbing in the arms of another of the *Garoul*. The one the Loup identified as *sibling*, and Pack-brother, and Des identified as *Jake*. Which was the only reason the Loup didn't leap on him, and try to tear his throat out and drink down his power for touching what belonged to it.

"—and—and—then she was *c-changing*, and she had these *teeth* and—" Ruby let out another high, desperate sob as she looked over her shoulder and saw the Loup there, watching her with its teeth bared and hackles up.

"It's okay, Ruby," Pack-brother Jake soothed, grasping Ruby's upper arms and shaking her a little. The Loup growled a deep warning and stepped forward warily. Ruby screamed and shoved the Pack-brother away from her. He fell backwards with a squawk that pleased the Loup.

Served him right for daring to touch *Her*.

And that *Her* was *strong*.

That *Her* was also bolting, *again*, the white nightgown flapping behind her as she sprinted on near-noiseless feet, unknowingly toward the back staircase.

Barking once more, the closest to a laugh it would ever get, the Loup leapt over its fallen Pack-brother—"Heyya, Des, what the hell?" he demanded querulously—and gave chase.

❖

Ruby ran and ran, and still she could hear the—*it*—the *wolf*—panting behind her.

She could smell it following, a scent like wet dog and wild things. So she kept on, till her sides were in stitches, and her lungs were filled with battery acid. She flew down a curving, narrow staircase that ended in a huge kitchen of spotted white marble, dark wood, and gleaming chrome. There seemed to be a million doors to choose from, even if there were only three, but Ruby didn't hesitate. She picked the one directly across from the staircase, darted to it, undid the latch, and pulled it open.

She found herself at a dead end in a huge pantry-like room, filled with cans and barrels and jars. It *was*, in fact, a pantry. She moaned high in her throat and turned around, hoping like Hell it wasn't too late to backtrack.

It was.

The wolf was sitting at the foot of the staircase, tongue lolling out of its mouth in a grin. And why *wouldn't* it grin?

Dinner was served. Ruby backed deeper into the pantry among the empty lower shelves. The wolf barked like a dog, getting to its feet and obviously preparing to leap.

Ruby screamed. It was suddenly airborne, flying toward her like a shadow brought to life, mouth still lolling open. Ruby could see, beyond its tongue, fangs that made her flinch backward, though she had no more *back* to flinch *to*. She crouched down to make herself a smaller target, sobbing.

The wolf landed at Ruby's feet and bounced up on its hind legs, paws landing on her shoulders, and it licked her face. Ruby screamed again, and got a mouth full of wet wolf-tongue for her troubles.

"Augh! God! Yuck!" she shrilled, turning her face away. Seeming not to be put off by this, the wolf licked her neck, her shoulders, her breasts—any part of her it could reach.

"Stop!" Ruby yelped, sitting hard on the bottom shelf, which gave away under her weight and spilled them both to the floor. The wolf landed heavily on Ruby and continued to lick and paw at her, barking like an overgrown puppy.

Ruby scrambled backward on her aching ass, wedging herself under the shelves and against the wall. The wolf followed her, cramming itself in with her. It whined once then licked the hands she held out to ward it off.

"Des!"

Both Ruby and the wolf started at the sound coming from nearby. Too nearby for the wolf, who growled as it turned to face the door, hackles raised once more. Three figures appeared in the doorway:

The first was a woman seemingly of Ruby's own height and age, dark-skinned and lovely in an old-fashioned floral maternity dress, watching her with compassionate eyes. This woman had answered Ruby's questions about her illness and even about Des's injury, but not about where Ruby was, why she was there, or when she could leave.

She was accompanied by a man who could have been as young as thirty-five or as old as fifty, Ruby honestly couldn't tell. But he was dressed in an even more old fashioned linen suit. But for his age and gender, he and Des could have been identical twins.

Last was a tall, lanky young man, perhaps a few years younger than Ruby, standing with his hands in his pockets until he raised one to wave at her cheerily. He was dressed in an Acapulco shirt and cargo shorts. His face was pleasantly forgettable but for his striking hazel eyes. He was the young man she'd run into when she was being chased. Or had *thought* she was being chased.

Sniffling and wiping her spit-and-tears wet face, Ruby touched the wolf's back with a shaking hand, instinctively seeking comfort. Its fur was spiky but soft, its pointed ears laying back toward her.

"D-Des?"

The wolf looked back at her with intelligent dark eyes and barked once. Ruby yelped again, more tears leaking out. Tears that once more got licked away.

"You're Des?"

Another bark.

"And you're *not* gonna eat me?"

Two barks.

Ruby sniffled again and sighed. "I hope that's a 'no'."

The wolf—*Des*—whined again and faced Ruby, burying its warm, furry muzzle between her breasts. Great, dark, strangely *gentle* eyes stared up at her, and she couldn't look away.

Without thinking about it, Ruby reached up and patted the wolf's head. It barked that happy, puppy-bark again.

Ruby sniffled and closed her eyes. But instead of darkness on the backs of her eyelids, she saw George's face coming toward her, only it was too long, too narrow and dog-like, too *toothy*. And it'd been changing as it got closer, hadn't it? Blue eyes turning green, then yellow, skin sprouting hair in patches, brows and cheeks growing thicker, cruder, heavier…

Then she'd been in pain unlike any she'd felt before, tearing through her shoulder and the vulnerable junction where neck met shoulder. And she'd screamed, and still the pain went on, until the world went so red, it was black, and then everything had gotten hazy and confusing.

She had disturbing dreams she couldn't quite remember. Then a period of waking and a period of sleeping that felt less like a coma and more like actual sleep. Then, finally, early this morning, a true waking up.

She'd awoken in a strange bed, next to a stranger who looked little better than death warmed over, and to other strangers who were kind to her, but evasive about how she'd gotten to the mansion she'd found herself in, and why she'd been so sick.

But these other strangers were absolutely mum on how she'd gotten the faint, but ugly, jagged scar on her collar, just below her neck. Yet Ruby had known, hadn't she? That scar was in the same place she'd been bitten in that awful nightmare she'd had where someone broke into George's apartment and shot him. And would have shot Ruby, if not for—

For Des, she thought, finally connecting her face to the one who had appeared in that awful nightmare. The sharp, almost feral face that'd calmly told her that she was *Queen of the Werewolves, or some ridiculous bullshit. Only it wasn't bullshit, was it? At least not the part about the Werewolves. Oh, God. This can't be true. It just* can't.

Can it?

❖

"But it is, isn't it?" Ruby asked quietly, scratching behind Des's Loup's ears. The Loup, for its part, butted its head against her hand, eager for more. Des may have been enjoying it as well. "It's all true."

"What, hon?" Phil knelt down and reached out a hand to the Loup who, attention whore that it was, whuffed and poked its muzzle out for scratching.

"I'm a werewolf, now, aren't I?" Ruby's round eyes darted from the Loup, to Phil, then closed on more tears. "George b-bit me before he died, and made me like Des. Like you?"

Phil sighed. "Yes, honey, it's true."

"I thought that was all a dream. A *nightmare*." Ruby started weeping again, and the Loup forsook Phil's scratches to lick away the tears once more. Ruby laughed a little but didn't stop crying.

"I fucking hate dogs," she said, then started sobbing, hugging the Loup close and burying her face in its soft black fur.

❖

"So."

Ruby sniffed and shifted in Des's arms, but didn't otherwise respond.

"This pantry's not exactly the Ritz-Carlton, huh?"

Warm and now dry on her neck, Ruby scrinched up her face and wound her arms even tighter around Des's waist. Des looked up at their audience.

It'd been almost half an hour since the Loup had tracked Ruby to the pantry and nearly twenty minutes since Des had reverted back to her Hume-form. Now, her brother, father, and stepmother stood watching them expectantly. Feeling more than a flash of annoyance at their intrusion, Des spoke directly into Ruby's ear. "Wanna get outta here?"

"No."

Well, it was *an* answer.

"Not even for chocolate pudding?"

Ruby snorted a little. "I hate chocolate pudding."

"And dogs?"

"And dogs."

"Hmm." Des smiled into Ruby's hair. "How about a nice, big steak?"

"I—" Ruby sat up, blinking at Des and looking her over. "You're naked."

Des shrugged.

Then Ruby looked up at their audience and flushed.

"Disappear, guys," Des ordered, and for a wonder, they did. Even Nathan.

Ruby looked at Des, surprised. "Are you, like, the um, Werewolf Chief?"

Des laughed. "Ah, no. That'd be, well, *you*."

"*What?*"

But Des was maneuvering them carefully out from under the shelves. Ruby clenched her arms tight around Des's neck, and Des stood up.

"*Jesus*, you're strong," Ruby said breathlessly, her eyes saucer-wide.

"You don't know the half of it. Now, how 'bout that steak, *chica*?"

Des strode out of the pantry without waiting for an answer.

❖

It was really throwing Ruby for a loop, that Des *didn't* care about the whole naked-thing. She easily carried Ruby into the kitchen, talking about meat and how hungry they both were the whole way, all while utterly bare-assed.

And indeed, Ruby *was* hungry, her stomach informed her loudly. Still, Des's nudity was distracting.

They saw no one in the kitchen, though Ruby was soaking in the surroundings carefully. The house seemed to be truly a manor, huge and vaulting, with buttresses and wainscoting and things for which Ruby didn't have a name. Even the kitchen was ridiculously huge, with a brick oven, a fireplace, and a giant gas stove with more burners than Ruby had fingers.

The only deviation from all the chrome and reflecting surfaces was a huge marble counter and the wooden stools that surrounded it.

". . . none of that Worcester sauce bullshit, either," Des was saying as she gently sat Ruby down on one of the stools directly across from the enormous oven. "Just good, old-fashioned steak, with a little salt and pepper for seasoning." Des grinned, showing small, even white teeth with very pointy canines. "How *do* you like your steak, by the way?"

"Um…very well-done."

Des chuckled. "If you say so. Me, I like it tartare or rare."

"*Yuck*. My father used to eat his steak that way." Ruby made a face. "He used to say: 'Ru, *min blomst*, run it through a warm room then bring it to me.' He's lucky he didn't wind up with intestinal parasites or something."

"My kinda man. And I don't say that often." Des winked then strode past Ruby to one of three huge Sub-Zero refrigerator-freezers. She opened the middle one and began rooting through the shelves, muttering to herself. "Let's see, we've also got pork chops, ribs, filet mignon—God, Nathan's such a pretentious ass—veal cutlets, ah, I think these are Swedish meatballs, chicken breasts, turkey breasts—ooh, halibut! Tuna steaks, swordfish steaks, pork loin, lamb shanks—"

"Steak'll do," Ruby said absently, wondering how someone could be so comfortable while being so *naked*. Not that Des had anything to be ashamed of. She was small, sporty, and lean, all whipcord muscle and prominent bone structure. Not as hairy as one might expect of a woman who was actually a…well, Ruby didn't want to think about what Des actually was and left it at: *Well, it's obvious she doesn't shave…anything.*

"I could eat all of this and then some. I'm fucking *starving*," Des announced, taking out what seemed to be a small pile of steaks. She kicked the fridge door shut with her heel, grinning. Ruby quickly raised her eyes and grinned back.

"All right, that was steak, well-done, for the lady," she said in a horrible English accent. Ruby smiled just a little as Des strode over to the stove and dumped the meat on the center of it. Then she was rifling cabinets and drawers for a skillet, oil, plates, and utensils.

Gold-plated utensils.

"Are all werewolves this rich?" Slipped out before she could catch herself. Des snorted.

"Nope. Nathan's Pack, the Coulters, is one of the oldest Packs still in existence in North America. He's their Alpha—leader, that is—and this is his house we're in, and his steak we'll be eating," Des said wryly, though there was an off note there Ruby couldn't decipher. "Anyway, when you hear the term 'old money,' that pretty much describes the Coulter Pack. Callum, the founding Coulter, was part of the Clan Coulter, in Scotland, seven hundred or so years ago. Rumor had it his mother was a sort of faerie maiden or some horseshit like that." Des snorted again, rolling her eyes at Ruby as if, in a world that contained werewolves, *faeries* were just over the top.

"No one ever really knew or even talked about it in Callum's company, since he was a bastard and had been abandoned on his father, Bran Coulter's, doorstep. We also know that Callum was driven out of the Coulter lands at the age of seventeen for being a demon." Des clicked the stove on and added oil to the skillet. "Seventeen being the median age for the *Garoul-born*—um, kids born to, uh, werewolf parents—to go through the, ah, physical changes that lead to them, uh. You know. Becoming true shapeshifters."

Ruby frowned. "So you're saying that werewolves gain their *powers* at *seventeen*?"

"Sometimes earlier, sometimes later, but yeah." Des carefully put a steak in the skillet. It immediately began to sizzle, filling the kitchen with a scent that made Ruby's stomach growl again. "Like, I came into my, uh, powers, at fifteen. My brother, Jake—you met him, the tall, hippie-looking guy in the Acapulco shirt—didn't come into his powers until he was nineteen. Neither did Nathan. It's been kind of a Coulter tradition since old Bran's granddaughter, Rebecca. At least until *I* came along." Des shrugged.

Ruby took a moment to put two and two together then asked hesitantly: "Is Nathan . . . your father?"

"Shocking, ain't it?" That wry grin popped up again. "That a guy like that could ever produce a mutt like me?"

Ruby smiled. She'd only seen the man she presumed was Nathan Coulter for a few moments, but he'd seemed as different from Des as up was from down, physical resemblance aside. "I wouldn't know, I mean all of this is pretty strange to me."

"Yeah. I keep forgetting how new you are. Here I am, telling you the Coulter family history when you probably have more relevant questions." Des stole a glance at Ruby then focused on the steak again, prodding it with a meat fork. "You can ask me anything, you know? Anything at all, and I'll do my best to answer it."

Ruby blinked. Then her mind conveniently went blank. "Um," she said, blushing and frustrated. "I'm still trying to believe all of this is *real*. I don't even know *what* to ask!"

Des turned the steak over and sighed. "That's understandable. When I first found out, I was such a wreck, I didn't even question it, I just shut down, for a while."

Ruby's eyebrows shot up. "You mean you haven't always known you were a werewolf?"

"Nope." Des smiled at Ruby. "And that's not exactly the PC term, *werewolf*. We call ourselves the *Garoul*, or *Loup-Garoul*."

"Politically correct werewolves?" Ruby snorted.

"Hey, don't look at me!" Des held up her hands and laughed. "I'm fine with the term *werewolf*, but then, like I said, I wasn't exactly to the manor born. Nathan didn't even know I existed till after my mom died nearly nine years ago. She was a Hume. Um, Human."

"I'm sorry for your loss," Ruby said softly, and Des's smile slipped.

"It was a long time ago," she replied lightly, waving a dismissive hand. "I'm over it."

Secretly doubtful, Ruby was willing to let it go but felt she had to say something. "I know what it's like to lose a parent. I mean, I was just sixteen when my dad—"

"What was it? Heart attack?" Des interrupted to ask. "Stroke?"

"I wish it had been that quick. For his sake." Ruby sighed bitterly, remembering how brave her father had been, even as he wasted away. How he always found a smile for her, even when it'd become obvious he wasn't going to go into remission before the cancer killed him. "It was stomach cancer, and he lingered for a long time. Too strong to succumb, but too weak to win the fight, by the end."

Des whistled, looking back at the steak. She prodded it with the meat fork. "Jesus, that's fucking horrible."

"Yes, it was," Ruby agreed with a limp smile. "I was a kid, and I thought it was the end of my world. But it wasn't. Just the end of my childhood."

"Was there any other family for you to stay with?"

Ruby shrugged and traced a random pattern in the marble countertop. "My mother had walked out on us when I was nine, no clue where she was. Her side of the family was all elderly spinsters and widowers, and didn't want to be burdened with a grieving teenager. My dad's side of the family all live in Denmark. And except for my cousin, Peter, I've never even met them in person." Shaking her head, Ruby tapped the terminus of the pattern with one fingernail. "I sued for emancipation and won. Got my GED instead of finishing high school, worked for a while to save up money, then I applied to college. Got in, and eventually got my degree in Human Services, and wound up working for a few places before I got an offer from Lenape Landing Technical College. I accepted it and moved out here. The rest is history."

Des snuck a glance at her. "How'd you meet George?"

Ruby's eyebrows shot up again. "He was the president of L.L.T.C. He hired me personally."

Gaping, Des faced Ruby, who was once more struck by how comfortable and matter-of-fact Des was about her nudity. "You're shitting me! George was the president of a college?"

"You didn't know?"

Des shook her head. "All I knew about him was what the Council—um, a legislative group made up of all the Pack-

Alphas—told me. He was the Wolf of Wolfs, the Alpha of the Alphas."

"The Untamed Heart." Ruby nodded absently as the phrase popped into her head from nowhere. Then she shrugged when Des looked at her blankly. "Sorry, go on."

"Nothing else to say, really. He had ruled the Packs and the Council for longer than even *Nathan* had been alive. He was approaching his final years, and his eyesight was failing him. He needed a guardian. Someone who'd take on all comers and keep them busy for long enough for George to Change and recover from the strain of Changing so *he* could fight." Des paused and plated the steak, then added more oil to the pan and dropped another steak in. "Changing shapes takes a lot out of you. Especially the older you are. And George was *old*."

Ruby did the math and didn't quite like what she came up with. "So, you were basically his Human, uh, his *Garoul* shield?"

"Hole in one!" Des brought the plate with the steak over to the counter and put it in front of Ruby. "Voila! Steak a lá Des."

Hungry though she was, Ruby wouldn't be side-tracked. "And you were all right with that?"

"Well, I didn't exactly have much of a choice, did I?" Des said harshly, her dark, dark eyes flashing challenge and defiance. "It was either that, or—"

When Des closed her mouth on the rest of what she was going to say, Ruby leaned forward. "That, or what?"

"Nothing. Never mind," Des mumbled, that fire in her eyes guttering. She pushed the plate closer to Ruby. "Eat up, Ruby Knudsen. Trust me, you're gonna need your strength."

Knowing when the battle was at a stalemate, at least for the moment, Ruby nodded and took the fork Des offered. "That sounds ominous," she quipped, hoping it'd make Des smile. Her hope was entirely in vain. What she got was a warm, calloused hand covering her own and squeezing. Des's hand was scarred and square. A fighter's hands.

"It'll be tough for awhile. But you'll get through this," Des said reassuringly, which had the exact opposite effect on Ruby. When someone like the sort of person Des seemed to be was offering such gentle comfort, things must've been dire, indeed. "Don't worry too much."

Easy for you to say, Ruby thought unhappily, cutting a piece of steak and popping it in her mouth. It was sizzling hot and just the way she liked it. She chewed then sucked in mouthfuls of air to cool her scalded tongue. "Ow, *shit*, that's hot!"

At this Des *did* smile. It was a rakish smile with more than a hint of something wild and *untamed* in it.

Ruby returned it with a hesitant one of her own.

The rest of lunch passed in almost comfortable silence broken only by the sizzle and pop of the steaks in the skillet.

❖

In the end, it took a bit of coaxing to get Ruby to leave the kitchen. She'd come to view it as some sort of haven from the world that now awaited her. But Des wasn't having any of it. She finally strode around the counter and took Ruby's hand and tugged her.

Ruby resisted, frowning, but Des quirked an eyebrow, shrugged, and tugged once more, hard. Ruby toppled off her stool with a yelp into Des's arms.

"Hiding in here won't make what you are go away," Des said, looking Ruby in the eye till she turned away, flushing. "You're going to have to get used to the fact that you *will* be meeting some *damned* strange people over the next few months. There's no getting around that. My father, stepmother, and brother are the least of your problems, and they're the most normal Loups you're likely to meet."

Ruby bit her lip. "I don't understand why I have to meet anyone," she mumbled truculently. "Can't I just go back to my job and my apartment and try to be as ordinary as possible?"

Des hung her head for a moment, frustrated and trying to keep a lid on it. "You could. At least until the next Full-Moon Waxing. What're you gonna do when the Change is upon you, huh? Pretend it's not happening?"

"The thought had crossed my mind," Ruby said flippantly, but she tilted her face up in a mulish sort of way that rankled Des just as bad as Nathan ever had.

Des glared, tipping and turning Ruby's chin toward her. "This isn't a joke, sweetheart."

Ruby laughed, but she had tears in her eyes. "Yeah? Well, you coulda fooled me. In my opinion, this is the biggest joke the universe ever played!"

Praying to whatever gods watched over temperamental Loups, Des sighed. "Look. When the time comes for your first Change, you'll likely be *gone*. You'll be the wolf. You will hunt. You will *kill*. And you will *feast*. Like I said, there's no getting around it." She tried to pin Ruby with her gaze, to convey the utter seriousness of what she faced. "You probably won't be able to control *when* you Change for months—maybe *years*. Whenever the Full Moon is out, you'll just be *gone*. That's just the way it is for most new Loups. Wouldn't you rather be somewhere safe when that happens?"

Ruby smiled mirthlessly. "And that place would be here?"

"No place safer," Des said plainly. "Anything that wants at you will have to get through me, and if it does, then it'll have to get through Jake, Phil, and Nathan. And even *I* wouldn't take on Nathan on a dare."

Blinking against eyes that were once more welling up, Ruby tried to turn her face away. But Des wouldn't let her.

"Don't you understand? *I had a life!* It may not have been the best life, but it was *mine!*" Ruby exclaimed, her voice shrill with barely repressed hysteria. "And you took it away from me!"

Des narrowed her eyes. "I didn't take *nothin'* from you, sweetheart."

"You know what I mean, damnit! Your *kind*! The *Garoul*! If you think I'm going anywhere with you or your family, you're crazy!" Ruby slapped Des's hand away from her face and crossed her arms over her chest. "I demand that you let me go."

"You *demand?*"

Ruby nodded. Then she flinched backwards when Des took a step toward her, smirking.

CHAPTER SIX

F or time immemorial, the *Garoul* have run with the Moon, and though we've worn many different names over the eons, they've all meant the same thing: shapeshifter," Nathan began pedantically.

Des rolled her eyes and leaned back against one of the library's comfortable sofas. Above her, actually sitting on the sofa, rather than on the floor, Ruby stared dully out one of the windows, the sunlight and shadow playing across her mask-like face.

She hadn't said a word since Des had gotten her in a fireman's carry and marched her to the library. Hadn't really moved since Des deposited her carefully on the sofa.

"You're gonna sit, and you're gonna listen. It might just save your life, someday," she'd said and Ruby, glaring up at her with wet eyes, had hauled back and slapped her in the face. *Hard.*

Torn between laughing and wanting to slap her right back, Des had simply shrugged, wiped away the thin trickle of blood from her nose, and folded into a full-lotus at Ruby's feet.

Now, she covertly scented Ruby. She smelled the same as she had in George's apartment that night, except for one subtle change. Where she'd once smelled of Hume, she now smelled like a Loup. Young and untried by her first Change, but a Loup nonetheless. Like fresh rainwater and the forest.

She also smelled of fear, deep unhappiness, and tears.

When Des put a gentle hand on Ruby's calf, the tear-scent intensified.

"Don't touch me," Ruby said quietly. But Des didn't move her hand, nor did Ruby move her leg.

Nathan looked between them and sighed. "But I can see where the history of the *Garoul* might pale in comparison with the worries you now carry," he said, actually managing to sound sympathetic. He approached the sofa slowly, brow furrowed. "Surely you must have some questions, child?"

"Will I be allowed to leave?"

Nathan glanced at Des, who shrugged stolidly. This whole mess about keeping Ruby at the manor until the Contests had been decided, for good or ill, had been Nathan's plan. Now that it was backfiring, Des planned to lean back and enjoy the show.

"I'm afraid that's the one thing we cannot allow you to do, as yet, young lady. There are those who wish you harm, and—"

"Haven't I been harmed enough?"

Nathan actually winced. "We do not know who sent the assassin after George, but we have reason to think they would have no qualms about sending one for you as well. Here, at least, we can protect you."

"Because you did such a bang-up job of protecting George?"

This time, it was Des who winced. Nathan, however, stepped over the question without so much as a glance at Des. "Now that we know the lengths to which this unseen enemy is willing to go, we believe we can be more effective at guarding you. Especially with you being *here*."

"If that's the case, why didn't *George* stay here?"

For this, Nathan seemed to struggle for an answer, finally settling on: "George was singularly determined to live his life the way he wanted to live it, regardless of the danger."

Des looked up at Ruby to gauge her reaction and found that dark, accusing gaze on her. She bore up under it, though it was tough.

"How long will you keep me here? What happens to my job and my apartment while I'm here?"

Des looked at Nathan, who waved a hand as if to say *go ahead*. So she took a breath.

"George was a very important Loup, Ruby. I told you he was the Alpha of Alphas. The Wolf of Wolfs, right?"

Ruby nodded grudgingly.

"Well, among the *Garoul*, that kind of position is usually passed along through the blood."

"Like dynastic succession?"

"Uh, no. More like blood transfusion, only more…bestial."

"*What?*"

"When he bit you, Ruby, he passed along his Death-right to you. That includes his position, his power, his possessions—everything." Ruby's eyes widened and Des forged on, running her hand down and up Ruby's calf in an effort to soothe her. "Basically, he made you our Queen."

Des braced herself for the explosion she was sure would follow, only it never came.

Ruby merely buried her face in her hands then ran them back through her mussed-up hair. "This has to be a joke or a dream. This can't be *real*."

"I assure you it is, Ms. Knudsen. And in light of that, I urge you to take the threat to your life *very* seriously," Nathan said gravely. "There are those who would contest George's choice of heir. There are those who would see you give away George's

Death-right and those who would take it from you through single combat."

Ruby was shaking her head. "No, see, I like that first option better."

"Neither option would allow you to keep on living." Des met Ruby's horrified gaze. "They don't call it a *Death-right* for nothing, babe."

Running her hands through her hair again, Ruby groaned. "What the hell am I supposed to do, then? I'm not gonna *give away* my life and I can't fight to save it—"

"Don't you worry about that. That's what *I'm* here for," Des said grimly, getting to her feet and sitting next to Ruby on the sofa. She took Ruby's hand, surprised when Ruby let her. "George swore me to be your defender with his dying breath. And I'm not gonna try to worm out of that. I'll take on all comers until they get the picture. *You're* the Dyre, and no one and nothing's gonna change that while I'm still alive."

By the end of this brief speech, Ruby was as wide-eyed as a newborn lamb.

"But..." she began hesitantly, rather hopelessly. "But you're so *little*."

A burst of low, rich laughter saved Des from having to formulate a response, and startled them both. For the first time in Des's presence—and probably anyone else's—Nathan Coulter was laughing his ass off.

❖

"Have I missed George's funeral?" Ruby asked as they walked up the front stairs. In each hand, she had a leather-bound book Nathan recommended she read. One was a history on the *Garoul* in general, and the other a history on North American

Packs, including something called the Carnahan Treatise, respectively. Both were rather thick and, upon a quick flip-through, she could tell they were hand-written and illustrated. "Do the *Garoul* even *have* funerals?"

"We do, of a sort. And no, you wouldn't have missed George's. After all, the new Dyre has to preside over the late Dyre's ceremony." Des smiled and Ruby blanched. She hated public speaking. The idea of doing so in front of tens, maybe hundreds of the *Garoul* was terrifying.

"So I'll be allowed out of the house to preside over the funeral?"

Des rolled her eyes and stepped onto the second floor landing. She was still stark naked, still completely unself-conscious about it. "The funeral will likely be held here. And you're allowed out of the house *now*. You have the run of the grounds, which are pretty extensive, for obvious reasons. You can also leave the grounds, as long as I'm with you."

"Me and my shadow?" Ruby asked, and did a little two-step. Des laughed and took her arm at the elbow.

"Come on."

Shortly thereafter, they were at the room Ruby had woken up in—the room she realized was likely Des's. She felt slightly awkward as they stepped inside.

"You're probably tired," Des said. Ruby realized she *was* tired. She'd been awake for only ten or so hours, but, yes, she felt rather drained. "You've had a lot to process and you've been down with the Fever for days. Plus, after lunch, you've probably got what Phil calls *the 'itis*."

Suddenly Ruby was laughing around a huge yawn. "My mother called it that, too," she said, muffled by the back of her hand. "Hey, can I ask you something?"

Des blinked at her and smiled. "Of course. Anything."

"D-does George have any family?"

Nodding, Des shut the door behind them and took Ruby's arm again, leading her to the bed. "He has a daughter and son, Evelyn and James." She paused and looked chagrined. "James is what the *Garoul* call a Latent. Meaning he's *Garoul*-born but lacks the ability to Change. It's a pretty rare condition, but it happens sometimes. And only to two of the *Garoul* who mate. It's never in recorded history happened to someone who's a half-breed."

"Like you?" Ruby asked, almost smiling. Des grinned, showing off those perfect, sharp teeth.

"Like me," she agreed. "Anyway, James is a Latent. I know he and George weren't particularly close, but Evelyn and George were like this." Des crossed the index and middle fingers of her right hand. "She's gonna be devastated. If we can find her to tell her, that is. She likes to stay off the grid. Last I heard she was running with an Eastern European Pack a few years ago."

Ruby sat down on the bed and folded her hands in her lap. "You said that all of George's stuff was mine, now, right?"

"Affirmative." Des sat next to her, still grinning. "The lawyers have no doubt faked a legit-looking will by now."

"Then I'd like to give all his possessions and his money to his children." Ruby looked down at her hands. "It's not right I keep the things their father owned and may have sentimental value to them."

Des snorted. "George was about as sentimental as a brick to the skull, and Evelyn was the same way, or so I've heard. She may take a few knick-knacks, but I expect the bulk of it'll stay in your hands."

Ruby took a minute to process that, remembering her own father, who was as sentimental as it got and had passed that trait on to his only child. "What about James?"

"He didn't want much to do with George when he was alive. Now that he's dead…" Des shrugged. "I dunno much about James. He might want the money. There's a lot of it. George always lived simply. I mean, there *is* the mansion, but he hasn't lived there since Evelyn and James left. "

"*Mansion?*"

"Yeah. Almost all the older Alphas and Pack-members choose to live in them, with plenty of acreage. George's came through his late wife, Nancy. When I asked him once why he didn't stay there since it'd be safer, he said it didn't feel right being there without her." Des made a face Ruby couldn't read. "Contrary old bastard. There was the easy way, the hard way, and *George's* way. And he never made it *easy* on ya."

"No, he didn't," Ruby laughed. "He used to ask me to read him books on philosophy and history then quiz me about them like I was his student or something. Though sometimes he'd have me read him Dylan Thomas. I really enjoyed those nights."

They sat in silence for a few minutes, each lost in their memories of George. Then Des swore and jumped up. "I'll be back in a second," she said tersely, padding toward the door. She let herself out of the room and didn't close the door.

"Oh-kay," Ruby said, turning on the bedside lamp, wondering if she'd said or done something wrong. Then she got up to draw the curtains closed against the late afternoon sunlight. A glance out the window reminded her how much land surrounded the Coulter home. A *lot* of it was wooded, which told Ruby she was outside the bounds of Lenape Landing proper. Maybe to the north or northeast.

The door behind her creaked and she looked around to see the wolf—Des—poking her snout around the door questioningly. She even whined a little.

Ruby found herself almost smiling. "And here I thought nature was calling."

Des came into the room and barked once, wagging her big, brush-like tail frantically. Then she trotted to the bed and stood on her hind legs, putting her forelegs on the bed and barking again. She gave Ruby a bright, expectant look.

Guess that's her way of telling me to get to bed, Ruby thought, drifting back across the room. She approached Des with considerably less caution than she'd displayed earlier and perched near the head of the bed after turning down the covers.

She and Des looked at each other, Des's tongue hanging out of her mouth, her tail still wagging. Ruby swung her legs up into bed, sliding them between the delightfully cool sheets. Before she could pull the covers up, Des hopped on the bed and darted under them.

Des turned around a few times under the covers, a warm, wolf-shaped lump, before settling on her stomach, submerged but for the very tips of her flaring nostrils.

"Comfy? Cozy?" Ruby asked wryly. Des whuffed and the covers churned with the wagging of her tail. Ruby chuckled. "Do all of the *Garoul* throw off as much heat as you do, or am I just lucky?"

Not so much as a whuff, this time. Des simply sighed.

Ruby laughed again. It was either laugh or cry at the strange mélange her life had so suddenly become. She laid down, shivering at the tickle of Des's soft fur all along her left side.

It was, she supposed, the same as sleeping with a dog in the bed. No real difference. Nonetheless, Ruby laid there, board-stiff with the covers up to her chin, until long after she thought Des was asleep. Suddenly a gentle paw came to rest on Ruby's arm, and like someone flicked a switch, she relaxed, all her tension flowing away like water.

She was asleep in minutes.

❖

If Ruby had expected nightmares to wake her up, she was wrong. In fact, if she'd dreamed, she didn't remember it at all, though the slight sense of disorientation and impending headache told her she likely *had* dreamed, and had a doozy of one.

Groaning, she shoved the covers off, shivering a little in the slightly cooler air of the room. Under the covers had been a furnace, thanks to Des, who was still sleeping, judging from the canine snores coming from Ruby's left.

In the pitch black of the room, the only thing to be seen was the clock-radio on Des's nightstand. It was 3:57 a.m. Ruby sat up, yawning and stretching.

Why am I up this late? Or this early? she wondered, and on the heels of that thought, her stomach yowled mid-stretch. Next to her, the snoring stopped with a snort and a sneeze. Then Ruby felt a paw on her thigh and Des whined as if to say, "please go back to sleep."

"Sorry, no can do. I'm really hungry," Ruby apologized, and her stomach growled again. Des whuffed and the paw disappeared, only to be followed by the light prickle of something sharp and a gust of humid air on her wrist, followed by a gentle tug. Ruby jumped and yelped when she realized those were Des's *teeth*.

Des whuffed again, terse and annoyed. "Oh, calm the fuck down," that whuff seemed to say. Then the tugging intensified.

Swallowing her fear—this was *Des*, after all, not just some random stray mongrel—Ruby inched toward the other side of the bed and the wolf lying on it. Immediately the teeth and breath disappeared.

Shaking, Ruby reached for the lamp she remembered being somewhere in the vicinity of Des's clock-radio and turned it on. She blinked in the sudden, soft yellow light and saw Des waiting by the door, tail wagging, tongue lolling as she looked back over her shoulder at Ruby.

She barked once, and Ruby sighed.

"All right," she said, sliding out of bed. The area rug was nubbly and cool under her bare feet. "But we'd better be going to the kitchen. My stomach thinks my throat's been cut."

Des barked again, darting out the door when Ruby opened it.

❖

"You're up early."

Ruby smiled, lingering in the kitchen doorway with Des at her heels. Philomena sat at the counter where Des had sat, drinking a large glass of milk. In front of her was a plate empty of everything but tiny meat-scraps and meat juice. But the whole kitchen smelled of meat so rare, it was practically tartare.

Ruby's stomach growled again, and Philomena laughed. "I guess that answers *that* question."

Whuffing again—"pardon me, coming through"—Des snaked past Ruby's legs and into the kitchen proper, trotting up to Philomena. Standing on her hind legs, Des put her front paws on Philomena's thigh and whined like a puppy. This was good for another bright laugh from Philomena.

"You know, if you were in your Human form, you could cook breakfast for yourself and Ruby," she noted. Des whined again and dropped to all fours, pacing to the middle fridge she'd gotten meat from earlier. She looked over her shoulder at Philomena, who rolled her eyes but levered her pregnant body off the stool with one hand on the counter.

"All right, okay," she capitulated. "I know when I'm beat. The sad puppy-face is too powerful for me."

This spurred a hesitant Ruby to action. She came into the kitchen, halting Phil with her hands held out. "You don't have to cook for us. I'm sure I can whip something up for Des and myself."

Philomena smiled. It was such a kind smile, it made Ruby ache for the mother she barely remembered. "That's all right, Ruby. You're just getting over a rather traumatic few days, and you're still no doubt tired. Sit. Take a load off, and I'll throw some meat on the skillet. Let me guess. Rare?"

Surprised, Ruby nodded. "How'd you know? Normally I like my meat well-done."

Philomena winked. "You're a Loup, now. Generally speaking, we tend to like our meat rare. The rarer the better, for some of us." She patted her distended stomach fondly. "Ever since the second trimester, I've been eating my meat rarer and rarer. The twins don't seem to want anything else."

Ruby watched Philomena stride gracefully to the refrigerator. Des backed out of the way then trotted to Ruby, settling at her feet with a sigh.

For the next few minutes, the only sounds in the kitchen were of Philomena humming as she bustled around the kitchen. Her nightgown was similar to the one Ruby wore, long and floaty, only a pale yellow like early morning sunlight.

She was a lovely woman, vital and seemingly approachable, impossible to be afraid of. So when Ruby finally got the courage to speak again, she asked the first thing that came to mind.

"When your children are born, will they be human-looking? Or, you know, wolf-looking?"

Philomena glanced at Ruby over her shoulder, grinning. "Why? Thinking of having little ankle-biters of your own someday?"

Trepidation forgotten, Ruby snorted. "Hell, no!"

Philomena chuckled. "I used to say that, too. But to answer your question, they'll be born in Human form. They won't achieve their wolf form until sometime during their adolescence. Probably by the time they're nineteen."

"Des said that the Coulter, uh, family, often didn't have their first, uh, Change, until they were around nineteen. Are you and she related?"

"Only very distantly by blood, more closely by marriage. I'm her wicked stepmother."

Des barked at this—a bark Ruby couldn't interpret, but apparently Philomena could, for she smiled wistfully. "That's awful sweet of you, Sug."

Des barked again then settled once more at Ruby's feet, seemingly content to wait for food to come. Ruby tilted her head curiously. "Do you understand what she's saying when she barks?"

"Of course, hon." Philomena dished up a steak and placed it on the counter in front of Ruby. Her dark, dark eyes were dancing. "You will, too, in time. By the end of your first year as a Loup, you'll understand what anyone in Loup form is saying. It's mostly a language of gestures and scents...and, *I* think, anyway, low-grade telepathy."

"Whoa."

"Yeah." With a smile, the next plate of steak went to Des, who yipped in seeming appreciation. "I think it's that way for most mammals. Ninety-nine percent of humanity being the notable exception. Most Loups and Latents have telepathic ability, to some degree or another. Yours, as a Dyre, will be the strongest in this part of North America. Of course, Dyres of other regions and Pack-clusters may have abilities which surpass yours, but there's really no way to tell that, yet."

Ruby took a few moments to digest this, absently cutting her steak into bite-size pieces.

"Will I have any other abilities that humans don't have? Super speed? Super strength? Laser-vision?"

Philomena sat across from Ruby at the counter, grinning wryly. "The first two."

"But no laser-vision? Bummer," Ruby deadpanned, then she sighed. "So how super-strong and super-fast will I be?"

"The average Loup is approximately five times stronger and ten times faster than most humans. As Dyre, you may be considerably stronger and faster than that. George certainly was, in his heyday."

Ruby frowned as the memory of George's death hit her all over again, but it reminded her of a question to which she still hadn't gotten a satisfactory answer. "Do you know why George chose me?"

Philomena's smile slipped. "Not for sure."

"Because I'm thinking it was just because I was there and he was dying," Ruby said, and Philomena frowned.

"I don't think you understand, Sweetie. George was dying, yes, but a Dyre can sometimes fend off death until he or she passes on his Death-right. George must have chosen you, in large part, because he felt you were up to the job. Otherwise, we'd all probably still be standing around his deathbed, waiting for him to name his successor."

Blinking back tears, Ruby looked down at her blurry plate. She popped a piece of rare steak—something she used to hate—

into her mouth just to have something to do. It was salty and delicious and seemed to burst with the remembered life and vitality of the animal it had been. "He was *so* wrong. I can't do this, and I don't *want* it."

"Well, want it or not, you've *got* it," Philomena said with maternal sternness that briefly threw Ruby for a loop. "George was the canniest of us all—putting him in the running for the canniest being on this planet. He knew what he was doing. Maybe all this came about sooner than he'd have liked, but he intended for you to wind up where you are right now."

"What about what *I* intended for me?" Ruby demanded, dropping her fork with a loud clatter. Des sat up whining, and Ruby unconsciously reached down to scratch between her ears. "What about the *rest of my life*?"

Philomena crooked one dark eyebrow. "What about it? Who says it has to change so much?"

Ruby blinked incredulously then laughed, torn between rue and genuine mirth. "Who says? I'm a fucking *werewolf*!"

"So am I. And I wasn't born one, I might add, just as you weren't." Philomena sniffed and placed her slim, shapely hands on the counter. "When I was Turned, I was working as a nurse in Chicago. I had few friends and no family to speak of." She shrugged, then sighed. "I was alone and overworked and running on automatic. Then on the way home from work late one night, I was attacked, and to make a gruesome story less so, I was left for dead. And I would have died, if not for the Loup who found me.

"She gave me a new life. A new purpose and new hope. She gave me a family and allies and friends, and people who'd always have my back, no matter what." Philomena paused, looking Ruby square in the eye. "If any of that sounds like something you've been lacking, you're not anymore. You have the power and resources of some of the most influential people in North America at your disposal. You have more friends than just Des, Nathan, Jake, and I. There are those of us, in the Coulter Pack and other Packs who believed in George's wisdom and his vision, and would unquestioningly welcome his successor with all the loyalty, courage, and canniness that is ours to give."

At these earnest words, Ruby gazed down at her plate again. If there were any way to reply to that, she didn't know what it was.

Suddenly, Philomena covered Ruby's hand with hers, startling Ruby into looking up. Philomena's dancing eyes smiled into her own.

"Don't worry. There's plenty of time to get all this sorted out and processed. For now, you need to keep up your strength. Eat," Philomena said gently, squeezing Ruby's hand.

As if in agreement with this assessment, Des licked Ruby's ankle.

"Gross!" Ruby groaned, pulling her legs up out of Des's reach. But she was almost smiling.

❖

"So, is it safe for me to go back to my apartment to get some extra clothes?"

Des, in human form once more, had stalked into the room naked, and right for her closet. Her wet hair stood in spikes and clumps from toweling and she knew she looked ridiculous, but it somehow didn't matter in front of Ruby, just like her nudity didn't matter.

As she pulled on a sports bra and boxers, she noticed Ruby watching her almost timidly from the bed. In the gentle light of dawn, she looked like a child in her white nightgown, with her bare feet and fluffy, fly-away curls.

Des swallowed and looked back into her closet, ignoring the way her stomach churned as she selected a t-shirt at random and pulled it on. The same for a pair of old skinny jeans. "Sure. Jake and I can take you to your place, and we can load up the SUV with whatever you wanna bring—clothes, photo albums, knick-knacks—all that good shit."

Ruby's silence was thoughtful. "So I'm really gonna be staying here, huh?"

Des pulled on her Doc Martens workboots and turned to face Ruby after taking a breath. She still had that child-like look that did funny things to Des's stomach. "Yeah. Safest place for you until we figure out where you're gonna put down roots."

"I don't suppose my old apartment is in the running for said place?"

"Not hardly," Des snorted, standing with arms akimbo. "The most defendable sort of place is a manor house with acreage around it and a fence. Someplace we can turn into a fortress for the next few months."

Ruby tilted her head in curiosity. She looked so defenseless it made Des's chest ache. "What's so special about the next few months?"

"Well, for one thing you'll be getting used to being a Loup, learning to be present in that form instead of a mindless, slavering animal. For another thing, there's the matter of the Contests. Most of the Alphas that'll be challenging your reign are on the up-and-up, and have nothing but North American Loups' best interests at heart, yadda-yadda. But a few would stop at nothing to be where you are right now. They've plotted and machinated and slimed their way as close to George as they could, and after all that, you got what they've been clamoring for, for a century."

"A *century*?" Ruby squawked. "How the hell old *was* George?"

Des shrugged. She honestly didn't know. "Dunno. Old. Older than Nathan, even, and Nathan's one hundred and forty-nine."

"Shit." Ruby laughed. "*Holy* shit."

"Yeah."

"How old are *you*?"

Des smirked. "How old do you think?"

Ruby pursed her lips. "Weeellll, you *look* like you're seventeen, except for your eyes. I'd say you were twenty-one, or twenty-two, but then, George looked only sixty-five or seventy."

Des smirked wider. "I'm not as old as that."

"Then how old *are* you?"

"I'm twenty-three."

Ruby frowned. "That's it?"

"Disappointed?"

"No, just...that's so young."

"How old are *you*?"

"Guess."

Des grinned. "Twenty-eight."

Ruby's mouth dropped open. "How—"

"I've always been able to guess how old women are." Des shrugged and hooked her fingers in the waist of her jeans. "It's my gift, it's my curse."

"Not your only one," Ruby said, nodding and swinging her narrow feet. "Jesus. How is any of this real? Am I awake? Or am I catatonic in a psych ward somewhere?"

Des approached Ruby slowly. When she didn't start or pull away, Des knelt at her feet and took her hand. "Look, maybe this is all some crazy dream, but if it's not, do you wanna spend the rest of your life living like you're waiting to wake up?"

Ruby's eyes filled with tears. "That's how I've been living my life for the past ten years. And it's worked for me."

"Has it?" Des snorted and Ruby blushed, looking away. But Des caught her by the chin and turned her face forward again. When their eyes met, a tear rolled down Ruby's cheek. Des caught it on the tip of her finger and licked it away.

Ruby's wide eyes went wider, more tears spilling down. Instead of catching these, Des kissed them away, licking the saltiness from her lips. Ruby drew in a breath as Des's mouth hovered near hers. Her breath stuttered fast, her scent soft and innocent like lilies, yet sharp and sudden as want. It was possibly the best scent Des had ever had the pleasure of inhaling, and she wanted more of it, even more than she wanted the feel and taste of Ruby's trembling lips.

She brushed Ruby's cheek with her nose, nosing her way south, to the junction of neck and shoulder, inhaling deeply. One hand came up to rest on Ruby's thigh, and the muscles under her palm jumped like nervous guppies.

"Des," Ruby breathed, winding her hesitant arms around Des's neck. "Oh, *God.*"

"Ruby-Ruby-Ruby," Des chanted against Ruby's skin before nipping it a bit more than playfully. Ruby gasped again, shuddering and drawn-out, and that want-Scent intensified. Des swore, breathing fast and shuddering herself. She slid her other hand down Ruby's neck, over the implacable solidity of collarbone, down to the heavy softness of Ruby's right breast.

"Oh!" she breathed as Des stroked her nipple then tweaked it lightly. Then less lightly, until it was a hard little peak under the soft cotton of her nightgown. And when Ruby parted her legs just enough to admit Des's body, Des was *right there*, her chest pressing close to Ruby's hot center, the home of that sharp, musky scent wrapping itself around her brain.

The nightgown was trapped between them, and this would *not* do. Des began rucking it up till it was at Ruby's thighs, and then she kissed her collarbone.

"I can't wait to taste you," she murmured, and Ruby moaned so huskily, Des nearly came right then and there. "Are you wet? I'll bet you're *so* wet for me"

Des slid one hand down to Ruby's inner thigh, where the muscles twitched and quivered, as if anticipating her touch. She was a mere few inches from the tantalizing heat that beckoned like a siren song, when Ruby suddenly scrambled back away from her and up the bed. She drew her thighs up and together, pulling the nightgown down to her ankles with her hands. Her eyes were wide and panicked, her face blanched.

"I—I—" she stammered, flushing so quickly and so intensely, it must have been painful. "You...what—?"

Before Des could begin to address the almost question, Ruby's eyes filled with tears again, and she leapt off the bed and bolted for the door, leaving only the scent of her arousal and panic behind.

Des, leaning on the foot of the bed, sighed and kicked herself right in the libido.

❖

Locked in Des's bathroom, Ruby met her own wide, wounded gaze in the mirror. She looked disheveled, breathless, and guilty, which was exactly how she felt.

She tried to run one hand through her hair, though her curls were a hopeless tangle, and she pressed the other to her chest, where her heart beat in time with the liquid throbbing between her legs. That throbbing was begging—no, *demanding* attention. Any attention at all, it promised seductively, and she'd be so glad she gave it.

Avoiding her own gaze, she hesitantly hiked up her nightgown and put her hand on her stomach. After a few seconds, she slid it down to the crisp curls where her thighs met...

"No," she said, loud and firm in the still, quiet bathroom, and drew her hand down her thigh, where it floundered.

"No," she said again, looking herself in the eyes, knowing the only reason she could do so was through the keeping of the promises she'd made all those years ago. Promises of self-preservation and of self-reliance. Promises to *herself* that she intended to *keep*.

Sighing, she looked away from the mirror and shucked the nightgown. It was time for a shower. A *cold* one.

CHAPTER SEVEN

Des sat at the bottom of the front stairs, scowling, playing with a Slinky, and occasionally glancing up the stairs. Ruby had been in the bathroom for forty minutes, with the shower running and the sound of soft, muffled sobs drifting out to Des's keen ears. *Oh, look at how I've gone and fucked this up*, she thought. Guilt only made her scowl harder.

The Slinky wobbled its slow, ponderous way down the three steps, and Des scooped it up to repeat the entire process over again.

After another few minutes, Des's nostrils pricked up—her ears a few moments after that.

"You're playing with the Slinky," Jake said. "This can't be good." Des looked up at him, still scowling. He held up his hands in placation and came the rest of the way downstairs, stopping at Des's step. "Hey, you're the one with the predictable tells, Lil Sis. Don't blame *me* for—oh, Des, you *didn't!*"

Flushing, Des looked away, realizing that she still smelled like thwarted desire and Ruby.

"Actually, I didn't. She panicked and locked herself in my bathroom before I could." Des said. "I guess it's a good thing at least one of us has some goddamn sense."

Sighing, Jake sat next to Des, his long arms dangling between his prominent knees.

"No one could blame you. She's—" Jake paused. "*Hot.*"

"Yeah. Like *you'd* know." *Slink-slink-slink,* went the Slinky, and Des caught it again. "Anyway, hot or not, she's still my charge. My fucking *queen.* And I came on to her like she was some barroom skank!"

"I don't think that's what you were doing," Jake murmured, catching and sliding the Slinky up his arm like a bracelet. He jingled it and smiled a little before looking Des in the eyes. "You're attracted to her. Any Loup with a nose could smell it. Anything with eyes could *see* it. But it's not just that, kiddo. You're solicitous of her. You treat her like she's something fragile and precious, and that's not the way one treats barroom skanks. And it's certainly not the way *you* treat *any* of the girls you take home. Am I right?"

"Maybe," Des groused, looking down at her boots. "But she's *not* just some girl I've brought home. She's—"

"Special?"

Des rolled her eyes. "I was gonna say 'our Dyre.'"

Jake's full smile shone out. "Even Dyres need love."

Des sat back as if slapped. "Hold on, a moment, Mr. Matchmaker. Who said anything about *love?*"

"Okay, okay, how about *intense like?* Whatever you wanna call it, Dyres need it, too. And for now, the only person she can trust and count on in her eyes is you. You're sworn to protect her, and on some level she can sense that."

Quirking an eyebrow, Des smiled bitterly. "So the only reason she'd want me is because I'm safe and convenient? Gee, thanks, Jacob."

"That's what I'm here for."

Des scowled again. "I *don't* wanna be her safety-fuck."

"Then *don't* be." Jake's smile turned crooked. "But you've gotta be patient, and that ain't exactly your strongsuit." He tilted his head and regarded her. "Give her time to adjust, to figure out who she is now, and what she wants. If it's you, go for it. If it's not, move on."

"Easy for you to say," Des muttered then growled. "Anyway, it's not like I'm pining over her, I just—you know. I'm not used to women fleeing my bed like I've got the fucking plague."

"A good pair of handcuffs *can* work wonders," Jake said, and Des elbowed him.

"Shut up."

"Make me."

"I don't make trash, I burn it."

"Then pick up your ashes and leave."

Des stuck out her tongue in reply, and Jake laughed. "Oh, *that's* mature."

Laughing, too, Des elbowed Jake again, and he put his arm around her, pulling her close. "It'll be all right, you know. It'll all work out, in the end."

"Promise?"

"Cross my heart and hope to die. May I eat a cow-pie if I lie."

Des heaved another sigh and laid her head on Jake's bony shoulder. "In that case, hold your nose and remember to gulp, not nibble."

❖

When Ruby finally emerged from the bathroom, she shivered in the cool air of the hallway. Before she could lose her nerve, she crept to Des's open door and steeled herself for a confrontation of some kind, for *something* she dreaded having to deal with.

She poked her head around the doorway, but she didn't see what she expected. Which was Des sitting on her bed, waiting. No, all she saw was her clothes, the ones she'd been wearing that awful night, neatly folded on the foot of the bed. Her wallet, Chapstick, keys, and cellphone were next to her underwear and even her sneakers, rather worse for wear and shapeless-looking, were on the floor just touching the duvet.

Letting out a relieved breath, she ignored the tiny bit of herself that was disappointed, entered the room and closed the door. Five minutes later, she stepped back into the hallway dressed, her hair pulled back into a sloppy, stubby French braid.

She made her way quietly to the front staircase, surprised she didn't get lost. Normally her sense of direction was pretty awful.

At the top of the staircase, she looked down to see Des sitting there by herself, leaning back against the stairs, her head hanging back, eyes on Ruby.

"Jake's pulling the SUV around," she said without inflection, then smiled a little. Ruby couldn't tell if it reached her eyes. "We'd better get going. The sooner we're back here, the better."

"Really?" Ruby started slowly down the stairs. As she drew closer to Des, she suddenly understood why she hadn't gotten lost. She'd been following a faint-but-growing-stronger scent like autumn wind, copper, and freshly ground cinnamon. *Des's* scent. Ruby didn't know whether to be horrified or pleased at this new superpower. "What's on the agenda for today? After I get my stuff, that is."

Des sat up, stood, and stretched. Then she hopped effortlessly down the last three steps and strode toward the front door.

"First thing's first, Nathan'll probably wanna give you some more background on Loup history and politics. You'll need it if you're going to be a good Dyre. Second, training. For both of us."

"In what?" Ruby called nervously. *This* Des, hard, matter-of-fact, business-like, was not what she'd expected after this morning.

"For you? Survival. For me? The same. Those Contests won't win themselves, after all," Des called over her shoulder, rolling them both. Then she paused at the door and looked back, her expression somewhat softened. "But for now, we grab-n-go, *chica*: Get the stuff you want before Nathan's Cleaners have had at the place."

Ruby blinked then scurried after Des, who crooked a wry half smile as she caught up. They walked outside together. "What're Cleaners?"

❖

"...and then Riley said, 'I dunno, but Abilene's a thousand miles *thataway*!' And then he started *running*," Jake finished, laughing as he pulled up to Ruby's apartment building.

Ruby giggled till she snorted. Not a pretty, ladylike little snort, but a raucous sound that made Des smile from the back seat. Jake was behind the wheel and Ruby was in the passenger seat. Every so often Ruby had gazed, shy and uncertain, into the rearview and met Des's stare. Des did her best to return that gaze reassuringly.

The truth was, she felt just as uncertain as Ruby clearly did. Not about her mission, no, but about the strange, powerful current that ran between them. Des had no idea what was going on in Ruby's head other than that disarming uncertainty, but she could still smell Ruby on her skin, that musky, lilies-and-innocence scent liberally tinged with *want*. She could still feel Ruby's pulse beating against her lips and taste her in the air.

She didn't know how much of that was memory, how much was Ruby's scent clinging to her, or if any of it was how Ruby would always smell around her. *Because she* is *attracted to me,* Des thought with frustration. *I* know *she is. I can* smell *it on her. So why the hell is she so afraid of a little recreational slap-and-tickle? Moon Above knows we could* both *use it.*

Des hopped out of the SUV, distracted by her thoughts. She nearly missed the startled, almost yearning look Ruby gave her as she accepted her hand and stepped down from the SUV. She also barely caught the shrewd look her brother gave her.

"Nice enough neighborhood," Jake said, and Des found herself looking around at the street for hiding spots and possible places from which an ambush could be sprung. Ruby's apartment building stood on the edge of Uptown and Midtown, on a street filled with similar dwellings and even a condominium. A small park was at the end of Ruby's side of the street, children playing under the watchful eyes of their parents and nannies. The streets themselves were lined with beeches and maples, the buildings made of neat red brick.

"There's kind of a Stepford-vibe going on," Des noted, her nose wrinkling in a wolfish shrug. "And there's not enough cover."

Jake rolled his eyes and Ruby huffed. "Sorry, I didn't ask George whether or not it had adequate 'cover,' before I moved into my fancy, rent-controlled, mid-town apartment," she said sarcastically.

"Well, now you know, for next time," Des said, ignoring the sarcasm completely and shoving her hands into her pockets.

Together, they strode to the front entrance, Ruby in the lead, flanked by Des and Jake.

❖

"Neat place."

Ruby smiled a little as Des stepped around her into the apartment. Jake, on the other hand, followed her in, shutting the door behind him and locking it. "Thanks. It's not much, but it's home," she said, though she realized even as she said it, it wasn't exactly true anymore.

Not that Coulter Manor was home after only four days, most of which she'd spent unconscious, but it felt like it fit more than the apartment had in some indefinable way.

Which wasn't to say she didn't feel a sense of house-pride. The apartment was gorgeous: one bedroom, one bathroom, roomy kitchenette, roomy closets, wood floors, exposed brick walls, picture windows that let in so much natural light, Ruby rarely bothered with electric lights in the daytime.

George had been the one to recommend her for this place. He'd been friends with the owner and gotten her a deal on the apartment. Otherwise she'd never have been able to afford it.

At the time, she'd wondered at George's kindness, but not too much. She hadn't wanted to delve too deeply in case she didn't like what she found.

Little did I know, Ruby thought as Des stalked around the apartment like she was casing the joint. Jake, meanwhile, was examining the contents of Ruby's bookshelf, running his finger over bindings and the occasional photo. Almost all of them were of Ruby and her father at different stages of Ruby's childhood.

Wrapping her arms around herself, Ruby tried not to feel invaded and stripped bare.

"Would either of you like some tea or something? I also have frozen pizza," she said, putting on her hostess-with-the-mostess smile. Des grunted a 'no' and peered between the blinds out of Ruby's north-facing window.

"Actually, I could do with some OJ, if you've got it," Jake said, pausing to look at her and smile. Ruby returned it, relaxing a little.

"OJ, it is." She went into the kitchenette and emerged a minute later with a tall jelly glass of orange juice, which Jake accepted graciously, murmuring his thanks and taking a big gulp. He licked his lips and grinned.

"You and your dad?" He nodded at the largest photo on the top shelf. It was of a six year old Ruby in her self-chosen Halloween costume, holding the hand of a lanky, sandy-haired man, framed in the doorway of the old house on Rosen Street.

Re-noticing this picture for the first time in nearly three years, Ruby shuddered visibly, and Jake frowned. "You okay?"

"Yeah, no, fine," she said, turning away from the picture. "Yep. That's me and my dad."

"You made a cute werewolf," Jake said. "Still do."

Taking a deep breath, Ruby forced herself to smile and face Jake again. "I was a kid. I thought werewolves were cool."

"We *are* cool," Des said, crossing the room to have a look at the photo, barging past them both. "Huh. Your dad made a pretty kickass vampire."

"God, please tell me those aren't real, too?" Ruby shuddered again when both Des and Jake avoided her gaze. "Oh, that's just *perfect*—werewolves and vampires and unicorns, oh, my!"

Des snorted. "There's no such thing as unicorns."

"Yeah, because that'd be both ridiculous and unbelievable," Ruby interjected.

"At least, there are no such things as unicorns *anymore*. They were hunted to extinction by groups of hard-hearted but virginal poachers about a thousand years ago," Jake added off Ruby's questioning look. "It's actually a really sad story. Makes *The Last Unicorn* look like a feel-good romp."

Shaking her head, Ruby went to straighten a small photo of her in her mother's arms on the day of her birth, but when she touched the slightly dusty frame, it was like sticking her fingers into an open flame. She let out a small scream, jerking them away and putting them in her mouth. The photo tumbled to the floor, the glass cracking.

For a few moments no one said anything, not even to ask Ruby what the hell had just happened. Then Des sighed. "I take it the frame is silver or silver-plated?"

Ruby nodded, fingers still in her mouth, still throbbing hot and cold.

"That's what I thought," Des said gently, squatting to look at the picture. Then she reached out and picked it up.

A look of pain crossed her face as she stood up. Her entire hand was turning red as she carefully placed the photo back on the shelf. When she took her hand away, Ruby could see angry blisters already forming.

Ruby took her own fingers out of her mouth to see blisters forming on the tips of her first two fingers as well.

"So it's true?" she asked. "I mean about the allergic-to-silver thing."

"Yeah," Des said, examining her fingers, then dismissing them with a shrug. "Some of us are more sensitive to it than others. But I never met anyone more sensitive than *me* until now."

"It's because you're the Dyre, you know," Jake said, taking another sip of his orange juice. His gaze went from Ruby to

Des, and back again. "You're the epitome of all that is Loup—*the* Garoul. The very essence of who and what we are. It stands to reason silver would affect *you* more than any of us."

Ruby turned away again, cradling her wounded hand to her bosom. "Just when I manage to forget, to pretend I'm still a normal person with a normal life…"

After a few seconds, she felt Des's strong hands settle on her shoulders. "It'll be okay," Des murmured. "It's gonna take time, but you'll see."

Ruby shook her head. "I don't think anything's ever gonna be okay again," she replied with a shiver. Then she turned and quickly kissed Des's cheek, feeling flames of embarrassment creeping up her neck. But she brazened it out, looking a very surprised Des in the eyes, anyway.

"Thanks for what you did. With the picture, I mean." She tried to smile again. "I'm gonna go pack."

Then she pulled away from Des and hurried to her bedroom, shutting the door.

❖

Des stood there, face alternately flaming and blanching, hot then cold.

Jake slung an arm around her and pulled her close.

"You sure you don't wanna pitch for the other team? We're way lower maintenance."

"You pitch enough for that team for us both. Remind me how many girls you've even been with? Is 'less-than-zero' a number?" Des said snarkily, shoving Jake's arm off. Jake laughed, immediately putting his arm back around her. This time she didn't shove it away, but dug her short, blunt nails into his wrist.

Jake hissed in a pained breath then let it out. "Fewer than you have, but definitely more than my boyfriend." He removed his arm and eyed the closing punctures on his wrist. "You're such a feral little beast."

"And proud of it." Then what he'd said caught up with her and she goggled up at him in surprise. "Boyfriend? As in a guy you've had sex with more than once or twice and haven't kicked into the wind?"

Jake huffed, still rubbing his wrist. "Keep that up, Little Miss Attitude, and you won't get to meet him."

"Forget *me*, has *Nathan* met him? Does he approve?"

Jake snorted. "Of *course* not. Thinks he's too old for me."

"*This* from a Loup who's almost one hundred years older than his babies' mama?" Des asked disapprovingly. "That's richer than Nathan is."

"Indeed." Jake finished his orange juice in one long, breathless swallow. He then strolled into the kitchen, Des on his heels. "He thinks James is too reckless and iconoclastic for me, and that he'll be a bad influence."

"Moon Above, you're like, forty-eight years old! I think you're pretty well beyond peer pressure-type bullshit!" Des said, leaning on the kitchenette counter while Jake washed his glass. Jake was always considerate, a trait he no doubt inherited from his birth parents.

"Well, you know how dear ol' Dad is." Jake glanced at her with shared long-suffering chagrin. "Anyway, James is pretty wonderful. He's like a much-needed breath of fresh air and sanity."

"I take it, then, he's not a Loup?"

Jake glanced at Des again. "Actually, he is. He's a Latent." And while Des was still reeling from that, Jake took a deep breath and plunged ahead. "He's also George Carnahan's son, Des."

Des's mouth dropped open, and Jake sighed.

"He's George's son, Jenny-Benny, and it's getting pretty serious between us."

Des closed her mouth and shook her head once. "How serious?"

Putting the now sparkling-clean glass in the drying rack next to the microwave, Jake faced her and leaned against the sink. "Serious like we're talking about living together. Or we were, before George died."

Des winced. "You mean before *I let him* die."

Jake reached out one long arm and took her hand. "You did your best. Jamie'll understand that."

"*I* don't even understand it, Jake!" Des laughed bitterly. "And clearly my best wasn't good enough."

"Maybe it wasn't," Jake agreed, shrugging. "But it was all you could do. There's no such thing as one hundred ten percent."

"But there *has* to be, now. For me to keep her safe," Des said quietly. "I can't let her end up like George, Jake. I *just can't.*"

"Then don't."

"It's not that simple!"

"Isn't it?"

Des blew out an irritated breath. "Were you always this cryptic and annoying, or is this something you learned from James Carnahan?"

Jake grinned.

❖

Ruby shut the bedroom door on the rest of their conversation and leaned against it. After a minute of letting tears stream down her cheeks, she wiped her face with the sleeve of her shirt and started to pack whatever she couldn't bear to leave behind.

❖

Shortly thereafter, Ruby emerged from her bedroom, red-eyed and lugging two huge suitcases and a large, empty tote bag. Des and Jake each took a suitcase. Ruby smiled at them, though in obvious pain, and went to her bookshelf, pulling on a pair of woolen gloves so that she could pluck her framed photographs off the shelves.

Des felt her own smile begin. *She's learning.*

Ruby put the photographs, along with a few books and several photo albums into the tote. Shouldering it, she looked around the living room once, her eyes hooded and grim. "I'm ready," she said finally, turning toward the door without another word. Des and Jake shared a look and a shrug, following close behind.

❖

"I don't think I'm ready for this," Ruby whined, letting Des push her into the manor's gym. "I think I still need to bone-up on the funeral rites for George."

"The funeral's not till the next Full Moon."

"Yeah, well, I've got a lot to learn, still. You and Nathan have made that abundantly clear."

Des snorted but didn't let go of Ruby's upper arms. She just pushed Ruby faster, across the gym, toward the sparring mats. "Who gathers, builds, and fires the funeral pyre?"

Ruby frowned in thought. "Well, in George's case, since he was the Dyre, each of the Alphas gather wood from the Lenape Hall property the day before the funeral. On the night of the funeral, they take turns adding to the pyre in descending order of length of reign, until the pyre is approximately two feet by three feet by seven feet. If appropriate, the family and friends of the deceased Dyre can scatter flowers and keepsakes on the pyre, as well." Ruby paused, thinking of her copy of *The Rights of Man* that George had given her, then she discarded that sentiment. The book was simply too precious to her. As were all of the books George had given her. It would have to be flowers, then.

"After the funeral rites are performed and the eulogy given," Ruby continued, "the new Dyre then fires the wood. When there's nothing left but ashes, the mourners can each claim a handful to keep or scatter, as they so choose."

Des whistled, wide-eyed and impressed-looking. "Yeah, you should totally keep hitting the books. Your knowledge of our ways is abysmal."

"Look, just because I got one question right—hey!" Ruby squawked as Des changed up her grip and spun and levered, yanking Ruby over her shoulder in an infamous judo throw Ruby'd seen in a hundred movies.

Landing jarringly on her back on the blue mats, Ruby involuntarily blew all the air out of her lungs then gasped in another breath.

"Welcome to Ass-Kicking 101," Des said while Ruby lay there panting. The world spun and quadrupled, and Ruby groaned. "I'm Professor Desiderio, and for the next few weeks, your ass is grass, and I'm the lawnmower."

Ruby groaned again, closing her eyes. "We have to do this for the next *few weeks*?!"

"At least until you're warmed up and ready for Nathan, yeah."

Ruby's eyes flew open. "No. Fucking. Way!"

Des—all four of her—grinned, wide and white. "Yes. Fucking. Way!"

In the day since Ruby had gotten settled into her room at the manor she hadn't seen Nathan Coulter. But she'd seen the results of his training with Des in the bathroom they shared, which included Des limping, wincing, and putting red meat on various deep-tissue bruises and contusions. Meat that she had a habit of then gnawing on and eating. Raw.

Ruby shuddered. "No, I can't see that working out well for me, at all."

Des laughed and dropped effortlessly into a full lotus next to Ruby, who was still panting. "I promise he'll go easy on you till you show that you're ready for something a little more advanced. He's a, uh, really good teacher. Better than I am, that's for damn sure. Really patient. But he figures you'll respond better to me, at first." She cast an oblique look at Ruby, who blushed and looked away.

"Come on, let's get you to your feet, and we can start with some basic ready stances."

"Right. And then you'll throw me around some more?" Ruby grumbled as Des stood up.

"Bingo, kid. Up and at 'em. Soon begun is half done."

Ruby rolled onto her side, ignoring Des's hand up, and got to her feet.

❖

Sitting on her bed, Ruby sighed in the warm air.

It felt divine after the ice-cold shower she'd taken. Three hours spent in close proximity to Des, having those rough hands on her arms, hips, and legs had been confusing and frustrating at turns. All she wanted after being pummeled and flipped, which Des called 'learning to fall correctly,' for hours was to take some ibuprofen, lay down, and wait for the aches to go away.

But she couldn't. George's wake was in two hours and she had to get ready. Standing up and shedding her robe, she went to the bureau and selected a clean pair of underwear and a bra. She had a decent blouse and a pair of slacks she'd worn to her job interview at the college. They were several years out of date, and probably too small, but they were wearable. However George deserved better than for his eulogist to be bursting at the seams of her old, sprung interview clothes.

And that thought brought back the realization that George—the closest thing to family she'd had in a long time—was dead. Horrifically so. And never mind he'd turned her into a werewolf. He'd always been there for her. He'd been like the grandfather she'd never had a chance to know.

And now she was expected, in the midst of her grief, to give his eulogy and honor him at a wake, something she'd only done for her father, then officiate at his funeral the first evening after her Change.

Ruby sat on her bed again, face buried in her hands, tears filling them like a cup of sorrow.

❖

Des stood outside Ruby's door, hand raised to knock. She'd been able to smell Ruby's sadness from across the hall, and it'd bothered her and the Loup to the point of distraction. So, half-dressed in a black pullover sweater and her boxers, her hair still wet and sticking up every which way, she dithered at Ruby's door, afraid to intrude on what was obviously very private grief.

But then that scent of sadness and despair reached an awful crescendo, and before Des could stop it, the Loup was bringing her hand down on the wooden door. Des held her breath. For nearly a minute, it turned out, but then she was letting it out as a muffled voice said, "Come in, Des."

❖

Ruby finished belting her robe and looked up as Des peered around the edge of the door then slipped in, shutting it. She looked rather ridiculous in her baggy, oversized sweater and baggy boxers. "What's up?"

Des smiled limply. "Actually, that's what I came to ask you. Are you okay?"

Returning the limp smile, Ruby sighed. "Not really. You?"

"I've been better."

Nodding, Ruby waved Des over and made room at the foot of the bed. Des hesitated for a few moments then sat, neither close nor far from Ruby, staring straight ahead at their reflections in the vanity mirror. Ruby, on the other hand, stared at Des.

She wasn't a pretty woman. Handsome might have been a better word. Or rakish. Her features were glass-sharp, but regular and pleasing. Her body seemed to be all whipcord muscle, barely a spare ounce of fat on her. Not Ruby's "type," in general, not that there'd ever been anyone before or after Casey Hampton, but still disturbingly attractive. She drew Ruby's eyes like the moon drew the tides.

Ruby could feel Des's gaze on her via the mirror, and sensed her discomfort.

"You're staring," Des said.

"I know. Should I apologize?"

Des finally looked over at Ruby, her dark eyes intent and intense, brimming with some emotion that made Ruby want to look away. But she didn't. She held that gaze, not wanting to be the first to break it.

Neither, apparently, did Des, for they sat there staring at each other for the better part of a minute, until Des put her hand on Ruby's knee and Ruby drew in a quick breath. Des immediately stole it with a brief kiss that tasted like toothpaste and surprise, as if Des, too, couldn't quite believe what was happening. And indeed, she pulled away before Ruby could respond, leaving behind a tingling ghost of her lips on Ruby's and the barest, most fleeting caress of the tip of her tongue.

When Ruby opened eyes she hadn't been aware of closing, Des was looking back at the mirror. But her hand was still on Ruby's knee, and Ruby covered that hand with hers, looking down at the way their fingers linked together. The way they contrasted like an old Benetton ad.

Then Des cupped her face with her other hand, tilting it back up. "It'll be okay," she whispered, her eyes darting from Ruby's eyes to her lips. "I promise."

"You can't promise something like that, Des." Ruby tried to turn her face away, but Des wouldn't let her.

"It *will*. Even if I have to *die* to make it okay, it *will be okay*. I swear."

"Don't say that!" Ruby said, blinking back tears unsuccessfully. Des leaned in again, kissing those tears away. The same minty taste, minus the surprise, but with the salt of Ruby's tears added. This time the kiss was long enough that Ruby had a chance to respond. Instead of pulling away, like a quiet, but insistent voice in her head and heart was telling her to do, she met Des halfway, leaning into the kiss and returning it with such ardor that she was both startled and a little afraid of what it meant. They kissed until the need for oxygen separated them, and their kisses were more shared panting than anything else. They both drew in shuddery breaths, Des leaning her forehead against Ruby's, stealing small, chaste pecks as they caught their breath.

"Tell me what you need, Ruby. Anything. And I'll give it to you," Des exhaled, squeezing Ruby's fingers again.

"I need…" Ruby began, but she found she didn't know how to finish. "I don't know what I need, Des."

"Do you know what you *want?*" *Or who?* went unsaid.

"I—" Ruby let out a breath and shook her head once. Des immediately let go of her and sat back, looking away. "I know I'm just displacing grief in order to not feel scared and confused and *sad*, and that kissing you feels good—*so* good, I can't help but wonder how doing *other things* with you might feel."

Des almost smiled, almost looked up. "But that's not enough, is it?"

Ruby sighed and looked down at her hand, fragile-looking without Des's. "A long time ago, I made myself a promise that I'd never get tangled up with anyone again. It only causes pain and anguish, for a few short moments of almost-but-not-quite-happiness, and manipulation and lies."

"Who hurt you so bad?" Des looked up, her eyes measuring and compassionate. Ruby recoiled as if slapped. "I mean, it must've been *someone*, if that bullshit you're saying actually makes sense to you."

Ruby sat blinking, then blinking back more tears quite suddenly, trying to find a way to backpedal, but she couldn't. Not after a minute of thinking, during which Des took her hand again and squeezed it.

"You can tell me," Des said in a low voice. Ruby shook her head. "C'mon. We've all had our hearts broken."

"And I'm not looking to have it broken again. By anyone."

Des frowned. "What if I told you I wasn't out to break your heart?"

Ruby snorted and stood. "Is anyone ever out to break hearts? Of course not. That doesn't keep it from happening." She strode to the door and opened it without looking at Des. "I need to get dressed for the wake."

After nearly a minute, Des stood and approached her. "Not everything has to be hearts and flowers, Ruby. Sometimes two people with the right chemistry can just be friends that fuck."

"Maybe in *your* world."

"*Your* world, now, too."

Ruby's met Des's steady gaze with narrowed eyes. "I have to get ready," she said again. Des crooked a half-smile and continued past Ruby, into the hall.

"When you're ready," she said with infuriating certainty. "You know where I am."

Ruby rolled her eyes. "That's a lot of assuming you're doing."

"I don't need assumptions, when I have *this*." Des tapped the right side of her nose. That half-smile became a full grin at the look of confusion on Ruby's face. "I can smell your pheromones a mile aw—"

Blanching, then blushing fiercely, Ruby slammed the door in Des's face and leaned against it, breathing hard and near tears once more.

❖

Des's triumphant grin faded as she caught the bitter-salt scent of tears coming from behind Ruby's door. It quickly eclipsed the scent of want and need that had clouded the air like a musky perfume not moments before.

Des kicked herself again. Where the hell was the smooth operator she used to be around beautiful women? Where'd *that* son of a bitch disappear to? Des raised her hand to knock, then froze an inch away from the thick, stained wood.

What, exactly, could she possibly say to make anything better for Ruby? *Sorry I shattered your illusions of privacy?*

Sorry your heart got broken once upon a time? Sorry you want me and you're too scared and paranoid to do anything about it?

"Sorry I couldn't protect you from all of this," Des whispered, flattening her hand against the door and leaning her forehead next to it for a few moments. The wood was a cool, implacable boundary between her and the woman who would be her queen. It was only two inches thick, but it might as well have been a million miles.

CHAPTER EIGHT

W hen Ruby finally emerged from her room, she was quiet and seemed somehow smaller than she should have in her ill-fitting clothes with her hair scraped back from her face and wound into a severe knot at the nape of her neck.

Des felt a twinge of guilt and opened her mouth to apologize, perhaps, but Ruby was looking down at her meekly folded hands, her face closed and miserable. So Des held her peace and offered her arm, which was ignored. Then she led the way to the front stairs, where Nathan, Jake, and Phil waited.

Nathan, in his exquisitely tailored charcoal suit, already looked distracted and unhappy. Jake, in his black business casual wear looked pensive—probably thinking about his newly-orphaned lover—and Phil, in a black-and-burgundy velvet maternity dress, looked tired and stressed out.

Des could relate.

It was going to be a very long evening.

❖

The wake was to be held on George's estate, the one left to him by his late wife.

"It's the only place large enough to hold all the mourners," Nathan Coulter had said with a barely perceptible shrug. "We expect there to be hundreds."

Ruby's eyes had widened till it felt like they would fall out of her head. "Will I have to meet every one of them?" she had asked, remembering her father's wake and the interminable time spent accepting condolences and shaking hands.

Nathan had frowned. "Briefly, but yes. Mostly, they'll simply want to get a look at you and make themselves known to you, whether as allies or enemies."

"*Enemies?*"

Smiling thinly, Nathan had spread his hands. "You're the queen of the most powerful Pack of Packs in the world. You will, naturally, have your detractors and enemies."

"But the most important thing to remember, Sug, is that we're here for you," Philomena interrupted to say, glaring at her mate. He'd simply shrugged again. "You can count on us to have your back."

"Damn right," Des had added, opening Ruby's door and and offering her a hand into the SUV. Their eyes had met, and Ruby was the first to look away at what she saw. She couldn't afford to reciprocate or even notice.

Shortly thereafter, she was sandwiched between Des and Jake, staring at her hands as the black SUV zoomed through the chill evening, stirring up vivid orange and red leaves in its windy wake.

"Nervous?"

Ruby smiled wanly at Jake. "Yes. No. Tired, mostly. Too tired to be as anxious as I usually am when faced with public speaking."

"You'll do fine," Des said, nudging Ruby with her elbow. "Just picture everybody in their underwear and your nerves'll disappear."

Ruby snorted. "The last time I tried that, I started giggling and nearly ruined my presentation."

Des and Jake exchanged a glance and Ruby frowned. "What?"

"Well," Jake began delicately, and Des jumped in with. "See, the thing is, George's wake is gonna be kind of an Irish one, George being Irish, and all. It was one of his requests."

"It'll be solemn enough in the beginning, just like Phil and I described to you, ad nauseam. But once the alcohol starts flowing…" Jake shrugged.

"All bets're off," Des finished, then grinned. "Loups'll generally look for any excuse to party hard. And when it comes to celebrating life in the midst of death, no one parties harder."

"Besides which, the North American branch of the *Loup-Garoul* have a problem with holding their liquor." Jake shook his head. "If the drinking starts before your speech, which it almost certainly will, you'll have to shout to be heard over the reminiscences about George."

Imagining herself straining to be heard above the mournful howling of a bunch of drunken werewolves, Ruby sighed. "That makes me feel better and worse at the same time."

"Don't worry, *chica*, you'll do fine," Des promised, rubbing Ruby's arm briefly. "And anyway, Loups aren't big on speeches. Most of them'll be waiting for yours to be over so they can get to the *serious* drinking and reminiscing."

Ruby smiled just a little. "George had a lot of friends, didn't he?"

Jake nodded. "And his fair share of detractors. But one thing friends and detractors alike had in common was a deep respect for him. He did some pretty amazing things in his time as Dyre. Some damn near *impossible* things, some might say."

"Such as?" Des asked.

Jake rolled his eyes. "Didn't you have to study this at one point?"

Des sighed. "You know how I was when I first found out I was a Loup. I wasn't interested in studying *shit*, except for all the lore surrounding ways of lifting my, ahem, curse. And no, there's no way out of it, Ruby. Sorry," she added at the look of excitement on Ruby's face, which immediately fell.

"So," Ruby said when the silence had dragged out, "I have pretty big shoes to fill."

Jake smiled apologetically. "That's up to you to decide."

"But there's plenty of time for you to decide later. For the first couple years, you're going to be learning and exploring," Philomena said from the passenger seat, smiling at Ruby. Next to her, Nathan nodded without taking his eyes off the road.

"I would advise you to make the best of that time and learn well," he said with quiet gravity.

"But no pressure," Des added, rolling her eyes.

❖

Sitting on the steep, forested Lenape Hill—as in *the* Lenapes, Lenape Landing's first family—with a master view of the city below, Lenape Hall had once been the seat of upward social mobility. Nancy duBarre Lenape-Carnahan had held salons and parties and other gaieties in the Hall, once upon a century.

Then she'd passed away from silver poisoning that had looked like mere organ failure, and the Hall had fallen into quiet disuse. George, it seemed, had never liked the old pile, closet Marxist that he was. And with his beloved Nancy dead, he'd seen no point in continuing on there.

But for the grounds- and house-keepers, the Hall had seen few visitors in nearly one hundred years. George had, it was said, only kept the Hall in case either of his children had wanted to take up residence, but it seemed neither had. Evelyn was always traveling, never staying anywhere long enough to put down roots, and James, though he'd stayed in Lenape Landing, had chosen to live in the penthouse of the LaMarque Building, down on Lakeshore Drive.

The driveway of Lenape Hall was nearly half a mile long and lined with cars of different socio-economic levels, from beaters to Bentleys. Nathan drove them past all these, right up to the steps of the Hall, where several young men and women in the red jackets of valets waited to park the SUV.

"Are they, um, Loups, too?"

Des nodded.

"Volunteers," Jake chimed in. "Thierry LaFours's Pack, most likely."

"I can see they've come up in the world," Des sniffed, looking for a moment *exactly* like her father, or so Ruby thought. Then Des opened her door before the tallest young LaFours could, hopping out with a hard look for the boy, who couldn't have been more than seventeen. He ignored her glare and held out a hand for Ruby at the same time Des did.

Ignoring them both, Ruby slid toward Jake's door and accepted his hand. He tipped her a stage-y wink and offered her his arm. She took it, blushing at the knowing look on his long face. Together, followed by Nathan and Philomena, and finally a sulking, hunch-shouldered Des, they climbed the shallow steps to the ivy-covered portico.

❖

Another LaFours, judging from his canny, streetwise resemblance to the valets, opened the door for Ruby's party. She tried to smile at him—a Loup who appeared to be her father's age at the time of his death. He returned the smile and bowed slightly.

"DyreMother Ruby," he murmured respectfully.

Ruby paused briefly, and Jake stopped a second later before he continued guiding her forward by the elbow. "Best get used to that," he whispered as she tried not to look cowed. "Especially from Packs like the LaFourses, that practically worshipped George."

Ruby squinted up at Jake. "Why worship?"

Jake smiled a little. "You've read about the Carnahan Treatise?"

Ruby nodded hesitantly. Lining the forever-long front hall were Loups three deep on either side, all staring at her like she was the second coming. Hope, wariness, and awe were written on nearly every face. Nearly. "I'm still trying to understand it, actually."

"Well, basically it involves the leaders of the smaller Packs, in part. The Carnahan Treatise gives the Alphas of those Packs the same voting power and Rights of Challenge as the more powerful Alphas. That included Thierry LaFours, who was little more than a half-breed bastard of the Quebec LaFours Pack when the Treatise went into effect. After it went into effect, he defected, along with dozens of other half-breeds and turned Humes, to the U.S. He was the first new Alpha to be accepted onto the Council of Alphas based on a Right of Challenge. When the Carnahan Treatise spread to Canada—not his native Quebec, unfortunately, LaFours moved the base of his Pack back up north, to Ontario."

"Is he here, tonight?" Ruby asked quietly, trying to smile as she met the eyes of the crowd that stared at her unabashedly.

"Of course. He and George were great friends, after a fashion." Jake nodded to someone in the crowd. "Thierry LaFours was the Loup many assumed would get George's Death-right."

Ruby swallowed and saw with gratitude that the crowd was thinning out, and they were nearing a staircase that was Loup-free. "So, I take it he won't be any too glad to see me."

"Are you kidding?" Jake snorted. "Thierry's *not* interested in being Dyre. He's got the largest Pack on the continent. He has all that he can do keeping a bunch of rowdy cast-offs and *orphelins* in line, never mind a goodly portion of the world's *Garoul*."

Jake led her past the staircase, as what he said sank in. "The *world's*?"

"Mm-hmm."

Stunned into silence, Ruby let herself be guided down the hall, to a large room that appeared to be almost haphazardly lined with full shelves of books. Behind her, Philomena and Nathan spoke quietly. Behind *them*, Des grumbled and swore to herself.

The latter made Ruby smile, for some reason. A real smile that somehow put a different color on her situation and she kept that smile on as she entered the room with her head held high.

❖

Edging her way past Nathan and Phil, Des grinned when she saw Ruby pause at the doorway to the library then tilt her head up, set her shoulders back, and straighten her spine till it was a ramrod. Des felt a surge of pride at the sight and realized she'd been despairing of Ruby even having a spine to straighten.

Then she felt a niggle of worry. A good game-face was only half the battle. The rest of said battle was psychological warfare with the Alphas who waited in the library, and Ruby may or may not have realized this.

No, there'd be no Rights of Challenge issued tonight, but based on Ruby's performance in the next few minutes, quite a few might be issued in the near future.

Ruby let go of Jake's arm and stepped ahead of him.

Okay, so far, she's off to a good start. Going in on Jake's arm might have made her appear weak, Des thought. At that moment, Jake glanced back at her and gave a discreet thumb's up.

From behind her, Nathan and Philomena waited like silent guardians—not of Ruby, but of Des, and she somehow drew strength from that, straightening her own spine and shoulders, drawing herself up to her full five feet, two inches.

She then caught up to Jake and together they followed Ruby into the library.

❖

Ruby had been told to expect anywhere from ten to fifteen Alphas to turn up to pay their respects to George. What she got was twenty-seven of thirty Alphas, meticulously dressed in rather dramatic, goth-looking ballroom chic, all talking quietly among themselves, so engrossed in their conversations that they seemed not to notice her.

And they continued to not notice her.

And continued.

And continued.

After several minutes, Ruby had to admit to herself that these leaders of Loups, these Alphas, were using one of the most childish, least subtle mind-games she'd ever been prey to. And she *had* been prey to it, working at the crossroads of academe and human resources.

The question was, what to do about it? Clearing her throat would make her seem like a beggar, as if she was pleading for attention. But standing around waiting for them to finally notice her would make her seem subservient and none too decisive or bright. There was only one thing for it, then. Ruby would do what she did at awkward Christmas parties and meetings where she was one of the lowest ranking employees attending.

She scanned the room carefully until she noticed someone she hadn't seen before. He was leaning against the south-facing wall, gazing out the window into the blustery night. Unlike the other Alphas in their impressive finery, this Loup was dressed in a simple, if notably antiquated fashion.

He wore a black morning coat with a matching vest, a white shirt and black cravat, and gray trousers. His overall appearance was rather Byronic, with shoulder-length, silvering dark hair, and pale skin. He was neither tall nor short, brawny nor skinny. His profile was brooding and handsome, as of someone who'd just stepped off the windswept moors of a Bronte novel. Most importantly, he was the only person in the room not talking to someone else.

Taking a breath and putting on her brightest smile, Ruby strode across the library, past the other Alphas, all of whom fell silent as she went by, turning measuring gazes on her. She ignored them as they'd ignored her, and made her way to the Alpha looking out the window.

When she got close to him, she picked up a scent like cloves and nutmeg, earthy and strong.

"Such a lovely night for such a solemn occasion," he said as she approached, his faintly accented voice pitched low enough that it was only meant for her ears. Nodding, she joined him in gazing out at the night.

"Indeed, it is. George would've loved a night like this," she replied fondly, remembering all the times they'd forsaken reading to take walks out in the weather. "He loved the fall."

"Yes, he always did have a fondness for the season. He especially loved autumns in Lenape Landing. He said it brought out the beauty in even such a homely urban sprawl as this."

Ruby tilted her head in curiosity. "Did you know him well?"

A small smile graced his broodingly handsome profile, and the Alpha shifted his stance a bit. "You might say that. He was like a father to me." He turned to face Ruby full on and held out a large, rough-looking hand for shaking. His dark, dark eyes were long and direct. "But I've forgotten my manners. My name is Thierry LaFours. And you must be Ruby Knudsen, our new Dyre."

❖

Scowling, Des watched Ruby chat with Thierry LaFours.

LaFours held out his hand, and Ruby seemed surprised, hesitating before she finally smiled and took it. LaFours returned the smile and raised her hand to his mouth, kissing it like he thought he was Valentino. Des could see Ruby's blush from across the room, and no doubt so could every other Loup present. Indeed, the chatter that had filled the room at their arrival had dried up.

Every eye was on Ruby and LaFours, some covertly, some not so much. Des wondered if *her* eyes were the only ones that felt as if they were about to throb out of her skull with rage.

LaFours didn't let go of Ruby's hand, the entire time they spoke, nor did she seem to want him to. In fact, she seemed to be *charmed* by him.

A covert sniff in Ruby's direction confirmed that yes, she was finding him charming, all right. She was, in fact, *attracted* to him.

And the feeling was most definitely returned, judging by the heavy scent of musky pheromones spreading from their direction. No doubt the rest of the Alphas smelled it, too. Perhaps the only person who didn't realize the strong mutual attraction between Ruby and LaFours, was *Ruby*.

Something had to be done about this.

"Okay, well, now you know she's bi," Jake muttered out of the side of his mouth, and Des elbowed him hard. "What?"

"Am I the only one who's alarmed by the idea of our future queen getting hormonal with Thierry-fucking-LaFours?"

"Yes," Nathan and Jake said. Philomena sighed. "Honey, there's no need to be jeal—"

"*Do not* finish that sentence," Des said from between gritted teeth, stalking away from her family toward Ruby, ignoring the horrified glances and shying-away that happened around her. She was used to it, after all.

Time to play bodyguard, she thought grimly, meaning to either march Ruby away from LaFours or LaFours away from Ruby. But before she could get within ten feet of them, a hand landed on her shoulder.

"Perhaps you'd best leave them to it, eh? Our little queen will need all the allies she can charm," a despairingly familiar voice said. Des shuddered, then shrugged the hand off without turning around.

"You don't get to talk to me about *our* anything, sweetheart, let alone our Dyre. And the next appendage of yours that touches me'll come back to you in a box with a ribbon wrapped around it," she said coolly, quietly, trying her best to keep a lid on her redirected rage and hold the Loup by the ears, so to speak.

Behind Des, Holly Black Lodge laughed, a clear, crystalline sound of grace and beauty—also despairingly familiar. But then, Holly had always professed to find Des amusing, something that should've set off warning bells in Des, once upon a time but hadn't, to the detriment of many.

"Tsk-tsk, Jennifer. Is that any way to speak to an Alpha?"

Biting her lip just shy of making it bleed, Des turned to face Holly, steeling herself for the shock of seeing her again after more than three years.

The steeling didn't help much at all. Not when Holly looked even better than she used to, if that was possible. Her features were still strong and regal, her skin still like burnished copper, her eyes even darker and more fathomless, her hair still a long skein of black silk that seemed to merge with her simple black gown.

No doubt her legs still go up to the moon and her tits still don't quit, Des thought with desperate gallows humor. "I'll talk to who I want, how I want."

"*Whom*, my love, *whom*," Holly corrected with absent fondness, her smile all perfect teeth. "And you won't win anyone to our queen's cause with that attitude, will you?"

"Fuck off."

"Still ever the piquant wit, I see." That smile of hers grew improbably wider. "You're exactly as I remember you, you know."

Des snorted. "What, you mean a murdering, rabid pup you tossed away as soon as you were done with her?"

The smile didn't so much as falter, and the Loup within Des wanted to bury its fangs in Holly's pretty, slender neck.

"I mean," Holly said quietly, her eyes wide and intent as she stepped closer to Des. "I mean you're still magnetic, still…" she sucked in a breath, scenting Des, her eyes gone hooded. "Still *mine*."

"Ha! And *you're* still delusional!" Des spat. "I don't belong to anyone, but *especially* not to *you*, hon."

"That's not what your scent is saying, and not what the entire Crow Nation would say," Holly replied, unperturbed. She held her hand out to Des, giving her a black business card with silver lettering. "And when you're ready to accept that, there's still a place for you among the Skins. There always will be."

"Yeah, and I know just what that place is, so *fuck* the Skins, and fuck *you*," Des said with what she considered remarkable aplomb, ignoring the business card, and the fact that her scent was giving her away like a jailhouse stoolie.

Holly sighed and quicker than even Des could follow, had shoved the card into the front pocket of Des's jeans, despite the way Des practically jumped back. The motion startled Des into taking a deep breath, and she could smell that whatever else Holly Black Lodge was, she wasn't a liar. Desire rolled off her like heat—*hell, maybe she's* in heat, Des thought with helpless hilarity. Not far under Holly's very real grief—for some reason, the Skinwalkers of the Crow Nation had revered George, though the Black Lodge Skins were the only ones to deign to become part of the Council of Alphas—was want and need, and it was all focused on Des.

Des took another startled step back.

"You'll call me," Holly said, and it was a prediction, not a request. Those dark eyes flicked over Des's shoulder to Ruby and LaFours, whom Des had completely forgotten for the past few minutes. "They make a striking couple, don't they?"

And before Des could toss a glance over her shoulder to see what action had prompted *that* remark, before Des could respond with another contemptuous *fuck you*, Holly had darted in and pecked her lips. This close, her scent was sweet and warm, like jasmine and honeysuckle. It was overwhelming, and Des whined low in her throat.

"Don't keep me waiting, *Des*. I've learned my lesson. Three years without you was long enough."

And with that, Holly was swishing back into the crowd of staring Alphas, probably already wheeling and dealing some poor stooge into an ill-considered scheme that'd benefit no one involved except the Skins.

"Who was *that*?" Ruby asked in a curious, wary voice. Des scowled, blinking away the frustrated, angry tears that wanted to spring up in her eyes.

"That was Holly Black Lodge. My wife."

❖

And with that bombshell dropped, without so much as glancing back at Ruby, Des stalked out of the room, shouldering past Nathan, who seemed concerned as he watched her leave.

"Let her go," Philomena said quietly, but somehow, Ruby could hear her as clearly as if she was standing next to her. "She handled that better than we could have hoped, but she needs to be alone for a bit."

"And in the meantime, we can murder that *woman*. It'll be quality family time," Nathan said pleasantly, but with an edge to his voice.

"Nobody's murdering anybody," Jake said to both of them. "Let's try to get through this night with a minimum of bloodshed."

"No one thought it was a good idea for Callum Coulter's great-great-granddaughter to marry into the Skinwalkers. But like her father, and every Coulter before him, she's headstrong and unbending," Thierry murmured from next to Ruby, startling her and reminding her that they'd been conversing. Ruby shook her head.

"Des is…is *married*? To *that…person*?" Ruby demanded, looking into the crowd of Alphas, all of whom were now genuinely talking among each other. She couldn't see which way the sultry female Loup went, which was strange, considering that ridiculously plunging neckline and the way her gown clung to a figure Ruby would've once killed to have. But she seemed to have blended into the crowd quite seamlessly.

"Yes. It was the scandal of the Packs. Callum Coulter, may he run with the Moon, wasn't a particularly peaceful Loup, and in his time, he made war with the Crow and several other Nations." Thierry paused, staring off in the direction Des had gone. "Despite their rather thick veneer of civility, the Coulters were a vicious, cruel, bloody-minded, bloodthirsty Pack. They've brought more war and death to this land than any of the other European Packs. They are utterly loyal to each other and few else, and they'd fight and die at the drop of a hat. That Nathan Coulter and his father before him put so much faith in George was, frankly, a miracle. But George had their respect for good reason. He never lost it. And now, you have it, as well." Thierry looked at her and smiled, taking her hand and kissing it once more. "Don't lose it."

Blushing, Ruby nodded and Thierry smiled. "Good. Now, if you'll allow me to act as your temporary escort, I can introduce you around the room. Everyone's just dying to make you feel uncomfortable and out of your element."

"In that case, it'd be rude of me to keep them waiting," Ruby said, glancing at the door Des had fled through. Her first instinct was to go after Des, but then what? What could she possibly say to Des to make her feel better? Why would Des even want to see her now?

So Ruby took Thierry's arm and let him lead her into the murmuring crowd.

❖

Des had lost track of how many turns she'd taken, but she wasn't terribly worried about being lost in George's mansion. After all, she could simply scent her back-trail and make her way back to the wake.

The wake where her charge waited, but not unguarded. No, she had Thierry LaFours for protection, and he was probably as vicious in a fight as Des, if not more so, considering he was an Alpha. The wake where her family waited, and worst of all, where her wife waited, was no place she wanted to be.

Why hadn't it even occurred to her that Holly would be here? Had she simply blocked out the possibility altogether? Or had she hoped that Holly would keep her distance and let things be?

Or had Des, not-so-deep down, *wanted* that little run-in to happen?

Shaking her head, Des finally halted her march through George's house and looked around. She appeared to be in some sort of drawing room, filled with old-fashioned paintings of people in their finest finery, smiling canny, wolfish smiles. They all had the same ash-blond hair and narrow, fine-featured faces, a hallmark of the area's original Lenape tribe since their intermingling with the infamous, riotous duBarre family.

"Huh. You guys must be *the* duBarre Lenapes."

"And *you* must be Des," said a low, thrumming baritone that was somewhat muted. Starting, Des spun around in a semi-circle, one of her switchblades drawn, as she searched for the source of the voice. Her nostrils twitched as she tried to pinpoint the direction the voice had come from.

She scented something behind a painting of a particularly horse-faced Lenape, but the artwork slid aside to reveal a tall, brawny man stepping out of a secret passageway. He bore more than a passing resemblance to George, from his wavy blond hair to his long, solemn features and penetrating blue eyes. He wore steely blue-gray business casual wear with a white carnation pinned to the lapel of his jacket. He stepped into the drawing room, closing the wall behind him.

"Somebody's gotta be," Des said to him. "And you must be James Carnahan." Des twitched the switchblade shut and back up her sleeve. "My condolences and my sincerest apologies."

James nodded. "Thank you." He drifted absently toward the pianoforte that dominated the right side of the room and sat heavily on the bench. "I heard it through the grapevine that you took care of the perpetrator?"

Des wrapped her arms around herself and sighed. "I killed the muscle and his backup. As to who was behind the assassination, I don't know. They weren't out to kill merely George, so much as end the Line of Succession. They tried to kill his successor, too."

James's eyes widened and he sat back, reaching into the guts of the pianoforte. He felt around and after a few seconds came up with a black labeled bottle. Without ceremony, he uncapped it and took a long pull. "That's goddamned disturbing."

"I'll say."

James smiled weakly, rather blearily, and offered Des the bottle. With only the slightest hesitation, she crossed the room, sat next to him on the long bench, and took it. The label was so old, she couldn't make out what it said, but the amber liquid inside scalded her tonsils and sinuses. "Fuck!"

Laughing quietly, James took the bottle back for another long pull. "Dilettante. So what're you doing here, instead of in Mother's library, squiring our new queen around and helping her navigate the uncertain waters of Loup politics?"

Esophagus still burning, Des sighed again. "Why on Earth would Ruby need me for *that* when she's got Thierry LaFours to do it? He knows more about Loup politics than I ever will."

"Hmm."

"Yeah, 'hmm's' right."

They sat sharing the bottle in heavy, distracted silence for several minutes. Then, Des asked, "So, what're your intentions toward my brother? Is this true love, or are you just sport-fucking him till the next guy comes along?"

James choked on his mouthful, and Des smirked, reclaiming the bottle from him.

❖

The dinner at the wake was really no different than all the rubber chicken dinners for the school, to which George had requested Ruby accompany him, except for the complete lack of chicken, rubber or otherwise.

She found herself warming to some Alphas, such as Beau Madrigal-Chen, a smallish, bookish, quiet sort who'd staked out a corner earlier, much as Thierry had done, and stayed there. He reminded Ruby of several academic types she'd met over her tenure at the school, humbly-suited and self-effacing.

Most of them made little or no real impression on her at all, nearly two dozen blurred faces with pasteboard smiles and condolences, as well as congratulations.

But some left Ruby cold, among them, Clara Kitchener. She'd looked Ruby over once, as if measuring her and finding her wanting, then drifted away without even a polite word or handshake. Even stolid Thierry had seemed nonplussed by her behavior, and had hurriedly ushered Ruby off to meet Samson Dawes, an affable giant of an Alpha, who pulled Ruby into a bear hug and told her she was "all right, for a Humie."

And so, by the time Thierry had taken her once around the room and declared their mission an "overall success," Ruby's head was almost spinning trying to remember names and faces, as well as kindnesses and slights.

"Are you in need of a little refreshment?" Thierry asked. Tired and dazed as she felt, it did *not* escape her notice that Thierry's hand had migrated from her elbow, to the small of her back, at some point during the evening. And stayed there, too.

She smiled, fighting off a yawn. "Do I look that out of it?"

Thierry returned the smile warmly. "You look lovely, but perhaps a tad wan," he offered, and Ruby laughed. Thierry joined her with a few discreet chuckles. At least until his eyes darted over Ruby's shoulder. Then his smile turned wry.

Ruby glanced over her shoulder and saw Des sauntering into the library with her arm slung around a tall, solid man who could've given Samson Dawes a run for his money. This man also had his large arm draped around Des's bony shoulders and between the two of them Ruby could smell the alcohol fumes from across the room.

Although, I am *a werewolf, now, so that's not saying much about their drunkenness* or *my sense of smell*, she thought. Then scowled at the picture these two inebriated Loups made.

"I suppose this means that Jamie's off the wagon. Again," Thierry noted casually, though with measurable worry in his soft, rich voice.

"And it looks like my guardian is off that wagon with him."

"James?" Jake's voice rang out above the general din of small-talk, and heads turned. "James, are you—"

"Drunk?" the man asked, grinning in a way that put Ruby in mind of George at his merriest. "My love, whatever gave you that idea? And why didn't you ever *tell* me your sister is so—so—"

"—awesome," Des finished decisively, certainly. "I'm *awesome*."

Jake pinched the bridge of his nose then sighed, approaching the pair. "Forgive me the lapse in my descriptive powers." He looked back and forth between his sister and his lover, and finally settled on the former. "You know you can't hold your liquor, Jenny-Benny."

"Ah-ah, she's half-Scots: don't underestimate her, dearest," James declared grandly, his baritone filling the library. He obviously looked the room over, finally settling his attention on Thierry. "Uncle Theo!"

"You *know* that guy?" Ruby whispered from the corner of her mouth as the drunken man sauntered their way, and Thierry chuckled.

"'That guy' is George's son."

Ruby blinked and squinted at the approaching man. At third glance, yes, he was *clearly* George's son: a slightly blonder, finer-featured version of him. And those eyes, even clouded by alcohol, were still the same piercing, canny blue.

"It's been a month of Sundays, Theo!" James Carnahan exclaimed, grabbing the older Loup for a bear hug that actually made little creaking noises. Thierry, for his part, took the embrace in stride, returning it with a few pats for solidarity. "Where've you been?"

"Ah, here and there, Jamie." Thierry extricated himself from the embrace but still held on to James and looked him over. "Well, you still wear blind, stinking drunk rather well."

"Of course I do. I'm a duBarre, a Lenape, *and* a Carnahan. And who's *this*? You've brought a date? It's about *time*, old man! Enchanted," he purred, and thereafter became the second man in Ruby's entire life to kiss her hand.

"Actually, you can put your charm away and pull on your best manners. This young lady is our new Dyre, Ruby Knudsen. Ruby, allow me to introduce you to Ellery James Lenape-Carnahan—"

"Only my mother ever called me *Ellery*. To everyone else, I'm simply James or Jamie. I *do* hope I may be so to you," James said, fairly dripping charm despite his uncle's imploration. But his eyes, bleary and reddened though they were, were quite solemn.

"Um, of course," Ruby stammered, glancing at Thierry, who merely shrugged. "And please, call me *Ruby*."

"I certainly will, Ruby," James said, his grin flashing out quite suddenly. "And even on this awful occasion, congratulations are in order. You must be someone very special if Dad chose to pass his Death-right on to you."

Ruby's own smile turned pained. "That's a matter that's still up for debate. I didn't even know that Loups existed till after I was bitten and had been in a coma for three days. And I still don't know even the half of Loup history or science or customs. Some might say I'm in over my head." She sighed, catching Jake's approach out of the corner of her eye.

Now there, she wanted to say, *there's someone who could handle this office with knowledge and sensitivity. Jake would be a good Dyre. Better than me, at least. But then, a capybara with a head injury could probably do a better job than I would.*

"History? Science? Custom? Pah!" James dismissed them, then with the confidence of the truly sloshed slipped his arm around Jake. Jake elbowed him, but smiled, and James tugged on Jake's ponytail. The resulting: "hey!" earned Jake a kiss on the shoulder. "None of that stuff necessarily makes for a good leader. Just an informed one. Dad, it so happened, was both, but he didn't start out that way. He studied Loup history for *years* before he attempted making any sweeping changes or decisions."

Ruby snorted, wishing she'd taken Thierry up on his offer to get her refreshment. She felt she could use a drink, herself. "It'll be all I can do just to make it through the next few weeks alive, from what I've hear—"

Just then came a loud tinkle and a trail of pain blazed itself across Ruby's right cheek. Another exploded low in her back. Yet another drilled into her shoulder.

She hadn't even begun to react to the pain with anything other than sheer surprise when she heard more tinkling sounds followed closely by screams of fright and bellows of pain.

Then something *solid* slammed into her and Thierry, knocking them both to the floor. Ruby hit her head *hard*, and the world grayed out before she could even be dismayed at the fire-roses of agony that had, mere instants ago, bloomed in her shoulder and her lower back.

❖

Des was already ripping off her clothes mid-Change when she hit Ruby and LaFours like a ton of bricks. But not quite fast enough, it turned out. LaFours took a bullet to the head, and Ruby took at least a bullet to the shoulder. A *regular silver* bullet, not a silver nitrate bullet.

Des had seen this ploy before, and it was a simple, but deadly one: overwhelm Loups for long enough to incapacitate them, and put silver bullets in their *hearts*.

Growling, Des shrugged off the last scraps of her clothes. She stepped toward one of the open spaces that used to be picture windows, and egged on the last of her Change, reveling in the sweet agony of freedom. Seconds later, she was preparing to leap at the window—through which bullets were still flying, when something grabbed her tail and yanked.

Still growling, she whirled around, ready to take a hand off some stupid fuck, only to find James, crouched over an unconscious Jake, holding his hands up in surrender. They were both covered in blood. Jake's blood, judging from the gaping, smoking, cauterized hole in the center of his chest. Far too close to the heart that was now beating slowly and arrhythmically.

James's eyes were wide and frightened, tears gathering.

"*Please*," he said shakily, in a smaller voice than Des would ever have thought him capable of. "There's so much *blood*. You have to help me get him somewhere safe so he can heal...*please*, Des."

Des and the Loup—as merged in intent and psyche as they'd ever be, looked toward the broken window, then at Ruby, who was already groaning and twitching.

Torn between her deep desire to drink the blood of whomever was trying to kill them and an equally deep need to get her queen and her Pack-brother to someplace defensible, Des hesitated. And in that moment, growls started to sound from all over the library, including one very familiar one. A moment later, Nathan streaked past her, a large black blur with dark eyes. He spared a glance for Des and Jake, then he was gone, his growl turned to a howl of rage.

Phil? Des thought, keen despair nearly washing away her reason. Then she shook her head once, an iron denial of the worst possible scenario. *Nathan would never have left Phil's side if she were hurt, or...or worse. No, he got her someplace relatively safe. That's his job, after all. And* my *job is to look after Ruby.*

Ruby.

Right.

It was painful, going full-Hume again so soon after turning full-Loup, leaving Des feeling weak and shaky, gasping, panting, and coughing, but she did it.

"You're okay, you're okay," James crooned in a low, soothing, urgent chant, and Des couldn't tell if he was talking to her or to Jake. She shuddered, and opened her eyes. Her vision was blunted, limited, her sense of smell seemingly faded to nothing. Every bone and muscle ached and screamed, but she ignored the cacophony of pain and got to her knees. Among the ruins of her clothes were her switchblades and one of her guns. Then she glanced to her left and saw Ruby, bleeding and pale, utterly defenseless.

No contest as to what got picked up when Des got to her feet. The only thing that mattered in this moment was Ruby.

"You can get us somewhere deeper in the house, right? Somewhere defensible?" She croaked, glancing at James, who was still holding Jake close, still keening. Des crouched down as low as her aching, wobbly knees and Ruby's leaden body would allow.

"Yes, I...yes." James nodded, looking over at Des. "I know this place like the back of my hand. No one knows it better."

"Good." Des hefted Ruby carefully, pleased when the unconscious woman moaned in her arms. That meant she was not only still alive, but close to consciousness. "Then let's get outta this shooting gallery."

James sniffed, dazed and shocked, but he nodded then carefully gathered Jake up in his arms. "Moon Above," he kept muttering, then, having gained his feet, he crouched down low, copying Des to avoid the sporadic gunfire still coming through the windows.

"What about Uncle Theo?"

Des blinked and looked at LaFours. A sluggish puddle of blood formed under the back of his head, and he was as pale as the Moon Herself. "What *about* him?"

"Des, we can't leave him here. He's hurt."

"So's nearly everyone in this room!" She looked around at the Alphas in various stages of change and injury. She felt a sudden pang as she realized one of them might be Holly, then another quick scan showed Holly was nowhere to be seen. She might be somewhere in the stacks, huddled down and safe, or she could be out with Nathan, hunting down whomever had dared attack the Council of Alphas on the night of George's wake.

In either event, it wasn't any of her business. Her business was Ruby and Jake.

"So which of us is gonna carry *Uncle Theo*, huh?" she demanded, but James had already slung Jake over one broad shoulder in a fireman's carry, and was crab-walking his way toward LaFours.

Thierry went over James's other shoulder with little more than a grunt from James, who then began a steady, quick beeline for the door. Des gaped for a moment, then adjusted Ruby into a similar fireman's carry, reminding herself that *Latent* didn't equal *weak*.

Then she was making her own beeline in James's wake, shuffling around the bodies of the wounded and dead, and trying not to think about Philomena Simms or Holly Black Lodge.

❖

The huge front hall had emptied since the last time Des had been in it. Once the shooting had started, no Loup had wasted time getting the hell out or finding someplace to hide. *They had the right idea*, Des thought as a bullet flew down the hall mere inches past her face. She swore and ducked.

"C'mon. Back to the drawing room," James grunted, already weaving his way down the hall. With one last glance at the library, Des followed him.

When James paused at a section of wall decorated with a mosaic of a wolf, Des drew up alongside him, about to demand what the hold-up was. But before she could, James said, "Could you depress the wolf's eyes?"

"What?"

James gave her a stern, no-nonsense look. "Just do it. Quickly, before someone comes along and sees."

Frowning, Des swallowed her temper and pride and did as she was bidden. She pressed the large, gray eyes of the mosaic wolf, and a section of wall slid away, dusty, chill air coming from a steep, narrow, unlit stairway within.

"I know my way around the secret places in this house with my eyes closed. So, I'll go first. Do your best to follow and step where I step. Oh, and there's a button at about eye-level—*your* eye—on the right wall that'll close the way behind us."

James stepped easily past her with his double burden, and made his way up the steps sideways like a crab.

"Now might not be a good time to mention my claustrophobia," Des muttered to herself, hefting Ruby and stepping into the secret stairway. Ruby shifted a bit on her own, another good sign. With the last of the hallway's ambient light, Des could just make out, at eye-level, a stone lighter than the others surrounding it.

A second later, the entrance slid shut, leaving them in near-total darkness, thick enough to stymie even a Loup's cunning eyes.

"Keep up," came James's annoyed, strained voice from a little way above her.

With a sigh, Des obediently inched along, uncomfortably aware that she carried the fate of the Loup world over her shoulder.

PART III: ...LONG LIVE THE DYRE MOTHER

"So I walked back to my room and collapsed on the bottom bunk, thinking that if people were rain, I was drizzle and she was a hurricane."

—JOHN GREEN

CHAPTER NINE

*H*ome, again. Home, again, jiggety-jig," James puffed
as they stepped into the drawing room once more. He
*immediately headed for a pair of settees near the pianoforte
and laid his uncle down on one and his lover on the other. Then
he stood between them looking lost and helpless. "What now?
They need medical help, right? Or will they heal up on their
own if given time?"*

*Des shrugged, laying Ruby down on a couch then nodding
toward the pianoforte. "Dunno. But we're gonna move* that *big
fucker in front of the door, just in case."*

*"Yeah, that's a good idea," James agreed, stretching once,
till his back cracked.*

*The two of them wheeled the instrument to the door and
blocked it in a matter of moments. Afterwards, James went back
to the settees, finally settling at Jake's side and taking his limp
hand.*

*"Baby, come back to me," he whispered, tears welling in
his eyes again. "I need you. I* love *you. Come back. Please…"*

*Des looked away, feeling like an intruder in a private
hospital room. She found herself staring moodily back at the
secret entryway, and thinking of Phil and Holly, and even*

Nathan, who could take better care of himself than anyone Des had ever met.

"Des?"

"What?" She started, looking back over at James, who was still sitting, still holding Jake's hand. "What's up?"

"I said, 'You're going back down there, aren't you?'"

"Maybe."

James nodded. "Thought so. If you can find Dr. Simms..."

Des nodded back, striding toward the secret entrance.

"Hey, uh, do you want my shirt, or something?" James offered delicately. "You're naked."

Des didn't even bother looking around, let alone stopping. "I do my best work naked." She heard him snort behind her. The stairway was more than just that, of course. According to a slightly breathless James, it ran as a series of stairways and passageways throughout the labyrinthine Lenape Hall. One could get from wing to wing, floor to floor, front end to back end of the Hall without ever having to leave the secret network.

To Des, whose sense of direction as a Hume was practically nonexistent, this sounded nightmarish. But she was pretty certain she could back-trail by scent the way they had come. The scents of gunpowder and blood proved stronger than her trail. Those got her to the mosaic even faster than she had been travelling, and finally she was groping for the stone lever that opened the wall. Before she pressed it, she bent all her hearing on whatever might be happening on the other side of the wall.

Nothing. At least nothing that her Hume ears could pick out.

She pressed the stone and quickly slipped out into the hall, then pressed the outer button again. The wall slid shut behind her once more with a dull, heavy click.

The front hall looked exactly the way she and James had left it, littered with the things people had been too frightened to pick up as they ran away. No bodies, though, or blood. Not here. Nor a living soul, either.

Sniffing, Des crept carefully down the hall and to the library. Except for the moans of the semi-conscious, she heard no sounds from inside, but that meant next to nothing. Loups knew quiet, *oh, yes. Wishing for her switchblades and pistol, Des peered around the post of the entryway and beheld the devastation that had begun not fifteen minutes ago.*

Most of the Alphas were still lying where they'd been felled, at least twenty of them. Most had been head-shot or heart-shot. The former were already starting to twitch and moan as their injuries healed. The latter would never twitch or moan or heal again. Among those, she saw Samson Dawes and Beau Madrigal-Chen, with bullets in their hearts. And other places.

Shaking her head, Des dropped to hands and knees and slunk across the floor, over the champagne glasses and dropped accessories, over spent bullets and around spent bodies, and through splatters and even puddles of blood, till she got to her abandoned weapons. She could only handle two of the three weapons at a time, so she took the pistol and the larger of the two switchblades, then she scented the air again.

Finding one scent in a cacophony of them, some of which included the anodizing scent of charred silver, was a bitch. But Des had to try. And while she tried, she slunk her way over toward the ten freestanding shelves of books. If there was anywhere to hide in a library, that'd be it. And sure enough, the closer she got to the stacks, the easier it became to single out not one particular scent, but two *of them.*

Only one of them smelled wrong, *somehow.*

Crawling as quickly as possible, Des passed all the shelves till she was at the aisle between the last shelf and a row of shot-out windows. Holly Black Lodge was huddled in the corner beyond the body with the wrong-scent. *She was covered in blood, the ends of her dark hair tacky with it. In one hand, she held a broken champagne bottle, and the other held a bloody carving knife that'd likely been part of the buffet.*

At first, she didn't seem to recognize Des, brandishing her weapons in tightly clenched fists. But then she blinked and relaxed somewhat, her shoulders shaking as she started to sob.

"What's happening?" she asked, tears rolling down her unusually blotchy face. "Why are they trying to kill us?!"

"Shh. They, whoever they are, may still be here, and they've got us outnumbered and outgunned," Des said quietly. For the moment, she ignored Philomena's body on the floor between them. She could do no more at the moment, than refuse to acknowledge it. "Are you okay?"

Holly nodded once, looking at the body. "If it wasn't for her and your father bringing me over here to chew me out over you, *I'd be out there—" Holly gestured at the wider room. "Dead. You saved my life. Again."*

Her full eyes began to brim over, and she let out a soft sob.

Never having been able to watch Holly cry, Des looked down, and found herself looking at the body, reaching out toward it hesitantly but unable to stop herself from doing so.

She had no idea what to expect of her hand and was surprised when she simply closed Phil's lifeless eyes and caressed her cheek. Her skin was soft and cool and strange—gray and bloodless.

"How long...?"

"Since this whole nightmare started," Holly said softly. "It was a heart-shot. She...she probably didn't feel it, it was so

fast." She sighed and another sob slipped out. "I'm so sorry, baby. So sorry."

"Has Nathan been back?"

Holly shook her head.

"Fuck." Des closed her eyes for a moment then opened them again. Phil was still there, looking less like she was dead and more like she was merely sleeping. But probably that was just Des's own wishful thinking. "Fuck. Nathan's lost his mate and unborn children in one night. He probably ran out there on a fucking suicide mission." Des buried her face in her hands, digging the heels of her palms into her eyeballs till they ached and burned. "Moon Above, this's all so fucked!*"*

And for the first time in her life since her mother died, Des felt like she might break down and actually cry.

But before she did, someone beat her to it, high and querulous—

❖

Des bolted awake from the memory couched in a nightmare—in a cold sweat and to the sound of crying.

From next to her in bed came a soft, petulant groan. "Baby..."

Heart still racing, Des pushed back the coverlet and rolled out of bed. "I know, I know, the twins are hungry again. I got it."

"Okay..."

Barely awake, Des stumbled across her room, to the twin bassinets.

In the thin moonlight peeking in from under the drapes, Des could easily see her little brother and sister, the former whimpering around the fist in his mouth, his big dark eyes opened wide and unseeing. The latter was still crying lustily, her tiny fists raised fretfully above her head.

"Ah, you're only crying so hard because you know you're gonna get picked up second," Des told her sister.

There was a soft knock at the door and Des smiled, scooping up a sibling in each arm. "It's open," she called just as softly.

The door cracked, spilling in gentle light from the hallway, and Ruby poked her head in, smiling. "Hungry?"

"Hungry," Des confirmed.

"Kitchen?"

"Kitchen."

Ruby's smile turned bright and fond as she made cooing noises at the crying, flailing child crooked in Des's right arm. "Then let's go-go-go! Whee!"

Des carefully, gratefully, handed Ruby the louder twin—who, as always, grew silent immediately once in Ruby's arms—and they were off to the kitchen.

❖

"How're those bottles coming, Big Sis?"

Ruby asked it quietly, practically crooned it at the twins, who watched her with wide-eyed wonder. Des grinned and tested each bottle then licked away the formula on her arm. "*Il perfetto!*"

"You hear that, guys? *Il perfetto!* Yes, it is! And all for you! Yay!"

Des brought the bottles over to the kitchen counter, where the twins were laid, tiny limbs all a-flail. Ruby kissed the bottoms of their little feet until they made those low, breathless, baby chuckles that still had a way of bemusing and surprising Des. The twins never laughed for *anyone* except Ruby.

"Here, let's get 'em fed *before* we play kissy-feet." Des tried to be gruff, but Ruby smiled up at her brilliantly, and it made her breath catch as always.

"Aw, but Big Sis, after bottle time, it's burpy-belly time, not kissy-feet time! Kiss-kiss-kiss!" Ruby followed word with deed, and the babies chuckled, waving their arms.

Des placed the bottles out of flailing reach and sat on the stool next to Ruby's. "You look ridiculous, by the way."

Ruby rolled her eyes, but continued kissing the twins' feet in an exaggeratedly noisy fashion. "Better than looking like a big ol' grumpy-puss. Besides, Winkin' and Blinkin' love it."

Her eyebrows shooting up, Des crossed her arms. "Winkin' and Blinkin', eh?"

"Mm-hmm."

"I guess that makes you Nod?"

"Or you," Ruby said, casting Des a sidelong glance and smile. This was the eighth set of placeholder names they'd gone through—Sonny and Cher being the most memorable—since The Purge, the night the Council of Alphas was all but exterminated. Everyone had been at Des and Jake to name their siblings, but neither of them were in any rush to do so, preferring instead to wait for Nathan to do the naming.

When he got back, that was.

After three days of not knowing whether Nathan would return or when, a hasty private funeral had been held for the twins' mother. In the fifteen days since that funeral, an ongoing search was being conducted for their father, who had not been seen by *anyone* since Des spotted him leaping through one of the Lenape Hall library windows. Temporary Alphahood had been conferred upon Jake in Nathan's absence. He and James now had the day-to-day running of Pack business divvied up between them.

The seven Alphas remaining who'd been Alphas *before* that awful night were all convened in Lenape Landing or its outlying suburbs despite the danger of this set-up. It was agreed that it was best for them to be at the Dyre's service, should she call for it.

"I don't know what I'd call them *for*," Ruby had confessed to Jake, James, and Des after one awkward conference call.

"Mainly, it's a show of solidarity on their part," Jake had said comfortingly. Then he'd frowned. "Even though I'm pretty sure Clara Kitchener still isn't really a fan of yours."

"Isn't a fan?" Des had snorted sarcastically, cracking her knuckles and glaring out the window. "I'm gonna have to put that bitch in her coffin if she becomes any less of a fan."

"Oh, I'm sure she won't be looking to do anything as stupid as *Challenge* Ruby. Not after The Purge, right?" James had looked from Jake to Des then to Ruby, who'd shrugged.

"Well, at least the other Packs are too busy choosing new Alphas through Right of Contest to want to Challenge Ruby's legitimacy. One good thing to come out of this clusterfuck," Jake had muttered wearily, nearly breathlessly.

Unlike Ruby and LaFours, whose bodies had quickly expelled the silver bullets, Jake was still recovering from the near fatal wound he'd received. The bullet had been close enough to his heart to damage one of his arteries, and it'd taken him days to expel the bullet and wake up, not that anyone had been certain he would. His weakness still showed in the small details, such as being unable to catch his breath sometimes, and his haggard, vaguely unwell face and slowly-fading pallor.

Then he'd shooed them all out of his office. Des and Ruby, at least, had obeyed, but James had not. From that day, on, they'd been handling the affairs of the Coulter Pack the way an Alpha and his life-mate would, as a team.

They spent hours of their days attending to Pack business, drilling Ruby in Loup history and protocol and law. She applied herself diligently and was proving to be an apt student, according to her teachers.

"Really, it feels more like we're reminding her of things she already knows, not teaching her something she has no familiarity with," James had told Des quietly one evening over dinner in the kitchen. At the other end of the counter, Jake and Ruby were discussing the finer points of Loup history like two old hands.

"Lucky you," Des'd said around a mouthful of steak. She, herself, was physically and mentally drained from trying to teach Ruby how to fight and defend herself. It was as if Ruby not only lacked any and all physical grace and instinct, but as if she was actively resisting trying to get them. She spent more time on the mat than she did on her feet.

And unlike the Ruby of before The Purge, this Ruby wasn't even sarcastic or disdainful, merely apologetic and absently self-effacing, as if none of it—the training, the conditioning, Des—were even blips on her radar.

It was maddening.

Well, at least she's good at playing nanny, Des brooded, watching Ruby tickle and kiss Winkin' and Blinkin'. *Moon Above knows Jake and I aren't exactly wards of the year. Between the two of us, we can barely keep the twins fed and diapered— and even* that *Ruby's done the bulk of. She's a natural mother. And I'm certain Thierry LaFours has noticed, if no one else has.*

Des frowned at the two bottles she'd just warmed up.

In the aftermath of The Purge, Jake had offered Thierry LaFours the Coulter hospitality during his indefinite stay in Lenape Landing.

Des didn't like it.

And it wasn't to say the man hadn't made himself spectacularly useful, spelling Des on Ruby-training duty.

Des *definitely* didn't like *that*.

And he'd even helped overhaul the manor's security system. The LaFours specialty was the tightening and breaking of security. Half the damn Pack were cops and the other half thieves, it seemed like. Thierry spent his free time patrolling the manor like any of Nathan's goons.

Des freely despised the man for it.

He'd also offered his extensive network of spies and stoolies in Ruby's service. She'd only asked they be used to track down any information on the conspirators in The Purge and to find Nathan Coulter.

So far, when it came to either of those things, LaFours's people, who even Des was willing to admit were practically the Loup FBI, were turning up nothing.

For the first time ever, Des was *worried* about Nathan.

"He'll be okay, Des."

Des blinked, and came back to the moment to find Ruby watching her, Winkin'—or was it Blinkin'?—in her arms, a bottle in hand. On the counter, the other twin was looking up at Des as if to say, *pick me up and feed me, already!* but not crying the loud, lusty cries of his sister.

So Des picked him up and fed him, and Ruby fed his twin. For a while, all Des could hear was the sound of the babies nursing, and everything was quiet and peaceful. A typical three a.m. at Coulter Manor.

"He's never come up against anything he couldn't handle. A team of assassins with silver bullets may just be that thing," Des said finally. "What if he's dead? What if he's on the run, too tired and wounded to fight, but too harried to get home? What if—"

"What if he's doing the same thing Thierry's spies are doing? Trying to track down the Loups responsible for the massacre?"

Des shook her head. "It's a nice thought, but..."

"But?"

"But, I don't wanna get my hopes up." Des shrugged and shifted her brother. "I already lost my mother. I don't wanna lose Nathan, too. I mean, we don't really get along, but he's one of my constants. He's always *there*, you know?"

Ruby nodded. "You love him."

Des sat back, shocked. "I..."

Ruby quirked a knowing eyebrow and Des blushed.

"Fine. I love him. There. Happy?"

"Ecstatic."

Des rolled her eyes and Ruby laughed.

"There's nothing shameful in loving a parent, Des." Ruby's smile turned wistful. "Even if the relationship with that parent is tumultuous and unconventional. Nathan is a good man. The kind you can trust with your life *and* your girlfriend."

Des snorted. "Trust me, Nathan and I didn't have anywhere near the same type. Hell, except for the fact that I'm here, and Winkin' and Blinkin' are here, I'd have thought the man was a eunuch."

Ruby laughed. "Well, it's good he found someone to love. After my mom walked out on us, my dad never found anyone else," she offered tentatively. Des tilted her head.

"You never talk about him. Is it painful?"

Ruby shrugged, this time, holding Des's sister close. "Kinda. But it feels good, too, to—you know, talk about him to someone—to keep his memory alive. To keep *my* memories of him alive." She hung her head. "I haven't had anyone to talk to about my father since George died."

Des bit her lip. "If you want, you can talk to me about him. And maybe sometimes I could tell you about my mom?" she said.

Ruby's eyes lit up. "You mean it?"

Nodding, Des found herself unable to meet the pure, simple joy that illuminated Ruby's dark eyes. It made her stomach do flip-flops, and her heart beat faster. "Of course. What're friends for?"

"Loaning money and providing alibis," Ruby deadpanned then laughed. "But do you mean it? *Are* we friends?"

"As fast as there ever were. We've bonded over many late nights and dirty diapers."

Ruby wrinkled her nose. "Too right. So, can I ask you something?"

"Shoot."

Eyes cast down at the baby in her arms, Ruby flushed. "Your wife…"

"Holly," Des said, and so saying, flushed herself.

"Yes, when did *that* happen? You're only, what? Twenty-three?" Ruby took a deep breath and forged ahead. "And does it have anything to do with why so many Loups seem so wary of you?"

Des blinked. Then she sighed, realizing that maybe the time had come to tell Ruby just who her protector really was. *I just didn't think it'd come this soon. Well, better it comes from my lips than anyone else's, I guess.* Des rocked Blinkin' for a few minutes, trying to figure out how to begin.

"You don't have to tell me, if you don't want to," Ruby said softly, frowning in concern. "Just know that whatever you tell me won't change the way I think of you. You're my friend, and you've saved my life more than once. I think the world of you, and *nothing* could change that."

Des blinked away a curious stinging in her eyes. "You may think that *now*."

"I *know* that. Always," Ruby said, her voice firm and grim, as if daring Des to prove her wrong. She reached out and caressed Des's cheek lightly. "I know it."

That unsettled feeling in her stomach and chest came back, and Des wondered if she needed an antacid or something.

"It's just…it's hard to know where to begin," she murmured, not wanting to disturb Ruby's touch. It felt nice.

But Ruby sat back, blushing, withdrawing her hand, anyway. "Well. Begin at the beginning. That's usually the best place to start." She smiled that gentle smile, but with a hint of wryness at the corners. "How did you find out you were a Loup?"

Des winced. "Ah, *that* beginning. Okay. Here goes. When I was fourteen, I was what you might call an at-risk kid." Des paused and snorted. "The fact is I was *rotten*. Always in trouble, running with a bad crowd. I was skipping school and failing every subject except math. And the only reason I wasn't failing that was because I aced all my math tests.

"I was a drinker and a partier and a stoner. I stayed out all night and slept all day. The only reason I wasn't sexually active was because I had no opportunity to be. Not that that stopped me from trying.

"Anyway, six months before I turned fifteen, I was in school—only because my mother had begged me to try harder, to at least hang on till high school was over—when I got called to the guidance counselor's office. "

❖

Des sat in the creaking, uncomfortable chair across from Mr. Tremblay and stared passively into his squirrely gray eyes.

"What's shakin', bacon?" she asked, when all he did was sneak glances at her and wring his neat, pale hands. "I haven't done anything lately. I've been a good little girl."

"Ah. Ah-ha-ha," he said—actually said, *instead of really laughing. "Yes, I'm certain you have. But, Jennifer, I'm afraid I have some terrible news...."*

Des rolled her eyes. "Who died?"

When Mr. Tremblay merely wrung his hands some more and looked at her pityingly, Des went cold. "Who died?" she asked again, even though she already knew. Why else would the news be coming from Mr. Tremblay, instead of from the one person whose death would actually matter to Des?

"WHO DIED?!" Des screamed suddenly, when Mr. Tremblay didn't answer right away. Startled, he took off his glasses and began to polish them with his tie.

"Listen, Jennifer, I need you to try and be calm—"

But he didn't get to finish telling Des what she should try and be. She'd already sprung and leapt over his desk, tackling him to the floor. She alternately screamed at him and throttled him.

Shortly after Des was tasered into immobility by a school security officer, Tremblay, with hand-shaped bruises already forming around his thin neck in a pretty purple ring, told the security guard who'd done the tasing, Officer Elizondo, that Jennifer had seemed much stronger than such a small young woman should.

"Like, Vulcan-*strength," he had said shakily, betraying both his youth and his overabundance of imagination. Officer Elizondo had merely rolled his eyes and made sure* not *to note that in his report.*

In the end, a social worker officially gave Des the news about her mother at the police station. She spoke with a dispassionate mix of wariness and weariness that Des was to come to know over the next several weeks.

"I'm sorry for your loss, Jennifer," the social worker said finally, edging her way to the door of the small room, which was used for the questioning of suspects and smelled like it: a mix of sweat, fear, and resentment.

"Yeah, whatever," was Des's numb reply. She hadn't looked up at the social worker once, but instead stared down into the cup of watery hot chocolate one of the PAs had brought her. It tasted like shit and did nothing to warm her cold right hand.

Her left hand, also cold, was cuffed to a table leg.

❖

It was an aneurysm, a different social worker told her two days later, this time in the bedroom of a temporary foster home. She shared it with three other girls who were sporadically attending the same high school as Des had.

Des hadn't been back to school since she'd tried to wring Mr. Tremblay's weedy neck. She'd been expelled.

"It was a time-bomb waiting to go off," the social worker, Flora Hart, had said with genuine compassion. Meaning the aneurysm. Flora Hart was, Des had sensed, still relatively new to the job. She looked it, anyway. "There was nothing anyone could've done to predict or prevent it."

"Okay," Des had said. Yet she secretly believed that the stress of working two jobs to support a child who treated her efforts with disdain and profligacy contributed to the time-bomb "going off."

Des knew that she'd killed her mother. Nothing ever could or ever would *change her mind about that.*

❖

Seven weeks after going to live in Santa Fe with her great aunt Clastine—older than dirt and tougher than nails—Des was still comfortably numb. She attended her new school without missing a day and avoided the kind of crowd she'd have been queen of at her old school. Her grades improved from straight Ds to straight Cs, but for an A average in Math.

She got a part-time job as a cart-wrangler at the local supermarket and managed to get neither fired nor written up. With her aunt's help, she opened a bank account and began saving her money for a rainy day. Maybe for college, though she had no idea what she was good for.

In other words, she was, for the first time since fifth grade, making an effort to be the kind of daughter her mother had deserved, even though it was too late.

She did her chores at Aunt Clastine's house without complaint, and was mostly left to herself. Aunt Clastine was of the mindset that children were better neither seen nor heard, and since Des managed to do both of those things most of the time, her aunt was satisfied that their arrangement would work. So was Des's latest case worker, another nameless, weary, wary woman whose lipstick was always smeared from worrying at her lower lip with large, square teeth.

One evening, after a perfunctory visit by the caseworker, Des was pushing her dinner around her plate and sighing. So much that Aunt Clastine, who could be counted on to ignore anything that wasn't outright mayhem or disobedience, looked up from her own efficiently cleaned plate and asked her what was wrong.

Des had opened her mouth to say, "nothing, ma'am." But what came out instead was: "Do you know who my father is?"

Aunt Clastine had sat back, the only indication of her surprise the raising of her drawn-on eyebrows. Finally, after a minute of stunned silence, Aunt Clastine had sighed and leaned forward, (elbows on the table, something she normally despised). "What did your mother tell you about him?"

Des fidgeted under the old woman's glare. "Nothing, except that he wasn't the man she'd thought he was, and she'd left him when she realized he'd never change."

Aunt Clastine snorted. "Well! I could've told her that from the beginning, and did!"

Des fought not to roll her eyes. "What was he like? What was his name?"

Smiling mirthlessly, Des's aunt took a sip of her water. "He was a proud, uppity man. Liked to put on airs. Neither tall nor short. Handsome enough. Real good at finding things." She frowned now. "Eerie-good. But he was an architect by trade, and he was in town to build a new office complex.

"His name was Coulter. Nathan Coulter."

Des's own eyebrows shot up. "A gringo?"

Aunt Clastine nodded. "Irish or Scottish or something."

"Huh." That explained why Des was so ghost-pale, even in the summers—except when she burned. Excited, now that she had a name to go with, she leaned forward. "Do you know where he was from?"

Aunt Clastine huffed. "From back East. Lenape Landing. And didn't everyone just make a big ruckus over that! Huh. Lenape Landing. Same as the ninth concentric circle of Hell, if you ask me. That city is a cesspool of corruption and decadence and—what's with all the questions about ancient history, Jennifer?"

Putting on her most innocent face, disinterested face, Des shoveled a forkful of peas into her mouth. "Nothing. Just curious."

"Well, curiosity killed the cat." Aunt Clastine stood up with her plate. "Now, hurry up and finish so I can wash these dishes."

"Yes, Aunt Clastine," Des said around another mouthful of peas.

Later that night, after a surprisingly short amount of time spent online, Des had not only found the one architect Nathan Coulter with a website, but she had a phone number for him. Probably for his office or secretary, but it was a number.

In slightly more time, she'd managed to suss out an address that was for one—one—of his homes. The one in Lenape Landing.

By eleven, Aunt Clastine was snoring.

By midnight, Des was buying a bus ticket.

❖

Lenape Landing was the largest city Des had ever been in, and even the air was different.

From the moment she stepped off the final bus, twenty-six hours after her initial boarding, she sensed her destination was like nothing she'd ever seen. And the evidence was all around her. The buildings were taller than in Santa Fe or Tucson, and the people moved faster, like they had mercury in their veins instead of blood. The streets were dirtier, with actual grime, not the ever-present dust and grit of the Southwest.

She walked around unafraid at four a.m. in the morning, duffle bag on shoulder, in an awed daze. She had her old trusty switchblade and could handle herself in a fight. She'd never before been afraid of the night or what it held, and she never would be.

Sun up found her in a twenty-four hour diner, slurping hot coffee and tearing into a breakfast of bacon, eggs, sausage, and pancakes. Spread out next to her plate was a local bus-map she'd brought with her from the depot. It confused her eyes, at first, but eventually she could trace a route from where she was, to the outskirts of Lenape Landing, where the larger homes and mansions were.

Breakfast safely put away, Des made her way to the nearest bus stop. Two hours later, despite rush-hour traffic, she was at the foot of Old Route 31, the last stop on the LL107 bus. From there, it was a half-mile walk to Nathan Coulter's estate.

❖

"Yes?"

Des peered up into the lens of the CCD camera, her finger still hovering at the intercom button she hadn't even pressed. She had, in fact, been dithering over whether she should even be there, and she was seriously considering making her way back to the bus depot and thence to Aunt Clastine's. She'd be in a metric shit-ton of trouble, she knew, but it might be better than the rejection possibly waiting behind the formidable gates at which she stood.

"Yes?" came the deep, patient voice again, and Des cleared her throat. No fear, she told herself, and she rolled her tense shoulders.

"Yeah, hi. My name is Jennifer Desiderio. My mother knew Nathan Coulter, and I'm here to see him."

"Do you have an appointment?"

Des snorted. "Do I look like someone with an appointment?"

"I'm afraid you'll have to make an appointment to see Mr. Coulter. He's a very busy man, and doesn't see anyone without an appoint—"

Des cut the voice off, irritation eclipsing fear. She'd come all this way, too far to be stymied by some voice in a security system. "Look, pal, I came here all the way from Santa Fe to see Mr. Coulter. Please tell him I'm here on behalf of Leandra Desiderio, and I promise you, he'll want to see me." Which may or may not have been a lie. After all, who knew how serious Coulter and her mother had been?

They may have just been fuck-buddies, *Des thought for the first time, shuddering.* Or it could be *he* left *her* because she got pregnant. Or—

Or a whole lot of things. There was only one way to find out.

"Please," Des said quietly, desperately. "It's really important that I see him, and maybe important for him to see me, too. Just tell him I'm Leandra Desiderio's daughter. If he doesn't want to see me after that, I'll lea—"

The gate slowly, soundlessly swung open.

With one last glance behind her, at the slice of Old Route 31 she could see beyond the trees and hedges, Des scurried inside before the gatekeeper changed his mind.

She followed the cobblestone path up to the mansion she'd seen through the gates, feeling smaller and scruffier with every step she took. But too soon, it seemed, she was at the open front door. A man stood framed in the doorway. He was wearing an expensive suit and looked like a male model, with perfect posture and narrow, handsome features. Going from the pictures she'd seen on the internet, this *was Nathan Coulter.*

This was her father.

Des glanced briefly down at her grubby, off-white "Born To Rock" t-shirt and denim cut-offs, and wished she'd thought to wear something a bit less her. *But she'd have to brazen it out.*

"Nathan Coulter?" she asked politely. The man crooked an eyebrow, his nostrils flaring slightly. Then he smiled a sardonic half-smile Des had seen in the mirror and in photos all her life.

"Yes," the man said in a low, pleasant tenor. "And you're Leandra's daughter?"

Des nodded. "Your daughter, too," she added.

"Yes, we do bear a rather strong resemblance to each other," Coulter said without any hint of surprise or dismay. "In fact, you look just like my mother."

Des shrugged, since she didn't know whether that was a good thing or a bad thing. Coulter crossed his arms and leaned against the doorpost. "How is Leandra, these days?"

"Dead." Des said, and Coulter's half-smile faded away, his look of absent amusement disappearing as if he'd taken off a mask. "It was an aneurysm. About four months ago. She didn't feel a thing, they say."

Coulter looked shocked and lost for a moment, then that mask came back on, minus the absent amusement.

"I'm sorry for your loss," he said stiffly, almost uncomfortably, then turned and walked inside. "Well, I suppose you'd best come in."

Des followed him inside, shutting the door behind her. It closed with a hollow boom.

❖

Here, Des paused in her tale. The twins were fast asleep and false dawn was lighting the sky. "Um, let's put the twins down for the night and I'll tell you the rest over coffee?" Ruby returned Des's crooked smile. Despite the tragic circumstances of the past few weeks, she'd been smiling more lately than she had since her father passed away.

"Okay."

They made their way back upstairs to Des's room. Ruby waited outside while Des put Winkin' and Blinkin' down, hesitant, as always, to enter Des's room when Holly was there.

It was still strange to think of Des as being *married*. She hardly seemed like the marrying type. Not a month ago, she'd been willing to start a friendship-with-benefits with Ruby on the premise that such friends could sleep together without any romantic feelings involved. Just for the fun of it.

Well, Ruby didn't know about *that*, but she *did* know she wasn't built that way. She'd only ever been romantically entangled with one person, and she'd fallen fast and hard. She'd thought those feelings were mutual, but they hadn't been. Casey Hampton had left her without so much as a backward glance.

In the end, it'd been easier and less painful to avoid anything that smacked of that kind of romantic entanglement, rather than have her heart so thoroughly broken twice in a lifetime.

"Alright, it's java time," Des said, shutting the bedroom door quietly behind her and interrupting the train of Ruby's thoughts. Ruby shook herself a little, and it turned into an all-over shudder. Des's lips pursed in consideration. "Are you okay?"

"Yeah, I'm okay. Why?" Ruby stretched long and wide, cracking her spine. Des eyed her worriedly.

"Nothing," Des said with a shrug, "it's just…the Full is in a few days, and you've already got the pre-show jitters."

"What do you mean?"

"Most of us don't get jittery until the night before the Full. But you've been all over the place for the past couple days. Groovin' and movin', hoppin' and boppin'. Like you've got bugs under your skin."

Ruby blushed, scratching her arms. "That's how I feel, most of the time. Like there're creepy-crawlies in my muscles, and my skin's too small. Like no matter how much I stretch and flex, I can't get comfortable."

Des nodded. "That sounds about right. Your body is getting ready for its first Change."

Ruby raised her eyebrows. "Will my voice get deeper? Will I get hair in funny places?"

"Smart ass," Des laughed. "It's nothing to be afraid of. It's just something your body does, now. In a year or so, you'll probably be able to control when the Change happens, even put it off entirely. Though that usually takes a few years longer."

Ruby sighed and started walking. Des followed her. "It all sounds so…"

"Weird?"

"Yeah. And painful."

"Well, it is, I won't lie. But you'll come through it like a trooper."

"You think so, huh?" Ruby grinned and Des grinned back brightly. Ruby's heart did calisthenics.

Be quiet, you, she told it, ignoring the way it just beat faster and made her feel hot all over. After three weeks of this, she was quite used to the sensation. She got it constantly around Des, and sometimes even around Thierry. She was afraid to question what the feelings meant but was even more afraid she already knew.

❖

The first few weeks at Nathan Coulter's home were an adjustment for Des, to say the least. She didn't know what she expected of a relationship with a father who hadn't even known she existed, but there seemed to be a thousand miles between them, even when they were in the same room together.

He didn't insist that they spend time together, though he didn't seem to mind when she joined him in the gym for exercise and training. He even began training her. Working out and sparring was the closest they ever really got to bonding.

After a month, Nathan's adopted son, Jacob, moved back home, ostensibly because he missed Lenape Landing, but likely to get to know Des. She didn't know whether to appreciate or be suspicious of him. But after getting to know Jacob "Jake to everyone" Coulter, she decided on the former. He was a cool guy—gay as the day was long, but without being annoyingly flame-y or bitchy—and always willing to spend time with her. He was also the one who drove Des to and from the expensive private high school in which Nathan had her enrolled.

Des made few friends there, but she didn't mind. She had Jake.

After three weeks in Lenape Landing, Aunt Clastine had come to visit Des and see how she was getting on. Surprisingly, she and Nathan got along well, despite whatever was in their shared past. In the end, Aunt Clastine signed over her guardianship rights to Nathan. In what would have probably been worth some celebratory family hugs with any other person, Nathan had calmly invited Des and Jake to his country club for golf. Jake gently suggested to Nathan they go shopping for a new civilian wardrobe for Des, first and foremost, which had resulted in Des getting a platinum credit card via courier a day later.

By the time Des turned fifteen, everyone had established a routine, of sorts. Nathan wheeled and dealed and designed buildings. Jake worked on his pre-doctoral opus, and Des went to school and stayed out of trouble.

It was stable until the morning Des had woken up feeling under the weather and headache-y. She had shuffled through her morning routine, picked over her breakfast, made her lunch—a rare steak sandwich and an apple—and dragged herself out to Jake's sporty red Prius.

"You look awful," he'd noted, starting up the car and pulling out of the garage. "Late night?"

Des had sighed. "Nah. I just feel crappy."

"You look *crappy."*

"Your face *looks crappy."*

"Witty comeback, on opposite day."

"Blegh," Des had replied then threw up her breakfast on Jake's dashboard. For several drawn out moments, neither of them had said anything. Just stared at the puke.

"What say we keep you home today?" Jake'd finally asked, backing the car into the garage once more and shutting off the engine.

"Blegh." Des added green bile to the puddle of used breakfast dripping from the dashboard and onto her legs. Then she passed out.

❖

"Well, well. It lives."

Des woke up in her own bed to blurred vision, a temperature, nausea, and a pretty young black woman with short dreads, leaning over her and smiling.

"What the fuck happened to me? Who're you?" Des croaked. The woman's bright smile grew brighter.

"You ralphed all over your brother's car and fainted."

Des remembered that part pretty well. "I mean after that. Are you a doctor?"

"Of sorts."

That wasn't very reassuring. "So, what've I got? Flu?" Having never had the flu, Des could only go on what she'd observed and read. Sure sounded like the flu to her.

"No, not the flu," the woman said. "My name is Philomena Simms, and I'm kind of a...general practitioner. They call me on the rare occasions they get sick."

Des tried to sit up then flopped weakly back. "And who's they?*"*

"Oh, lots of people," Philomena said, patting Des's hand. "Your father can explain better than I can. In the meantime, you'll be weak for at least the next few days."

Des thought that over and found it to be unacceptable. She tried to sit up again. This time she made it, though she was sweating and the room was spinning. Philomena watched her with what looked to Des like a mix of amusement and disapproval.

"Where's Nathan? Or Jake? I wanna see them," Des said, pushing back the blankets covering her and surprised at the chill in the room. She shivered hard, and the room spun even more. "Ah, fuck.*"*

Philomena pushed her back down to the bed without any real effort, and pulled the covers back over her. "I'll get them for you. Just try and relax."

Des stared at Philomena hard, taking her measure then nodded.

When Philomena left the room, Des closed her eyes for a moment and didn't open them again for nearly a day.

❖

The next time she woke, she wasn't in her right mind. At least she didn't think she was. It was the middle of the night, and her bedside lamp was on its lowest setting. Laying on her legs was a dog.

No, a wolf.

It was ridiculously huge and heavy, yet its weight didn't bother Des. It was russet brown, and watching her with intelligent hazel eyes.

"What the fuck?" she rasped dryly, her parched throat clicking. The wolf whuffed quietly and leapt off the bed. It went over to the slightly ajar door and barked. A minute later, a smiling Philomena came in with a teapot and a cup.

"Is that your wolf?"

Philomena laughed. "Actually, he's his own *wolf. Perhaps if you're extra good, he'll let you pet him." She sat at Des's bedside and poured her a cup of tea. Meanwhile, the wolf leapt up on the bed again and leaned up to lick Des's face.*

"Eww," Des gasped in surprise. As if understanding her, the wolf licked her face even harder and faster. "Back off!"

Philomena laughed again. "All right, Jake, stop torturing Des and let me get this Feverfew into her."

Des started. "My brother's name is Jake, too."

"Hmm," Philomena said. The wolf finally stopped licking Des, turning around in a circle before settling at the foot of the bed. Then Philomena said, "Here. Sip this."

Des opened her mouth when the teacup touched her lips. Philomena's brew tasted vile. She would've spit it back into the cup, but her surprise at its taste made her reflexively swallow.

"Ugh. God, what is *this shit?" she demanded.*

"Feverfew tea. It'll bring down your fever and make the Change easier on you."

Des frowned. "What change?"

Suddenly Jake-the-wolf leapt off the bed again and paced around in front of the window, in the moonlight. He stood on his hind legs, pawing at the air for a few moments, then he seemed to…elongate. To stretch. *Des would've thought she was hallucinating, but for the sounds of cracking bones and the pained whines coming from the wolf.*

Soon, not just its body was rearranging itself, but its face, too. The features, aside from becoming elongated, were also flattening, becoming almost human.

Familiar.

"That Change," Philomena said drily.

"The fuck!" Des watched in horror as the wolf's tail shortened, the brush of fur disappearing into skin that likewise disappeared into the area just above its rump. In fact, the hair all over its body was being absorbed into its skin. Paws turned into long hands and black nails retracted, lightened, and became clear. The same happened to the wolf's feet.

Bones cracked as legs and arms lengthened and straightened, and the wolf let out a howl of agony that wavered until it became a human yell, hoarse and broken. Its snout shrank into the restructured bones of its face, and its ears pinned themselves back, rounding off and gaining lobes.

Finally, the fur on its head gained a wave, and lengthened until it hung halfway down an all-too-human back that was narrow and knobby of spine. And there, at last, in the cold, silver-white moonlight, stood a naked man, panting, shaking, and sweating, even in the seeming chill of the room. He braced his hands on his bony knees and groaned, his hair hanging in his face.

After a silent, charged minute, he glanced over at Des, and smiled tiredly.

"Hiya, Jenny," her brother huffed out breathlessly. For the third time in two days, Des fainted.

❖

Ruby gaped at Des, who smiled a little and shrugged.

"*You* fainted? *Three times*?" Ruby asked, and Des snorted.

"Okay, not the question I expected you to ask, but yeah," she said, crossing her arms. "It was a very trying time, and I was *sick*."

Ruby waved her hand. "Excuses," she joked, then grinned. "I totally didn't faint when you showed *me*."

"Yeah, you just ran like your ass was on fire, and your hair was catching," Des snorted again.

Ruby picked up her coffee and took a prim sip. "Well," she said, "you were intimidating."

Des preened a little. "Really?"

"Yes. Of course. You were a *werewolf*, Des. And a *big* one."

"Ah, go on," Des blushed. "I'm actually small for a Loup. You should see Nathan when he Changes. Big as day, black as night. Or Jake. Holy *shit* is Jake big. The size of a Shetland pony."

"Sheesh." Ruby shook her head. "So the next time you woke up, was Jake a wolf again?"

Des sighed. "No. But *I* was."

❖

She was having a dream.

No, a nightmare.

She was in agony all over, so acute and deep she barely felt it when she rolled out of bed and hit the floor.

She started screaming for help, but nothing came out of her mouth except a croaking whisper. The agony in her face ramped up another few notches, as it felt like every bone in her face was breaking and grinding against the tatters of muscles and nerve-endings.

The bone-breaking, bone-grinding pain spread down her body, to all her joints, even the ones in her toes and fingers. And suddenly her skin felt as if it was on fire, burning and itching and tight. She tried to scream again. This time, something loud and only marginally human came out.

Frightened, Des rolled onto her hands and knees, trying to get to her feet. She'd just made it when it felt like her spine was being split down the middle and her ribs began to cave in, before they began to arch and curve, and bell out, respectively.

Panting and moaning, Des could only lay on her stomach as pain rolled over her for what felt like eternity.

Scents and tastes began to wash over her: carpet cleaner, shoe-leather, her own sweat and fear, and other scents she'd had no idea she'd even noticed or catalogued. Nathan, Jake, and the sweet, spicy scent of the woman who called herself Philomena.

These scents were soothing, calming. They meant she wasn't alone. Indeed, she heard voices from all over. They were outside the house, inside the house, in Nathan's office and in the kitchen.

The kitchen smelled like food, and after two days of not eating Des was ravenous.

She opened her eyes and saw—

Colors, bright and bleeding.

The colors of her throw-rug, which far from feeling comfortable, suddenly felt scratchy and synthetic, and smelled like a chemical-dump.

The bone-grinding sensation reached a crescendo so sharp and high, Des thought her heart would just give out before it abated with a near audible click as every one of her bones stopped moving and grinding, and all but snapped into their new places.

Shaking her head, Des got to her feet—all four of them.

All four of them?

"Oh, fuck," she said softly, and it came out as a soft, resigned whuff.

CHAPTER TEN

D amn."
Des raised her mug in a wry toast. "Damn, indeed."
Ruby sighed, leaning on the counter across from Des, her elbows on the table and her head in her hands. "So that's what I have to look forward to?"

"In all its glory, yes." Des reached out and rubbed Ruby's shoulder. "But you get used to it. And it hurts much less over time. Granted, it'll never be Shangri-La, but it gets better. And by the time you're Nathan's age, it'll barely take any time or hurt at all. According to him, anyway."

Ruby sighed again. "God, this is all so scary. I keep expecting to have a breakdown at any moment over all of this, but then I don't."

"And probably won't." Des shrugged at Ruby's look of surprise. "You've had nearly a month to get used to the idea. Plus, you're stronger than you seem to think."

"I don't *feel* strong," Ruby said doubtfully. "I feel like I'm living in a bubble of denial, and I'm gonna be up shit-creek when it pops."

"You won't be. You'll have me and Jake and Thierry LaFours, I suppose, to walk you through it. Before and after."

Ruby nodded, and they finished their coffee, each lost in her own thoughts for some time. "What's it like? Being a wolf, I mean."

Des smiled. "Pretty much the best damn thing in the world. Everything is so bright and alive and *electric*." She shivered happily, her smile turning into a sharp, canny grin.

Ruby sighed, glancing away for a moment, willing a sudden blush to fade. "I just don't know if I can do this. I mean, not just being a werewolf, but being the *queen* of the werewolves. I've seen some of what Jake's been handling and it's daunting."

"Which is why you'll have us to help you. And believe me, the only big priority you've got now is finding the party responsible for The Purge. And you've got plenty of Loups on the case. Namely Thierry LaFours." Des sniffed disdainfully. "I suppose if anyone can find the mastermind behind that, it's him and his Pack."

Ruby tilted her head questioningly. "You don't like Thierry very much, do you?"

Shrugging, Des looked away from Ruby. "I'll admit there're Loups that I like better."

"Is there bad blood between you?"

Des opened her mouth to speak, then shut it with a snap, turning slightly to face the back staircase. A moment later, Holly Black Lodge came down the stairs on cat-quiet bare feet, wearing a white, silken negligee and nothing else. Her long dark hair was artfully messy, and her eyes seemed to sparkle as she spotted Des.

"Couldn't sleep?" Des asked, standing up. Holly smiled her sexy, knowing smile and insinuated herself into Des's willing embrace. They kissed briefly.

"Couldn't sleep without you. Your bed's so lonely when I'm by myself, Holly pouted. Then she looked at Ruby. "You don't mind if I borrow my wife for a while, do you, DyreMother?"

Inwardly Ruby cringed. Being called "DyreMother" made her feel every minute of her twenty-eight years and then some. She had a feeling Holly did it on purpose, but the woman had never been anything other than outwardly polite and respectful to her.

"Of course I don't," Ruby said, putting on her most friendly smile. And what else could she say? *Yes, I mind terribly, Des is mine?* Hardly. Ruby's chance at making Des hers, if such a thing could be accomplished, if such a thing had been her wish, had passed. No amount of late-night bonding would change that.

"C'mon, love, let's go," Holly murmured, taking Des's hand and pulling her toward the stairs. Des started to follow but glanced back at Ruby questioningly. Ruby's fake smile turned genuine.

"Go on. We'll finish our conversation some other time."

Des frowned and resisted Holly's tugging. "It's not that I don't want to tell you, it's just kinda hard for me to talk about. I think I need some time."

"No, yeah, it's cool," Ruby said, waving Des off with false jocularity. "I don't want to monopolize your time. You've already done so much for me."

"When the DyreMother says go, we should probably *go*, Jennifer," Holly said, and this time, Des followed when she tugged. But not without looking back, still questioning. Ruby waved again, still smiling.

She held that smile until Des was out of sight around the curve of the staircase.

Then she groaned and buried her face in her arms, resting her wet, heated cheek on the cool, dry counter—

❖

—only to start awake when someone touched her shoulder.

In fact, she nearly fell off her stool, but for strong hands that caught and righted her.

"I'm so sorry. I didn't mean to startle you," a low voice said, and Ruby laughed a little, turning to face the owner of those hands.

"No, I'm the one who's sorry, Thierry. I didn't mean to fall asleep in the kitchen, and I certainly didn't mean to startle awake so easily." She squinted in the bright, early morning light and rubbed her eyes. "What time is it?"

"A little after seven," he replied, sounding amused. But for some reason, this didn't bother her. She stretched and yawned, listening to her stiff muscles creak.

"Des and I were up with the twins for a while, then she went back to bed, and I fell asleep in my favorite room of the house," she said sheepishly. "I guess I needed the sleep, but now I feel all stiff and cold."

"Well, perhaps we could go for a walk? That will loosen your muscles up and we could...talk." Thierry quirked an eyebrow and smiled rakishly. "Once around the manor, and then I'll make you breakfast." His smile did tingly things to her, almost in the same way Des's did, but with noticeably less intensity.

"A walk and breakfast?" Ruby hopped off the stool and took Thierry's arm. "You've got yourself a date, Mister."

Thierry took her other hand, bowed over it and kissed it.

Ruby blushed and looked away, but not before she caught the return of that wry smile.

❖

Des knocked on the office door and let herself in even as Jake's harried voice said, "Enter at your own risk!"

He sat behind Nathan's desk, typing away furiously on Nathan's laptop. But he looked up to Des for a moment, and he smiled. "Ah, *comment ca va?*"

Rolling her eyes, Des dredged up her rusty French. "Eh. *Ca va. Et toi?*"

"*Ca va.*" Jake stopped typing and rubbed his tired eyes. "Been reading reports from Thierry's guys all day. And they're all in French."

"Yikes." Des approached Nathan's huge desk and sat on the edge, across from Jake. "I don't know how you do it, man. I'd demand that their reports be in good ol' American."

Jake laughed wearily. "A good portion of the LaFours Pack doesn't even *speak* American."

"Well, they ought to after, what? A hundred years?" Des crossed her arms. "But forget them. I came to find out if there's any news about Nathan or the assholes behind The Purge."

Jake shook his head. "Not a damn thing. All we've managed to ascertain is that the assassins weren't from any pack in the U.S. There's evidence, however, that they may have come from somewhere in Eastern Europe."

"From the so-called 'Old World?'"

Jake nodded. "I haven't been able to contact Lazslo Kiraly, the European Dyre, directly, so we can't tell if they're declaring war or if this is an independent action perpetrated by a few terrorists. We just don't know. And until we have an acting Dyre, we can't officially bring up the matter with the Kiraly and his Council." He sighed tiredly, burying his face in his hands. His long hair fell forward and for the first time, Des noticed silver in it. Jake was young for a Loup, but as of three weeks ago, he had the worries of a Loup thrice his age. Not to mention the injury he'd suffered, and from which Des suspected, he might never fully recover.

"Well, the Full's only two more nights off. Once Ruby's had her first Change, she can start taking over some of her responsibilities." Des smiled her commiseration, but Jake merely sighed again.

"You and I know that the first Change is an arbitrary milestone in the Dyrehood. It doesn't mean one is more or less ready for anything than any other Loup." Jake leaned back in Nathan's chair, running his hands through his hair.

Frowning, Des picked up a framed photo of herself and Jake off Nathan's desk. In the photo, they were both mugging ridiculously: Des making her best monster face, and Jake caught in the middle of flipping his eyelids inside out.

She didn't remember posing for the photo, or who might have taken it. Certainly not Nathan. She couldn't remember ever noticing it on Nathan's desk before. But then, she'd usually avoided his office. Especially when he was in it.

This touch of sentimentality on Nathan's part surprised her, and made her feel a pang of something that was sharp and painful, and lived in the region of her heart.

We have to find him, she thought grimly, putting the picture down. *Once Ruby's had her first Change, once she's running the place, that'll be our first priority, Jake and me.*

"You're underestimating her because she's inexperienced," Des said softly. Jake blinked at her and smiled wearily.

"And you're *over*estimating her because you love her."

Des sat back so hard she almost fell off the edge of the desk. "Of course I love her. She's my Dyre."

Jake swung his bare feet up on the desk and leaned back until he was smiling at the ceiling. "That's not what I mean, and we both know it."

"Fuck what you *think* you know."

"If you want her, you'd better make your affections known before Thierry LaFours does."

Crossing her arms, Des huffed. "He can do whatever he likes. That's not going to get him Ruby."

"Oh, won't it?" Jake looked at Des for a second before resuming his contemplation of the ceiling. "She's young, lonely, scared, and clearly not used to the kind of attention and chivalry he shows her. And he's obviously intent on wooing her."

Des snorted. "Just because he wants to get his dick wet doesn't mean he wants to *woo* her."

"Don't be crude, Des. And who says he just wants to 'get his dick wet,' as you so classily put it? Who's to say his feelings for her aren't as strong as yours?"

"I'm telling you, I don't *have* feelings for—"

"Okay. Whatever you say. Just keep in mind that Thierry LaFours is pretty old school. The kind that will mate for life. So if anyone else was interested in Ruby, they'd better get on plighting their troth before she winds up out of reach forever."

Before Des could respond to that—with what, she didn't know—the door opened and James came in, bearing a tray of food and a bottle of merlot.

"Knock, knock," he said, grinning. "It's time for all good little Loups to have lunch."

"You're so good to me," Jake said, returning the grin and sitting up. James put the tray on the desk in front of Jake and leaned down to kiss him hello. And hello. And hello.

Des took that as her cue to make herself scarce, but Jake's words rang in her ears for hours afterward.

❖

That evening, Evelyn Carnahan-Prevost and her husband arrived in town.

James and one of Thierry's people, a silent, red-haired Amazon of a woman called Madeleine, went to pick them up from the airport, and were home a few hours later.

Ruby expected someone who either looked like Des or even Madeleine, perhaps, but Evelyn was a tall, cool, aristocratic blonde who could've graced any runway in the world with her high, prominent bone structure and long-legged stride.

When she stalked down the front hall of Coulter Manor, Ruby, who'd been waiting on the stairs in a sweatshirt and jeans, immediately jumped up and smoothed her rumpled clothes. Evelyn spotted her, and smiled a welcoming, hostess's sort of smile. In her casual khaki dress, and with her hair pulled back in a loose ponytail, she still managed to look elegant in a way that made Ruby feel rumpled and frumpy.

"Hello," she said in a low, Lauren Bacall sort of purr. Her nostrils flared delicately. "You must be the new Dyre."

"I must be," Ruby replied dryly, holding out her hand. But Evelyn merely came up the first few steps and kissed Ruby's cheeks, European-style. "Um…"

"Let me get a good look at you," Evelyn said, leaning back to look Ruby over. Ruby did the same, noting that Evelyn shared the same features as James, only feminized and finer.

"Oh, but you're so lovely!" Evelyn exclaimed, laughing. "Darling, come look at our new Dyre! Isn't she lovely?"

Ruby then noticed the man who had been trailing in Evelyn's wake along with James. He was tall, though not as tall as Evelyn, with sandy hair and pale, watchful blue eyes. He looked Ruby over in a way she didn't quite like, as if she were something he wasn't certain was worth acquiring. Then he smiled, and it didn't reach those watchful eyes.

"Yes, quite," he said dismissively, looking around him with an expression of weary disappointment. He ascended the stairs, gliding past Ruby without even introducing himself. He smelled of expensive leather and wool, some strange, astringent aftershave, and mulled wine. "Ellery, do be so good as to show us to our room. It's been a long flight, and we would like to freshen up."

James, a step behind his brother-in-law, made a face that only Ruby saw. "Of course, Julian. Evvie, let's go."

Linking her arm through Ruby's, Evelyn followed her husband and brother up the stairs, all the time chattering away about the flight in from Prague.

Not once did she mention George, and Ruby didn't have the heart to bring him up.

❖

With Evelyn and Julian shown their room, James excused himself and Ruby, taking her by the arm and leading her out of their room. She and James took the back staircase down to the kitchen.

"She's so elegant!" Ruby finally exclaimed, almost accusingly, to James. James smiled absently, looping his arm through Ruby's much like his sister had.

"Oh, sweetie, she's elegant when she *wants* to be, which is certainly not all the time. Before she settled for Julian, she used to gad about the world in khakis and tie-dyed shirts. Half the time, you wouldn't even know she was blonde under all the road dust she was covered in." James laughed and escorted Ruby to a stool, handed her onto it like she was a *lady* or something. Bemused, Ruby blushed and waved him away with a murmured *go on.*

Then she picked up on a part of what he'd said. "What do you mean *settled* for Julian?"

James grimaced. "Evvie and I have had our differences over the years, but the bottom line is, she's my big sister, and I adore her endlessly. I want the best of everything for her, and..." He glanced back at the stairs, his nostrils flaring. "...and Julian Prevost is *not* the best."

Ruby smiled in commiseration. "Well, he seems very..." she trailed off, at a loss for words that were complimentary.

"Exactly," James sighed. "He's an Old World snob who thinks because he's of the Elder Packs, that he's better than everyone. That includes my sister," James added grimly.

Ruby frowned. "If she's so beneath him, why marry her?"

"Why else, my dear? Power. Influence." Smiling ruefully, he sat next to Ruby. "All of which my sister has inherited and cultivated. My father's reign as Dyre was dynamic, if nothing else, and he carried a considerable cachet even across the Pond, upstart half-breed that he was." That rueful smile turned almost fond. "Evvie, despite her complete lack of interest in the title, was presumed by the European Council of Alphas to be the natural heir to the Dyrehood. The Elder Packs have never accepted that this is simply not the way it works for the North American Packs anymore. That the Dyrehood is not inherited by blood-kin. In their eyes, Evvie, being the eldest sibling, sound of mind and body, and most definitely not a poor, crippled Latent, like *moi*, would have been the heir-presumptive, so there was, and still is, a great clamor for her society. Julian was one of the clamorers."

"Oh." Ruby shook her head. Just when she thought she had a handle on Loup politics, she had a whole new set of Packs to deal with. Except for Nathan's Big Book of Begats and a few historical connections, she'd honestly never given a thought to the Loups of other continents. "So, he doesn't love her?"

James shrugged. "Evvie's *impossible* not to love, and I think Julian loves her as much as he's able. But I don't think he's *very much* able, when it comes to loving someone other than himself."

Ruby shook her head again. "Well, what's he going to do now that *I'm* the heir-presumptive? He already seems to not like me."

This time, James was the one to wave Ruby away. "He's like that with everyone. Which isn't to say that he *doesn't* despise you, but he despises pretty much everyone else, too."

"That actually makes me feel better." Ruby laughed a little. "At least I can rest assured he won't be sneaking into my room tonight to garrote me."

"What, and get his hands dirty? Heavens forfend!" James chuckled then cocked his head. "Ah, my liege approaches."

"I hate it when you call me that, Jamie." Jake yawned as he entered the kitchen, one hand up to cover his mouth. He looked disheveled and exhausted, but James cast a covetous eye his way nonetheless.

"That's not what you were saying last night...my liege."

Jake turned red and leaned against the doorway, resplendent in yet another Acapulco shirt and a pair of baggy madras shorts. His feet were bare, and his hair was loose around his slightly hunched shoulders.

"Other than treating Ruby to snippets of our sex life, darling, what're you up to?"

"Oh, just giving her the skinny on his Royal Doucheness, Emperor Julian."

"Ah, I see." Jake quirked a curious eyebrow at Ruby. "Has he told you about how Julian only married Evelyn for her money and influence?"

"Yep."

"Then you're all caught up." Jake shuffled into the kitchen and sat on Ruby's other side with a sigh of relief. As always, she noticed his pallor and slight breathlessness, and it hurt her heart. "At least on that front. I've only met him in passing, but from all accounts, Julian's a ruthless climber. I'm surprised he hasn't started ingratiating himself to *you*."

"He was downright hostile to her," James said, rolling his eyes.

"I guess he would be," Jake murmured thoughtfully. "But it's quite odd of him to *show* it, if he plans on getting you on his side. Through Evelyn, he's got considerable interests in the U.S. and Canada. It'd behoove him to have the Dyre on his side to make sure his wheels get greased."

"Grossest. Metaphor. *Ever*." James mock-shuddered and Jake laughed.

"Oh, c'mon, if it weren't for his personality—"

"—I still wouldn't fuck him with someone else's dick." James finished firmly. "He's got a face like a rabid weasel."

"James!" Jake burst out laughing again. James shrugged unapologetically.

"Evvie absolutely *hated* it when I used to call him her weasel-faced fuck-toy."

"I can't imagine why." Jake rolled his own eyes, now. "Still, there must be something to him that gets her going. I'll bet he's fantastic in bed."

"Not *even* with someone. Else's. Dick," James reiterated. At this, Jake subsided with his hands raised in placation. "Anyway, onto happier topics. Tomorrow night is *the night*, huh?"

Realizing he was talking to her, Ruby smiled a little. "Yeah. The moon's at its Full, and I'll turn into a werewolf. It'll be a mitzvah."

Jake slung an arm around Ruby, like she'd seen him do with Des a hundred times, and hugged her close for a few moments. "It really will. Granted, the Change itself is kinda uncomfortable. But once you get used to it—even *before* you get used to it, really—it's *so* worth it." He squeezed her shoulder reassuringly. "The trick is not to fight the Change. To give in to it, even urge it along. Go headlong into it. Remember the faster it happens, the sooner it's over, and the fun can begin."

Ruby mulled that over for a few minutes as Jake got up, stood behind James and wrapped his arms around him. James leaned back into the embrace and asked Jake how he was feeling.

"Like a walking shambles, as usual, these days," Jake said with a sigh. Then he smiled, leaning in to kiss James's neck just below his ear. "But definitely better now that I'm out of the office and with you."

"You're just saying that because you want to get in my pants."

"Am I that obvious?"

"You're poking a hole in the front of *your* shorts and the back of *my* jeans. Yes, you're *that* obvious."

Jake chuckled, kissing James's earlobe, where he whispered something that made James smirk.

"Sure ya got the energy, young buck?"

"At least twice as much as you do, old man."

"Get a room," Ruby said, good-naturedly. Jake peered at her from around James.

"Best idea I've heard all day. But whatever will you do without the pleasure of our company?"

Ruby thought of how Thierry always managed to find her before she'd been alone for too long, and she grinned. "I'll find a way to keep myself amused."

Just then the back door opened and Thierry walked into the kitchen, like Heathcliff straight in from the moors. He was frowning, but when his eyes met Ruby's, he smiled, and she smiled back.

James's gaze moved back and forth between them, and he raised his eyebrows slightly.

"'Keeping oneself amused'? Is that what the kids are calling it these days?" he asked dryly, then squawked when Jake smacked his thigh.

❖

Shortly after Thierry arrived, so did Evelyn, which put the kibosh on James's and Jake's plans to go to bed early.

Evelyn, James, and Thierry regaled Ruby with stories about George, some funny, some touching, some just plain *weird*, during which Ruby upwardly revised her estimation of Evelyn. She was a cool customer, yes, in the way George had been sometimes, but quite effusive once she warmed to her audience, which she did quickly. She and James fought good-naturedly over who would get to tell Ruby which stories, and tried to outdo each other in the telling.

Then she and James made a simple, yet delicious dinner of steaks cooked rare with onions while keeping everyone in the kitchen amused.

"Ellie, remember how scandalized Mother was when Dad decided to teach us to cook?" Evelyn asked James as he cut onions, popping pieces into his mouth every so often. She was seasoning the steak efficiently, rubbing it with herbs and squeezing lemon everywhere.

"*Do* I!" James laughed, smoothly, quickly dicing onions. "She kept moaning that that was what the help was for. But Dad kept insisting that we learn to do the 'basic necessaries' of life. Like cook for ourselves, keep our rooms relatively clean—"

"—and that time he tried to take us hunting with that ancient blunderbuss he called a gun, and Mother put her foot down, and said no—"

"—and then he did it anyway." James finished wistfully. "Not that Mother didn't know he was going to. I think she just felt she should put up a token protest."

"Well, she *did* get him that new set of rifles for his birthday, so I think she secretly approved," Evelyn said, waving one seasoned, blood-smeared hand gracefully. "At least of him spending time with us."

James popped another piece of onion into his mouth and Jake, sitting next to Ruby once more, sighed. "Go easy on those raw onions, babe. I plan on kissing you later."

"As if you care what's been in my mouth once we start making out." James snorted and ate another piece of raw onion just to prove his point. Then he turned to Evelyn. "Anyway, speaking of gigantic dicks, where's your lesser half?"

Evelyn gave James a stern look. "*My husband* is out hunting. You know perfectly well he prefers his meals on the fly."

"How *is* Julian, by the way?" Thierry asked, and Evelyn smiled at him.

"He's doing well, as always, Uncle Theo." She cast a dazzling smile on Ruby. "This past summer, we helped broker a peace treaty between several of the Eastern European Packs, including the Patsonos and the Kovacs. Julian's *amazing* when it comes to hammering out the fine details. I mostly just looked fabulous and said inspiring things."

Thierry snorted. "Don't sell yourself short, Evelyn. You've got something equally as important as good negotiating skills. You've got the common touch, something our dear Julian doesn't quite grasp."

"Like I said, he's a gigantic *dick*," James added, receiving another glare from his sister. "What? I'm just saying you could do better."

"What if I don't want better? What if I want what I've got, hmm?" Evelyn challenged.

James made a frustrated gesture. "Remember that really nice, cute hippie you used to see?"

"You mean *Carl*? The boy I went to *Woodstock* with?"

"That's the one! He was all right. He had *really* good drugs," James mused.

"Yes, *there's* a wonderful criterion for choosing a life-mate, his ability to get LSD under any circumstances." Evelyn rolled her eyes. "At any rate, he and I were just friends with bennies. He had the drugs I liked, and I let him fuck me. It was almost like a business arrangement."

James rolled his eyes, too. "The common touch, indeed," he announced to the room at large.

"Oh, don't pretend to be such a prude." She turned to Jake. "I could tell you stories about this one that would curl that lovely hair of yours. Have you ever heard the term 'daisy-chain'?"

"Now, now, we weren't talking about me, we were talking about dear Julian and you," James said hastily, shifting his glance between his sister and his lover.

Jake, far from seeming dismayed, blew James a kiss. "You think you're the only one in this relationship who's been in an orgy?"

This time, James's mouth was the one to drop open.

"I vote we stop this line of conversation," Ruby said.

Thierry nodded. "I second that motion."

"Motion carried."

Everyone looked up at Julian standing in the kitchen doorway. He was dressed in what, for him, was no doubt a casual outfit: a pair of gray twill slacks, loafers, and a white linen shirt. Ruby thought its simplicity probably cost more than her monthly salary at the college.

He sauntered into the kitchen, immediately heading toward his wife, whom he pecked on the cheek.

"Ooh, careful, darling, I've got blood on me." But she pecked him back carefully. "I thought you were off hunting."

"I was, but I wasn't terribly in the mood for rabbit and squirrel. I've grown so used to deer, after Hungary." Julian glanced at Jake and smiled condescendingly. "I don't know how you do it, Jacob. Running around chasing rodents to fill your belly. I should've gone quite mad."

"What can I say? I love the exercise," Jake replied sanguinely, smiling his own lazy smile. "And I'm not really up to running down deer, lately."

"Ah, yes. The Incident." Julian paused thoughtfully. "How're you healing?"

Jake's, James's, and Thierry's eyebrows went up.

"I'm getting there," Jake said. "I still tire and get winded easily, but I'm getting there."

"Thank you for asking," James added warily, peering at Julian as if suspecting he was a pod-Loup.

Julian waved a hand. "Frankly, we of the Elder Packs were horrified when we received word of what had happened. As a result, the Alphas, in their panic, have circled the wagons, as you Americans say, and clamped down on security. It's grown quite claustrophobic in the European Loup community. I must say, it's something of a relief to get away from all that.

"And we, of course, wish to extend our aid in any way that we may," he said smoothly. His speech had a practiced ring to Ruby's ears. But when she glanced around the kitchen, everyone else seemed to take his words at face value.

"Julian is right. We certainly wish to help in any way possible." Evelyn, at least, sounded genuinely interested in their well-being. Ruby saw the same earnestness in her eyes that James displayed when he was invested in something.

A silence that wasn't exactly comfortable fell over the kitchen, but no one seemed to want to break it. Finally, Julian said, "So, Ruby, you're now the Dyre of North America."

Ruby nodded warily and Julian fetched her a charming, if patronizing, smile. "And I suppose that with the Incident, everyone's been rather too busy to guide you in the traditions of leadership and ritual required of a Dyre?"

Put on the defensive, Ruby straightened her spine and sat up proudly. "I've actually been learning rather a lot about Loup history, ritual, and politics from Jake and James. I've also been able to observe Jake in his daily duties as the sitting Alpha of the Coulter Pack. It's quite fascinating."

"I see," Julian said, his smile unchanged. "But I don't suppose you've had your pick of advisors and tutors what with The Incident. Talented leadership must be thin on the ground, Jacob and Ellery aside," he added as an afterthought. "In light of that, I'd like to put myself at your service. I have over fifty years' experience serving as Beta to the Alpha of the Prevost Pack. I'm well-versed in matters politic, diplomatic, and historical."

"Jack of all trades, master of none," James muttered. Though everyone else ignored him, Ruby had to repress a smile.

"Thank you, Julian," Ruby said, stalling for a moment. Then she was speaking as if her unconscious mind had already known what to say. "I'll certainly keep your generous offer in mind. For now, I feel it's best to concentrate on getting my feet under me, so to speak. Once I've gone through the Change, I'll be in a better position to decide what's best for me and for my Packs."

After a nanosecond of pure and obvious shock, Julian was smiling once more. Then he gave a small, deferential nod. "Of course. I suppose it would be a bit hasty to do otherwise."

Silence fell again, distinctly uncomfortable. Evelyn was the one to break it this time. "Will you be joining us for dinner, dearest?"

Julian glanced at his Bulova wristwatch and shook his head. "I've already eaten. And I find I'm rather jet-lagged. I'm afraid I'll have to sit this dinner out. But do enjoy yourself, darling," he said, pecking Evelyn on the cheek again. Then he nodded to each person in the room. "Goodnight, all."

"Don't let the door hit you where Moon Above split you— ow! Goddamnit, Jake!" James turned an affronted gaze on his partner and rubbed his just-smacked hand. Julian, meanwhile, strode out of the kitchen as if he hadn't heard.

"*Must* you be such an asshole to my husband, Ellie?" Evelyn demanded in a hissed whisper, hectic spots of color at each high cheekbone.

James shrugged. "Oh, Evvie, he knows I'm just teasing," he claimed with a charming smile of his own. "Or he would if he had a sense of humor."

Evelyn sighed. "You do nothing but provoke him and provoke him. One day, he'll take the bait, and *then* where will you be?"

"Ready and waiting for him, of course." James had a dangerous glint in his eyes as he dumped a handful of onions into the frying pan where they immediately began to sizzle and caramelize. "I may be *just* a Latent, but I can defend myself."

"But you wouldn't *have* to defend yourself if you simply let the man *be*, love," Jake said softly. James looked over at him, and that dangerous glint was replaced by a look as fond and yearning as any starry-eyed lover.

"You're right. I *know* you're right. He's just *so* easy to needle, and so *worth* the needling," James groused. Then that charming smile made a quick comeback. "But for me, I was pretty civil, wasn't I? Don't I get a few brownie points for being civil?"

Jake grinned. "Compared to how catty I've seen you be, you *were* downright subdued, tonight. I'm proud of you." He leaned over the counter and James met him halfway for a light kiss on the lips.

"See?" James turned a righteous look on Evelyn, who rolled her eyes. "I was a perfect gentleman."

"Now, I wouldn't go that far," Jake interjected, and Thierry laughed heartily. James ignored them both. Ruby, however, found herself staring at Thierry. Soon, he was staring right back, a half-smile playing on his full lips.

"...not *my* fault your weasel-faced husband makes it difficult for one to be nice to him. And it's *certainly* not my fault he often mistakes condescension for cordiality. A sign of a bad upbringing, that," James tsked. Evelyn's mouth was a lovely 'O' of shock.

"He's...not...weasel-faced," she finally spat out.

James shrugged again. "All right," he conceded. "But he *is* condescending and badly-raised? So noted."

"You're such a spiteful bitch, sometimes, Ellie," Evelyn sighed, carefully adding the steak to the pan. It, too, sizzled and spat. The scent of cooking meat immediately filled the air, making everyone's stomachs growl. Then James smiled.

"*Only* 'sometimes'? Damn, I must be slipping in my old age," he said with real regret.

❖

Belly full, and her head swimming with stories about George, and Evelyn and James's strange, rather fantastical childhood, Ruby finally pleaded exhaustion at midnight. She and Thierry left the siblings drinking and reminiscing with an exhausted but indulgent Jake.

"You don't have to walk me to my room, you know. I'll be perfectly safe getting there on my own," she joked. Thierry smiled absently.

"I know. But I want to."

"And why is that?"

Glancing at her, his dark eyes shining with amusement, Thierry's smile widened. "Can you not guess?"

At this point, they'd reached Ruby's door and she leaned against it. Thierry stood in front of her and took her hands. He kissed one, then the other, and he looked long and intently into Ruby's eyes. "May I kiss you good-night?" he asked quietly.

Startled, Ruby could only stand there, gaping for a few seconds. Then she shook her head. "*Me? You* want to kiss *me?*"

"Among other things, yes." Thierry looked down for a moment, his smile turning sardonic and self-effacing. "In my younger days, I'd have asked your father and mother if I could perhaps court you." He looked up again, his eyes somber and direct. "But one must change with the times, or stagnate. So, I will make my intentions known to you and hope that you will at least consider them."

Ruby's eyebrows shot up. "Intentions? You have *intentions?*"

"Of course," Thierry replied, stepping closer. His eyes were hypnotic. "My intentions are to make you fall as madly in love with me as I happen to be falling for you and, in due time, make you my mate."

Now Ruby was *really* flummoxed. "I—you—what—?" she stammered. Thierry let go of one of her hands, caressing her cheek and tilting her face up ever so slightly. Ruby's breath caught, and she shivered. "There was someone once," she said. "Someone who claimed to love me too, but in the end, I just got strung along and wound up heartbroken."

Thierry's smile faded. "I'm so sorry," he whispered, his thumb brushing across her lower lip. The contact sent tingles up and down Ruby's spine, and her legs almost went wobbly.

"I was young and stupid. Despite all the warning signs, I let myself fall deeper and deeper, convinced that *love* would make everything work out in the end. Suffice it to say, it didn't." Ruby snorted. "And Casey didn't even want me. Not really. We never were together in a sexual way. *I* wanted to be, but after nearly a year of bullshit excuses and asking me to wait, Casey disappeared for three days, then came back drunk and beat up and making up all these lies. I was so sick and heart-sore, I just said, 'Get your shit and go.' That was that."

Thierry let go of Ruby's other hand and cupped her face in both of his.

"I am truly sorry," he murmured, shaking his head. "But I am not this Casey. I know what I want and how to take care of what I have, when I have it. And believe me when I say that I am not afraid or ambivalent in any way about wanting *you*."

And with that, he leaned in and pressed his lips gently, briefly to hers. His kiss barely felt like anything at all, but every part of Ruby sat up and took notice. Her exhaustion was eclipsed by the prickly heat that spread out all over her body, from the inside out, then back again.

She broke the kiss to look into Thierry's sea-dark eyes. She didn't know what she was looking for, but what she found made her brave enough to lean in for another kiss.

This one seemed to explode across her consciousness, and she gasped. Thierry took the opportunity to deepen the kiss, stroking his tongue past her lips and teasing her. Ruby heard a long, desperate moan that must've been hers, since it didn't sound anything like Thierry's low timber. Her hands had come up to rest on his chest. He wrapped his warm, strong arms around her and pulled her close. Closer, still, till her arms slid up around his neck.

He was only the third person she'd every kissed, and *this kiss* was far different from Casey's tentative, half-hearted ones or Des's languid, teasing ones. This kiss was demanding, yearning, and intense. It felt like the kiss she'd been waiting for her whole life. It was *perfect*.

As if a dam had been breached, ten years of repressed sexuality was suddenly released, flooding away her reservations and defenses. For once, her body was in control, and it wanted Thierry LaFours, it seemed, like it had never wanted anyone before.

She mirrored his kisses with innocently wanton ones of her own, aware that she didn't know how to kiss, not really, but beyond caring. She let him teach her what he liked and when she felt she'd given it to him, began to improvise and experiment.

Then, feeling bolder by far, she pressed her body against Thierry's. He was all wiry, tightly-coiled strength and heat, sheathed in long, solid muscle. He clinched her closer, shifting his stance, and she felt the hot hardness of him pressing against her stomach.

It was nothing she'd ever felt before, and those all-over tingles flooded, without delay or tangent, to the very place they'd originated. Wet, molten heat pooled at her core and she moaned again, running a hand up through Thierry's hair.

His kisses wended their way south, down to Ruby's throat where he mock-bit her, rumbling low in his throat. "You are lovely," he murmured, nibbling at the spot where her pulse beat. "So lovely."

"You don't have to say that."

Thierry kissed his way back up to her mouth. "I know I don't. But it's true, and you deserve to hear it as often as possible." He looked into her eyes and smiled. "Ruby Knudsen, you are lovely. The loveliest woman I have ever had the pleasure of beholding. And I've, ah, beheld my fair share of women."

He cleared his throat delicately and Ruby laughed. "I'll bet. You strike me as a man who could get any woman—or man—he wanted. So, what do you want with *me*?"

"The same thing any other man wants from a woman with whom he's falling in love, Ruby." Thierry took her hands again and Ruby's face went up in flames. "I want...*you*. Only you."

❖

Des lay wakeful in bed next to a deeply sleeping Holly, listening to the mini-drama going on across the hall.

"I want...*you*. Only you," Thierry said, and Ruby responded by kissing him, from the sound of it. The combined scent of their pheromones grew stronger and stronger, and Ruby shyly asked Thierry if he'd like to come in.

"I'd be honored," he replied, sounding like he genuinely was. Des rolled her eyes, anyway.

The door to Ruby's room opened and shut on their quiet murmurs.

Des rolled onto her side, facing away from the door, ignoring the burn in her eyes.

It's Ruby's life. She can do whatever she wants with anyone she likes. It's none of my business. I don't have a prior claim on her, do I? Of course not. In fact, she turned me down twice, Des thought angrily, though whether she was angry at Ruby or Thierry or herself she honestly couldn't tell. *If she likes dick so much, she's welcome to it. I'm just the hired muscle, and it's time I started remembering that.*

Closing her eyes, Des tried to focus on the sounds of the night coming from outside, rather than the soft, increasingly breathless laughs and gasps, interspersed with whispers, coming from across the hall.

She likewise tried to focus on the intermingled scents of herself and Holly, rather than the muffled scents of Ruby and Thierry...*intermingling.*

Finally, she pulled her pillow over her head and held it there.

Breathing was overrated, anyway.

❖

They fell onto Ruby's bed laughing and kissing, and Thierry instantly rolled them over so that Ruby was on top of him.

"Ow!"

"Sorry."

Ruby pulled her right hand out from under Thierry's shoulder. "It's okay. I'm left-handed, anyway."

Thierry grinned and pulled her down into another kiss, sliding his hands down Ruby's back to her ass, squeezing and kneading. Ruby straddled Thierry's hips and sat up, planting her hands on his chest.

"Can I tell you something?" Ruby asked suddenly.

"As long as you unbutton my shirt while you tell me," Thierry half-joked, running his hands up and down Ruby's thighs. "What is it?"

Ruby smiled a little, and slipped the first button through its hole. "Well, I've never...been with anyone. You know, like *this.*" She looked down at Thierry's unbuttoned shirt and well-defined, unsurprisingly hairy chest, and she sighed. "I may not be any good at this."

Thierry sat up and kissed her lightly. "Do you want to be here? With me?"

Ruby took a breath and for once, let herself admit to herself that *yes*, she wanted to be there. With Thierry. "I do."

Thierry smiled. "That's fifty percent of being together, right there."

"Really?" Ruby let Thierry pull her back down on top of him. He pushed up her sweatshirt and unhooked her bra, singlehandedly. *His fair share of women, indeed.* "And what's the other fifty percent?"

Thierry rolled them onto their sides and maneuvered off her bra and sweatshirt, then ran one finger down the curve of her breast. Ruby shivered and gasped.

"The other fifty percent I'd be happy to show you," Thierry said, searching Ruby's eyes. She shivered again.

"Show me," she breathed.

He did.

❖

They were still at it.

At false dawn, Des had yet to fall asleep. She'd changed and fed the twins all by her lonesome. For once Winkin', like Blinkin', mostly slept through both processes, thank goodness, so she had no trouble putting them back down for the rest of the night. Then she'd gone to get some coffee and brood out the kitchen window for nearly two hours.

Coming up the back stairs, she could hear Ruby's gasps of *oh, God...oh, Thierry...* And LaFours's breathy, panting silences.

Des could even hear, as she got closer to her room, the deliciously obscene sound of skin-on-skin. She almost saw red.

By the time she opened the door to her room, she was livid and turned-on, and Holly was awake, naked, and on display. And Des mostly forgot about Ruby and Thierry LaFours.

Mostly.

"You got started without me," Des mock-pouted. Holly grinned and arched her back invitingly.

"But I wouldn't dream of *finishing* without you," she purred. "Now get over here."

Des shucked her shirt, stepped out of her boxers, and approached the bed.

Ten minutes later, she was flopping back down into her pillow, angry at herself and embarrassed. From between Des's legs, Holly lay gaping.

"You called out *her* name while *I* was making you *come*?!"

Des flung an arm over her eyes. "Moon Above, it was an accident, Hol."

"Accident my ass!" Sitting up, Holly smacked Des's leg. Hard. After a few seconds, Des peeked out from under her arm. Holly's eyes were angry and hurt. "I've put up with your weird fixation on her for the past month, but instead of fading, it's getting more and more intense!" Holly put her hands on her hips. "Just what is it about her, hmm? Is it the *Geas* that's doing this? Are you confusing responsibility with desire? Or is it that you just want what you can't have?"

Des winced and covered her eyes again. "Honestly? I don't know, Holly."

"You don't know? What the *fuck* kind of answer is *that*?"

"The only answer I got."

Silence. Then Des felt the warm, familiar press of Holly's body all alongside hers and Holly's wet face buried in the junction between her neck and shoulder.

"Don't you love me, Des?"

At this, Des saw red again and pushed Holly away, jumping out of bed. "In case you forgot, I fucking *killed* for you!"

Holly sat up, her eyes still welling with tears. "That's not an answer, Des."

"Then what do you *want* to *hear*?" Des demanded, and those tears filling Holly's eyes fell. Guilt crashed onto Des like an anvil. Her voice was soft and desperate. "What do you *want* me to *say*?"

Holly shook her head. "If you loved me, you wouldn't have to ask."

Des swore and turned away. "That doesn't make any kind of sense."

"It actually does," Holly said, and her voice was a hard smile. The bed creaked as she got up. "If you loved me, you'd know that that's all I wanted to hear you say. But I guess the fact that you didn't say it was answer in itself."

Des ran a hand through her hair and faced Holly, who was rooting around in Des's closet. She came out with her wheeled Louis Vuitton suitcase, and Des felt something she couldn't define. It may have been anxiety, or it could have been relief. In any event, it made her heart beat faster. "C'mon, Hol, don't be melodramatic!"

"As soon as you stop being condescending." Holly slammed her suitcase on the bed, unzipped it, and stalked back to Des's closet. Now, the feeling Des was swallowing was panic.

"Uh, what're you doing?"

"What does it *look* like I'm doing?"

Des held her peace as she watched Holly carry an armful of her clothes—each item probably costing more than Des' entire wardrobe—and cram them into the suitcase. Then she began gathering her underwear and clothes from around the room where Des had tossed them. All Des did was watch. It was all she *could* do, since she couldn't lie.

"You're not even gonna try and stop me, are you?" Holly asked incredulously, as she pulled on her underwear. "Not even gonna lie to me, huh?"

Des started, then stammered. "I-is there anything I *can* say?"

"Do you still love me, like you did three years ago?"

"I'd still kill for you," Des said softly.

Holly sighed, looking over at her. "I don't *need* you to kill for me anymore. I need you to say you *love* me, and *mean* it." Des felt Holly's scrutiny as she searched Des's face and shook her head again. "But you can't say it because you don't feel it. And you never *were* any kind of liar at all."

Standing up, Holly dug around in her suitcase and came up with a pair of black slacks and a jade-colored blouse that looked like it was probably made of silk.

"And the kicker is, *she* doesn't even return your feelings! She's fucking Thierry LaFours *right now!*" Holly exclaimed, and Des winced again.

"I know that! You think I don't *know* that?" She crossed her arms over her chest and slunk dispiritedly to the bed, sitting on the foot. "I don't know what I'm doing, Hol. I really don't."

"And you think I'm going to wait around for you to figure out what you *want* to be doing is *her?* You've got another think coming, sweetheart." Holly slammed the suitcase shut and zipped it. Then she went back to Des's closet for her shoes. "I'm not going to wait around for someone who doesn't want me, no matter how much I love her. That's the difference between you and me. *I* have a *spine*."

And here Des had thought Holly no longer had the power to cut and wound her like a knife. "I'm sorry," Des said, sniffing back something that *couldn't* be tears, because Jennifer Desiderio did *not* cry. Not even at her own mother's funeral. "I'm so sorry."

"Still not what I need to hear." Holly gathered up her waist-length hair and twisted it into an efficient knot at the nape of her neck. In seconds, she looked more pulled together than Des felt on her best day but for her red, swollen eyes.

Des had never seen Holly so distraught. Not even that horrible night nearly four years ago, when Des'd had to choose between her best friend and her best friend's twin sister—to kill one, thus saving the other. No, Holly had awaited her fate with a reserve of calm Des could only marvel at, then and now.

Here she was, the same woman, come completely undone behind her hastily applied mask of calm. All because of Des.

Holly pulled her suitcase to the floor and stood looking at Des expectantly. "Last chance," she said stonily, and Des took a breath.

"If you ever need me for anything," Des said quietly. "*Anything*. You know where I am."

Holly nodded once and tilted her head up, pulling on her mantle of Alpha with visible effort. But pull it on she did, and when she strode past Des, she held her head high.

Des listened to her footsteps and followed the sounds of suitcase wheels down the front stairs. She heard Holly call for Angus Graham, long-trusted head of Nathan's security team. Her voice rang throughout the manor like a bell, no doubt waking anyone who didn't sleep like the dead. And Angus, who seemingly *never* slept, was at her beck and call in under a minute.

"I need a ride to the airport, double-time."

"To which gate, Mother Black Lodge?"

At this point, Des tuned out and crawled up her bed, to the pillows, which still smelled of Holly, expensive hair products and musky perfume that mingled and enhanced Holly's own personal scent. Des crushed the pillows to her face and inhaled, letting cotton absorb the tears before they could spill down her cheeks.

❖

"Oh, *Thierry*," Ruby breathed, arching up to meet the languid, controlled pistoning of Thierry's hips. She couldn't believe how amazing it *had* felt from the moment he first penetrated her—painful, yes, but not without a rather wide edge of pleasure—up to and through the current moment.

It seemed as if they'd been together like this for eternity, and could be together like this for at least an eternity more, until Thierry suddenly *stopped*, his head cocked at a listening angle as he frowned.

"What is it?" Ruby panted, and Thierry looked at her for a few moments before smiling and leaning down to kiss her.

"Nothing," he said softly. "Nothing more important than this."

And he drove into her with a powerful thrust that made her clutch at him with desperate arms and beg for release. He snaked a hand between their bodies and fingered her, till she came *again*. She'd honestly lost count of how many times she already had, calling out his name and weeping.

Shortly thereafter, Thierry finally let himself come, pinning her wrists to the bed as he did so, a low growl rumbling out from between his clenched teeth. Then he collapsed half on top of her, breathing hard, his heart racing directly above her own.

He should have felt heavy and uncomfortable, but instead, he felt...good. *Right*.

Yet he was considerate enough to lever his weight up off her, anyway. When he slipped out of her, her breath caught, and he kissed her teasingly, cupping her breast and stroking her nipple with his thumb.

Laughing a little, she nudged him till he rolled onto his side, and she rolled with him. Their legs tangled together, and for a long time he looked into her eyes.

"May I stay the rest of the night?" he asked, and she kissed him long and deep.

"Even if I have to tie you to the bed."

"I wouldn't be averse to that," he murmured, and his smile was pure sin.

❖

Des stared into the sunlight coming into the kitchen and gnawed absently on the t-bone that was all that remained of her steak. The eggs she'd fried to go with them, covered in hollandaise sauce, were cold and untouched.

She'd cried herself to sleep sometime after dawn in pillows that smelled of Holly, then woken up shortly after eight, wracked by an intense sense of loss that'd hollowed her out. Like a zombie, she'd dressed and gone to the kitchen, ignoring the soft snores coming from Ruby's room.

And in the kitchen she'd stayed, as the other Loups in the manor came and went making their own breakfasts before or after running errands. Even Jake had come in, looking pale and tired, to make breakfast for himself and a still-sleeping James.

He hadn't said anything to Des at first, merely come up behind her and hugged her shoulders, rocking her a little. "I'm so sorry, Jenny-benny," he'd said, and Des had smiled, hard and rueful.

"Not your fault my wife left me *again*." *Or that you were right about Ruby and LaFours.*

Jake had kissed the back of her head. "I wish I could make it better for you."

Des had grunted.

When Jake had gone back to his and James's room, Des had finally made her own breakfast and sat there gnawing on a bone like a lonely, old dog.

"Good morning!"

Des started. She'd been so lost in her own thoughts, she'd neither heard nor smelled Ruby approaching, though the woman made no attempts at stealth *ever*.

But really, how could I have missed her scent? Des thought as she glanced over her shoulder. Ruby was smiling bright enough to rival the sunlight coming in the window, and she seemed to glow in its light. *She smells so strongly of LaFours and sex, how could I have missed her scent?*

"You look awful!" Ruby gasped, stepping close to Des and putting a cool hand on her forehead. In the sun's light, Des could just make out the remnants of finger-shaped bruises on Ruby's wrists. "Are you okay?"

Des moved her head away and put the t-bone down. "I'm okay. Just short on sleep."

Ruby's hand flew to her mouth. "Oh, sugar-honey-iced-tea! I forgot to help you with the twins last night! I'm so sorry!"

"Whatever. I know you were busy," Des said flatly.

Ruby's eyes widened and she blanched. "How—"

Des touched the side of her nose. "The nose knows, remember? Besides, you're, like, twenty feet away from me. Less, even. I could hear you, even if I couldn't smell you," Des said, and this time, Ruby turned red.

"Oh, I—I—I'm sorry we disturbed you," she murmured, embarrassed and chagrined. She turned and fled the kitchen, for once barely making any noise as she did so. And Des wanted to call her back, to take back her tone, if not the words she'd said, but she was entirely too aware that she couldn't.

But then she remembered the faint hickeys dotting Ruby's neck, and she had to let her go. Back to Thierry LaFours, no doubt. But what could Des do about it? She had to find some small space in which to regain her self-control and the nice, protective wall of numb she'd had before Ruby had come into the kitchen.

Before Ruby had come into her *life*.

Des stood up and shucked her shirt, then peeled off her jeans and kicked off her boots. She strode to the back door and opened it. The sunlight hit her like a wall of cheerfulness and she growled, shutting the door and dropping to all fours.

A minute later, a black wolf bolted from the manor toward the treeline.

❖

In the bathroom she shared with Des, Ruby sat on the hamper, wanting to cry for no reason she could put her finger on.

By all rights, this morning had felt like the happiest morning of her life before running into Des. She'd woken up in Thierry's arms, his warm breath on the back of her neck, and she'd wanted to do something nice for him. To show him that she cared and was glad he'd stayed.

She'd decided to make him breakfast, and she hoped it wouldn't come out as inedible as her breakfasts usually did.

But then Des had been there, and suddenly everything that'd made the morning so wonderful had seemed wrong and shameful.

Ruby sniffed, wiping at her eyes. Suddenly, more than anything, she wanted a shower. She stood up, removed her robe and stretched muscles that were still sore from her assignation with Thierry, who was still asleep in her bed, then stepped into the shower.

She let the water get as hot as she could stand, then started on her hair, letting her tears finally flow and be washed away by the shampoo and hot water. As she was rinsing her hair, the shower door opened, and Ruby turned, thinking, for some reason, that she'd see Des smiling at her. But before she could see anything but a flash of pale skin, large hands were on her hips and a hard body pressed against the back of hers.

Soft kisses graced her right shoulder, and she closed her eyes, leaning her head against the shower wall. One of the hands on her hip slid around to her stomach, then lower, slipping and sliding on her labia, teasing inward, fingering her open till she shivered and sighed. She shuffled her feet apart, and Thierry sighed in her hair, bending her forward slightly.

"*Je taime, je taime, Ruby,*" Thierry whispered, and then he was inside her, sliding slow and deep until he could go no farther.

Ruby clenched her teeth and her muscles, sore yet still turned on. *Can Des smell this? Smell us wanting this and getting it?* Hot tears leaked out of her eyes faster and hotter than the water that sought to wash them away, and behind her, Thierry stilled, wrapping his arm around her waist.

"*Ma lumiere,*" he breathed gently, kissing her shoulder again. "What's wrong?"

He seemed to genuinely care, to want to know. But how could she tell him? *What* could she tell him, when she couldn't even tell *herself* what was wrong? "I don't know," she said truthfully. "I'm sorry."

"There is nothing to be sorry about," he said, still in that gentle tone. "Only tell me how I may fix it."

Ruby sighed, willing her tears to stop. It took several minutes, during which Thierry held her silently, patiently.

He's a good man, she thought. *He deserves a woman who doesn't let someone shame her about being with him. Because in the end, there's nothing to be ashamed of. Thierry is offering me his companionship, not just a friendship with benefits. And I have chosen to accept it. There is* nothing *wrong with that, despite what Des seems to think.*

"You can fix it by holding me tighter, and not letting me go," Ruby choked out, pushing back against Thierry and taking the hand that wasn't still stroking her gently. She pulled it to her breast, drawing in a shaky breath when Thierry cupped it. "Make me stop thinking and remembering what I don't wish to think about or remember." And, out of pure defiance, "Make me *scream.*"

CHAPTER ELEVEN

"So, tonight's the big night."

Too relaxed and blissed-out to be startled, Ruby looked up from her book of Loup genealogy—of which she'd not even managed a chapter in several hours—and smiled at James. "Hmm?"

James rolled his eyes and sat next to her on the couch, one of several in Nathan's sunny library, and plucked the book from her fingers. He scanned the title and made a face. "Ugh. Dad made us study this when Evvie and I were younger. Sheer-fucking-torture."

"It's not *that* bad."

"Oh, please. All those 'begats.'" James shuddered. "Ghastly."

Ruby laughed. "Well, it can be a little annoying. But Jake thought it might be helpful to know who begat whom."

James rolled his eyes again. "I love that man with every fiber of my being, but he's filling your head with all the boring stuff. There's more to be learned from a shameless gossip than there is from a 'begat.'"

"Oh, really? And where would I find such a gossip?" Ruby batted her eyes innocently, and James laughed.

"You're looking right at him." He made a small half-bow. "You'd be surprised at what I pick up, and what people tell me about the transgressions of others."

Ruby laughed again. "Well, if you can't say something nice, come sit by me."

"My kinda woman." James rubbed his hands together gleefully. "Pick a name, any name out of that Big Book of Begats, and I can probably tell you something juicy about them."

"Hmm," Ruby said once more, this time with much more consideration. Though the name she came up with was seemingly completely out of left-field. "Holly Black Lodge."

James whistled. "You don't beat around the bush!"

"When people are trying to kill you, life's too short to beat around the bush," Ruby said dryly. "So. What's *her* deal?"

James's eyebrows shot up. "Her *deal*?" He chuckled. "You'll have to be a lot more specific than that. There're a bunch of *deals* to that one."

"Well, for one thing, she and Des." Ruby gestured helplessly. "I mean, when did that all happen? For how long? And why did it *stop* happening? And why did it start happening again? And how long will it even last? What if—?"

"Whoa, whoa. Slow down, Questions McGee!" James held up his hands in surrender. "In the order that your questions were asked: About four and a half years ago. About a year. I can't be sure, on that one. And till this morning, apparently."

Ruby processed those answers then frowned. "What do you mean 'till this morning'?"

"Just what I said," James said with a shrug. "Des and Holly broke up again this morning, but I guess with you and Uncle Theo making us all jealous last night, you might've missed the fireworks. And—hey, where're you going?"

But Ruby didn't answer. She was crossing the library to the entryway, her book of begats forgotten on the floor.

❖

Des's room was empty, and so was the next place Ruby checked, Nathan's office. Well, it was empty except for Jake, who smiled his kind, tired smile and asked her what was up.

"Where's Des?"

Jake sighed. "If she's not in the manor, she'll be somewhere on the grounds. Probably in the woods, somewhere." Pausing, Jake steepled his long hands. "Ruby, you may or may not know, but this morning, Holly left Des. Again."

"I just heard from James." Ruby nodded impatiently. "That's why I'm looking for her."

Jake bit his lip and regarded her for long moments before speaking. "If she's on the grounds, she's likely in Loup form and probably looking for a little breathing room. When you can't find Des, it's pretty likely she doesn't *want* to be found."

Ruby shook her head. "I don't accept that."

"You kinda have to. If she doesn't want to be found, you *won't* find her, Ruby."

"But what if she *does* want to be found?"

Jake spread his hands. "Then if anyone can find her, I suspect it'll be you. If you're going to go looking, I'd suggest the western edge of the property. Des likes to watch the sun set while she broods."

Ruby nodded and turned to go. When she got to the door, she stopped and looked back. Jake was already typing away at Nathan's computer again.

"Thanks," she said, and he smiled without looking up from whatever he was working on.

"Any time. Good luck."

❖

Des was lying in the bit of woods encircling a copse, her belly full of rabbit and squirrel, half-asleep, when her

Loup picked up a scent and sound that had no business being there.

None, whatsoever.

"…sure pick a nice, convenient spot to hole up in," a voice puffed, then swore voluminously after a sound like branches cracking and a yelp. "And that's just perfect. I've probably sprained my ankle. I hope you appreciate what I'm going through to find you, Des. God, you're probably way the hell on the other side of the property and I'm here, lost, sprained ankle, talking to myself."

The Loup raised its head from between its paws and watched as Ruby hobbled into the copse, a disheveled, sweaty mess. Her hair was a fuzzy-curly corona, her jeans covered in grass stains, and her t-shirt twisted and askew. She was frowning so hard, she looked like she'd never seen a smile.

She was beautiful.

The Loup whined high in its nose, feeling lonely and depressed, and Ruby's head came up. She hummed and turned toward the direction in which Des and her Loup lay.

"Des?" she called hesitantly. "Was that you?"

Kicking themselves, Des and her Loup realized that just because she was untried, didn't mean that Ruby wasn't, herself, every inch a Loup. And a damned powerful one, at that. In the running to be the most powerful Loup in the world. Not to mention that this close to her Change, her sense of hearing and smell were going to be especially acute. Maybe even acute enough to find Des. After all, she'd gotten this far, and not by luck.

"If you can hear me, Des, I just found out about you and Holly. I'm so sorry. And I want you to know that I'm here for you if you wanna talk, or if you just wanna not be alone while you sort through stuff. I'm here." Ruby limped to the center of the copse, standing in a ray of sunlight that turned her hair auburn and made her eyes seem to glow. "I'm here!" she called out, loud enough that it echoed in the small, close space, then dispersed into the wide, open sky above.

And quite without Des's approval or input, her Loup slunk out from the bushes it'd been, in all honesty, hiding in. It whined again softly, so as not to startle Ruby, who smiled a little limply.

"Boy, I sure hope you're Des and not some random wolf looking for a meal," she quipped, and the Loup whuffed, sitting on its haunches patiently, waiting for Ruby to approach. Which she did, slowly, carefully, as if *she* didn't want to frighten *Des*.

When she was within touching distance, she held out her hand, and the Loup closed the distance between them, pushing her nose under Ruby's hand and licking a palm that tasted of sandwich and tree-sap. Ruby suffered the attention for longer than Des or the Loup would have expected.

"I'm sorry," she said again, scratching the Loup's muzzle, back up to its forehead, then behind its ears. "So sorry."

The Loup sighed and flopped down again, head between its paws. After a few seconds, Ruby joined it, tailor-style, with a sigh of her own. "I hope you realize," she stated primly as she smoothed her jeans, "that I don't sit on the ground for just anyone, Ms. Desiderio."

The Loup's tongue lolled just a bit. An almost-smile.

Ruby looked around them, taking in the trees ringing the copse, and the low, fragrant bushes. Above them, the sky was cloudless and golden-orange. The sun was on the wester.

"Well, it's certainly a beautiful spot, if a bit secluded and hard to get to," she said finally, almost-smiling, herself. "I can see why you come here."

The Loup shifted about until its head was resting on Ruby's lap. Ruby didn't comment, merely began stroking the Loup's head. As far as the Loup was concerned, it could stay like that forever, and for once, Des completely agreed.

❖

"When I was young," Ruby began as the sun sank below the horizon. "When I was maybe nine or ten, for a while my father worked as a logger in Northern California. By that time, my mom had left, and it was just me and him, on our own, travelling wherever there was work."

Des and her Loup grunted. They had clear memories of Des's mother holding down many different jobs, some of which involved commutes that were practically small journeys. And though Des hadn't thought of it that way at the time, that willingness to travel, sometimes to the ass-end of Nowhere, when sometimes the commute itself was as tiring as the job, to take care of one's child, was one of the highest forms of love.

No, Des hadn't realized that then. But she realized it now, and there had been times, even recently, when she'd wished with all her heart for just a little time to tell her mother thanks, and how much Des had always and still did love her.

Five minutes would have been enough.

Unaware of the tenor of Des's thoughts, Ruby spoke on. "We didn't make a lot of friends, but then, we didn't *need* a lot of friends. We had each other. When he came home from a long, tough day with splinters in his hands, and cuts and scrapes, he'd sit at the kitchen table. I'd get the first aid kit, tweeze out the splinters, and clean the cuts and scrapes." Ruby chuckled, smiling. "I'd cover him in these day-glo, little-kid bandages, trying to get every single little cut he had. And then he'd make us dinner, and we'd talk about our days. When dinner and the dishes were done, he'd help me with the rest of my homework.

Then we'd watch some television together—always old reruns of sitcoms from the seventies and eighties, and we almost always made up our own soundtracks and dialogue—then he'd tuck me into bed. I never wanted to go to sleep. I always wanted to spend some more time with him. It was never enough, I guess. And now, it never will be."

Ruby sighed again, and the Loup whined, leaning up to lick her hand. Ruby smiled down at it and ruffled its head-fur.

"I remember this one time, he taught me how to catch a calf."

The Loup blinked and Ruby laughed.

"This was when he was still working on the dairy farm, before Mom left. He'd get up at four thirty in the morning, tiptoe quietly into my room, pick me up so carefully I didn't wake up, and carry me to their bedroom. He'd tuck me in with mom, and that's where I'd wake up later, all warm and toasty and safe. I think I was six—maybe seven.

"Anyway, in case you ever need to know, the trick to wrasslin' a calf is not to tackle it, but to stroll up to it, and when it gets ready to run, it'll stick its tail up, like so." Ruby made a little flip-up motion with her free hand. "And when it does that, you sidle up beside it and grab the tail to hold on, then get the neck. And there! You've caught yourself a calf!"

"Bear in mind, of course, that I was too small to *actually* catch a calf. Smaller than the calf, even. But I've seen it done, and it works," Ruby said wistfully. "My dad was pretty awesome. I miss him every day."

The Loup whined, and Des thought about Nathan. She had never had the close relationship with Nathan that Ruby seemed to have had with *her* father, but since her mother died, Nathan and Jake had been the two constants in her life. And Jake had nearly died not a month ago, and Nathan . . . was Moon Above knew where. . . .

"Don't worry, Des. Thierry's people will find him." Ruby patted Des companionably. And both Des and the Loup, for their parts, were too depressed and worried to growl at the sound of LaFours's name.

What if Nathan never came home?

What if the twins grew up without *both* their parents?

Oh, so many horrible *what-ifs*. . . .

The sun was setting, revealing a night sky as pink and purple as some strange fruit. But Des took no joy in its beauty—no comfort in its familiarity.

The only joy and comfort she took was from Ruby's simple touch.

❖

Ruby must have nodded off, because she opened her eyes to full dark with stars overhead. Des was also asleep, with her head still in Ruby's lap, huffing wolf-y snores.

Ruby carefully attempted to stretch the kinks out of her stiff arms and back muscles, not wanting to wake Des. She felt wired and tired after an afternoon spent wandering the western part of the Coulter estate, then an evening spent talking herself hoarse about her childhood and her father.

She looked around the copse and scratched her arms absently. Then her thighs, around Des's head. The pines were tall and forbidding, where they'd been charming and picturesque in the afternoon.

She wanted to go *home*, and at some point in the past few weeks, that had become Coulter Manor. Coulter Manor was where she felt needed and even wanted. It was where her every friend was, where she felt safe, and where Des was. Ruby's stomach growled, long and loud, and Des snorted herself awake, raising her head and sniffing the air even before her eyes were fully open.

"Good evening, sleepy-head," Ruby yawned, trying once more to stretch away some of the kinks. Still no success.

Des barked and stood up, pacing around Ruby in a circle, sniffing her at intervals. Ruby got dizzy trying to turn her head every which way and follow Des's progress. "What? Do I have B.O., or something?"

Des barked again, twice, and looked up at the sky. Ruby followed her gaze and saw nothing but the same sky and stars, and the *rising moon.*

"Oh, shit," she breathed, and Des barked her agreement. "Should we get back to the manor before I *Change*? *Can* we make it back in time?"

Des whined, her intelligent dark eyes meeting Ruby's for a moment. Then she was trotting out of the copse, eastward. Ruby, itching, jittering, wired, and tired, followed, with one eye on the moon above.

❖

Half an hour later, the moon was directly overhead and Des and Ruby were within sight of the manor.

"Oh, thank goodness…" Ruby puffed, bending to brace her hands on her knees. Her face was shining with sweat, her t-shirt soaked, her hair a damp mess. "I feel like I'm about to keel over! You don't make hiking easy, super-wolf."

The Loup wrinkled its muzzle in apology, and started down the gentle slope that led, at last, to the manor, and Ruby followed. For a few feet, anyway. Halfway down the slope, she stopped and crumpled to her knees, hugging her torso and moaning.

Looking over its shoulder worriedly, the Loup trotted back to Ruby, whining and licking her face.

"I know, just a few minutes away, but I don't think I can, Des. Feels like a full-body cramp," Ruby groaned, clutching herself even tighter. "Feels like there's fire in my bones and battery acid in my muscles!"

That sounds about right, Des thought grimly, and the Loup agreed. *We're not gonna make it to the manor, but maybe that's not so bad. Maybe it's better for her to have her first Change out here, away from the prying eyes of the household.*

"Oh, fuck," Ruby breathed, toppling onto her side, shaking and drenched in sweat. And, right or wrong, Des knew they no longer had any choice about where Ruby would Change.

The Loup paced around Ruby, guarding her at this, her most helpless moment. Every so often, as Ruby shook and shivered and swore, the Loup licked her face comfortingly. Finally, after what seemed like forever, Ruby began rolling around and moaning. The cracking, creaking sounds of bones breaking and shifting began.

It was time.

❖

It was *agony*. Quicksilver-agony, racing along the marrow in her bones and filling every cell of her muscles. Even her skin was on fire, so much so that she unconsciously began ripping at her clothes. She managed to rip off her t-shirt and unbutton her jeans, which she kicked off along with her sneakers. The underwear, however, was a bit more of a problem. It got snagged around her knees and seemed content to stay that way. She managed to pull her bra up, but couldn't reach the hooks.

But soon enough, the underwear was gone, too. Des had simply nipped at the fabric and pulled till it tore, so nothing was against her skin but cool grass. It was somehow soothing.

Agony still steamrolled her, however, and soon had her laid out spread-eagled on the ground as her bones began to *move*. And break. This happened all over her body, but nowhere was it more agonizing than in her face and head. She clutched at both with elongating, warped hands in which the nails were turning black and the skin itself was sprouting coarse fur.

She screamed, and even that was distorted, sounding like the drowning gurgles of some dying beast. She rolled onto her side and, despite the urge to fight the pain, fight the changes happening to her body, she gave in to it. She not only let the pain come, she encouraged it, forced it deep into muscle and bone, giving it a home and making it welcome. She held it close, as close as any bosom friend, and let it reshape her.

Reshape her, it did, the pain ramping up to a fever pitch as every bone seemed to shatter, grind, and knit together into new, yet familiar shapes; every muscle arched and curved and humped up to suit the new frame they were wrapped around; and every hair follicle pushed more coarse fur through her skin. Then, with breath-taking rapidity, the pain was gone, leaving a strange lightness in its wake.

Ruby moaned and turned onto her stomach, panting and sweating and inhaling the night-scents she'd never really noticed before.

There was the intense scent of green, growing things, of grass and sleepy-smelling trees.

There was the low, rank, mouth-watering scent of animals, especially strong in the direction from which she and Des had come.

There was the loamy, rich scent of the Earth itself, and the slight, ground-salty scent of the earthworms and insects that moved through it.

And from the opposite direction of the animal-scent was the scent of *home*. Of Coulter Manor, with its confusion of scents, all of which were tantalizing and beckoning.

Finally, the most important scent of all, like cinnamon and wind and moonlight, like *Des*.

Ruby opened her eyes and saw green so intense it hurt her eyes, and she whined.

It's okay. It's just grass, Des said.

It hurts!

You can control how well you see, hear, and smell. You're already *controlling it. Just control it a little better.*

How?

I notice you're not howling in pain from hearing that's too sharp.

I—

Do what I do. Imagine all your senses as dials on an electronic board. Right now, your vision is at ten. Dial it back to five, and see if that works. Then do the same for your sense of smell, and I'm guessing that you've already got your sense of hearing under some sort of control.

Ruby hesitated, then did as she was bidden. She imagined a board covered in switches and blinking lights, all of which were in the green. But at the center of the board were five levers, three of which were up at a notch marked as ten. The notches went up to twenty, however, and Ruby shuddered, wondering what it would have been like if her sense of sight had been up *there*.

Then she recalled the task at hand and imagined all her levers resetting themselves to the fifth notch, which actually brought her sense of hearing up three notches. When all the levers were aligned, she let the image fade away, and risked opening her eyes to see grass neither more nor less intense than she was used to seeing it. She lifted her head and the next thing she saw was a black wolf watching her with black eyes. Its tongue was lolling and dripping in a huge smile.

Better? it asked her. Only, it didn't exactly ask. It *gestured-smelled-tasted* like the concept of *Better?*

Um...much. Thanks, Des, Ruby replied in like fashion. But even as she said her name, she blinked, and could see Des's Human form superimposed on her Loup form. It was like seeing two beings sharing one space and one consciousness.

The Loup shrugged, and so did Des's Human form. *It's like this for some of us. The Loup is like having another person in your consciousness, vying for control of the body you share. It can take a long time to gain even the barest control for some Loups, which is why it's so hard to fight off the Change at Full-Moon Waxing. But then there're the lucky sort, like you, and I'm guessing most of the Alphas, who are one with the wolf, for lack of a better term. You'll probably be controlling when you Change within a matter of months, unlike the years it sometimes takes the rest of us.*

See if you can stand up.

Ruby yipped and tried to get her legs under her. They were shaky, but otherwise fine. She didn't have any sense of dislocation or disorientation, no feeling of getting used to having four legs instead of two, with no hands to speak of. She was disturbed at how easy it was to feel at home in this body.

Despite her reservations, Ruby stood. And when she did, she discovered she was a full head taller than Des and a good deal larger. But Des didn't seem frightened of her, just respectful and a little uncertain.

And excited.

And the excitement was catching. It made Ruby want to run and jump and howl and feast.

Can we go to the kitchen? I'm hungry.

Des laughed, and it came out as several yelps. *You don't have to ask, DyreMother! We can go anywhere you want! However, you're a Loup, now. You might want to get used to catching dinner on the fly.*

On the—Ruby's eyes widened. *You mean...catch...other animals...and eat them...raw?*

Bingo.

That sounds—revolting, Ruby meant to finish, but her stomach growled again, and she realized the notion didn't sound as revolting as all that. In fact, it gave her hunger a keener edge. *Do-able. But how? I've never hunted anything in my life.*

Des grinned, her tongue seeming to loll practically to the ground. *I'll teach you.*

Ruby let her own tongue loll out. Practically to the ground.

❖

Okay, you smell that salty-tangy scent?

Ruby sniffed, her nostrils flaring wide. She *thought* she smelled something.

Turn your scent dial up to where it was before, Des said, a smile in *her* scent and voice. Ruby emulated it, or tried to, then reimagined the electric board. She slowly raised the scent dial to ten, and as she did the scent she *thought* she smelled bloomed into full, undeniable life.

That's deer, Des told her, licking her chops. *There are a few on the estate, but we don't hunt them. Tonight, we hunt rabbit.*

Rabbit?! Ruby exclaimed, her stomach growling ferociously. Des laughed. *I'd have to eat about a thousand of them before I felt full!*

Oh, I think you'd be surprised at how far a few rabbits can go. Des's muzzle twitched, a Loup-ine chuckle. *Besides, for the untried, such as yourself,* catching *a rabbit'll be tough enough. In some ways, tougher than deer. They're smaller, craftier, and better at hiding.*

Ruby sighed and sniffed the air again. Then she cautiously turned her scent dial up to fifteen and caught another scent, like sweet, new grass and fear. It made her mouth water and her tail wag.

Ah, I see you've caught the scent, Des chuckled. *And it's your lucky night. We're downwind of it, too! Now, the trick is to creep up on it slowly, silently, always being ready to pounce if the wind changes or you sense it's about to run. And remember, it's perfectly natural to err on the side of caution on your first try, but also don't be afraid to just go for it.*

Gotcha, Ruby was already creeping up the gentle, tree-lined slope, deeper into the woods, letting the scent of rabbit lure her, while she concentrated on making no noise. As clumsy as she tended to be in Hume-form, she was remarkably successful. She crept closer to the rabbit, which continued to nibble on grass unawares. Des hung back, watchful and patient, like any good teacher.

Suddenly, the wind changed.

The rabbit's nostrils twitched.

Ruby went for it.

❖

Des yawned, blinked, and hissed at the bright sunlight, turning her face into something warm and fuzzy and sweet-smelling. When her eyes got used to the filtered, yellow light, she reopened them and glanced around the copse, finding it undisturbed since she and Ruby had decided to rest there at dawn.

Ruby. Who was, to Des's surprise, curled up in her arms and snoring lightly. In fact, Des had a face full of Ruby's fluffy curls tickling her. Despite the chill in the autumn air, she was mostly warm, thanks to Ruby's body spooned against her own.

Oh...oh, shit, Des thought when she realized that while one arm was innocently pillowing Ruby's head and dead to the world, the other was draped over Ruby's side, hand cupping Ruby's breast.

It was warm and soft, and seemingly made to fit Des's hand. She ran her thumb over the peak of one already pert nipple almost helplessly. It responded by growing harder.

Des sighed softly in Ruby's hair, her breath hitching as she made herself stop, and carefully removed her hand, but a sudden hand on her own made her freeze.

"Don't stop."

Caught out, Des pulled her hand away and sat up just enough to see that Ruby's eyes were still closed. "I probably should. We're barely even awake."

Ruby smiled and opened her eyes, rolling over to face Des. She was blushing, but met Des's gaze candidly. "Speak for yourself. I never went to sleep."

Des blinked. "After last night? And this morning? We were out hunting and running the woods till dawn!"

Ruby let out a breath and laughed on the heels of it. "I know! Who could sleep after all that? My first night as a werewolf!" She laughed again and sat up, leaning in to kiss Des. It was a kiss wholly without artifice, a kiss of pure joy. But within seconds, it turned into something else entirely. Something hungry and desperate, under whose assault Des let herself be borne to the ground and straddled. Ruby pinned Des's wrists to the soft, dewy grass and kissed her breath away. For minutes, all Des could do was respond and respond and respond some more, sliding her hands up Ruby's thighs then coming around to squeeze her ass.

Ruby let Des's wrists go and ran her fingers through Des's hair, then pulled Des's head down, breaking the kiss. Before Des could complain, Ruby was nipping mock bites down Des's throat, following the line of her jugular vein, sucking on skin and humming while she did so.

"Oh, *fuck*, yeah," Des breathed, happily offering her throat in submission and subservience. It not only felt good, it felt *right*. As if this was the way it was *supposed* to be all along.

"Tell me what you want," Ruby murmured, kissing along her clavicle, gnawing it briefly like a dog with a bone. "Tell me what you *need*."

"You, Ruby, just...*you* "

Which Des sensed was the wrong thing to say as soon as she said it. Ruby froze and sat up. Her lips were kiss-swollen and her hair was a sunlit corona around her face. She was frowning.

"Wait. What about Holly?"

Des made a face, but other than a distant sense of regret, didn't feel much of anything else besides a near formless sense of concern. "What *about* Holly? Holly left me three years ago. I learned to live without her, and it was a lesson I never forgot. Even when she came back. Holly and I are over." She sighed. This was why she hated talking during foreplay. Even dirty talk. "What about Thierry LaFours?"

Ruby's face fell guiltily, as if she'd forgotten all about LaFours, and she sat back, seemingly as unconcerned with her nudity as Des was with her own. "I...I don't know."

Oh, how Des *hated* talk during foreplay. "Well, maybe you'd better figure it out before whatever this is goes any further," Des said with hard-won diplomacy, against her worse nature and the Loup's inward howl.

"But you were the one who said friends could have sex and it didn't have to mean anything," Ruby said, pouting. For some reason, that made Des angry enough to push her off and sit up. Ruby went, but not without reluctance, flopping down to the grass and crossing her arms like a child having a tantrum. "What? Now you're changing your mind?"

"Yes," Des said simply. Ruby stared up at her, obviously confused. "That's not what I want anymore."

Ruby pursed her lips. "Then what *do* you want?"

"I already told you. *You.*" Des crossed her own arms, more a defensive gesture than a truculent one. "I want you, and only you. I want you to want the same with me."

"We haven't even been out on a *date* and you're plighting troth?"

Des's eyebrows shot up. "We haven't even been out on a date yet, and we were gonna *fuck.*"

Ruby grimaced and tried to run her hands through her tangled hair. "That's different!"

"Is it?" Des snorted. "Look, you either want me or you don't."

"Of course I want you! I have from day-damn-*one*!" Ruby shouted, angry tears filling her eyes. "But I knew all you wanted from me was sex, and I was afraid I'd lose my damn heart over a few convenience fucks. Now, we're *finally* on the same page. I can finally be with you the way you want, only you *don't* want that anymore. *You're* looking for what, a relationship?"

Des hung her head for a moment then looked up again, letting her own confusion show. "Honestly? I don't know *what* I want other than for you to be mine, and me to be yours. It feels so *right.* Can't you feel it, too?"

Ruby wiped at her eyes, a look of dawning understanding crossing her face. "The *Geas*," she said softly.

Des groaned in frustration. "Not *everything* is the *Geas*, goddamnit!"

"Then what, Des? *What?*"

Des got to her feet angrily, finger-combing grass out of her hair. "Can't I just be falling in love with you without there being some x-factor forcing me into it? What, is it that you're not good enough to inspire that kinda feeling in someone? Or am *I* not good enough for *you*? Or is it that you want Thierry-fucking-LaFours more?"

"Now you're falling *in love* with me?" Ruby asked quietly, sitting up. She looked surprised and vulnerable and painfully young. Des could see the little girl Ruby had once been peering shyly out of her unguarded eyes.

The vision made her close her own eyes and fight the sudden pounding of her heart. It was a fight she lost, and so help her, she didn't really mind the losing.

"Yeah," she said simply. After nearly a minute of silence, she opened her eyes again. Ruby was still staring at her, but now she looked gobsmacked.

"When it rains, it pours," she murmured, shaking her head. "Thierry said he was falling in love with me yesterday."

Thierry would've said anything for a chance to fuck you, Des almost replied, but she bit it back before it slipped out. And anyway, she knew it wasn't true. Thierry LaFours had been a ladies man once upon a time not *too* long ago. But he was also a straight shooter. Like Des, he wouldn't *say* love unless he *meant* love.

Which meant Des's competition just got stiffer.

As if I needed that. He's an Alpha in good standing, and I'm me, a formerly rabid pup with no real ties to the Garoul *anymore, but for the damn* Geas. *I once blithely offered to sport-fuck my* queen, *no strings attached, incidentally making an ass of myself, and my ex-wife just left me for the second time. A real tough choice to make on Ruby's part, I'm sure.* Des sighed again, watching Ruby measure her. *Moon Above,* I'd *choose LaFours over me, too.*

"Look," Des began heavily, without inflection or hope. "I understand if you choose him, I really do. And I promise it won't change the job I do of protecting and training you, and that if you still wanna be friends, I'd…like that."

Ruby got to her feet without breaking eye contact. "What if I don't choose him *or* you? What if I choose *both* of you?"

Des narrowed her eyes. "I don't share. And I doubt LaFours does, either."

"It was worth a shot." Ruby shrugged, smiling. Then her smile faded. "This is a really weird time for me, Des. Really weird. Maybe not the time for me to decide which of you I want to embark on a committed relationship with."

Holding her peace, Des nodded stiffly. "Understood."

"Is it really?" Ruby approached Des slowly, cautiously, the way one would approach a wild animal. "Do you really get that I'm not trying to have my cake and eat it, too? That I'm not trying to string you along?"

Searching Ruby's eyes, Des nodded again. "I get it. You're dealing with a lot of new, crazy shit, and you don't need people professing their love, left, right, and center. Believe me, I get that." *I don't like it, but I get it.* "You're young, newly Loup, and you have wild oats to sow. But keep this in mind—" Des got into Ruby's personal space, and to Ruby's credit, she didn't take even a step back.

Des didn't say anything, only stared at her. "Keep *what* in mind?" Ruby ventured.

Des smiled and before Ruby could say anything else, she wrapped her arms around Ruby's waist. Again, Ruby didn't take a step back or pull away. She even slid her arms around Des's neck and inclined her head closer. Des, who never needed to be told twice, leaned in and kissed her gently.

"Maybe *he* deserves you, and maybe I don't," Des finally murmured, every word a brush of their lips. "Maybe, in the end, neither of us deserves you. But no one's gonna *love you* better than me. You'll always come first with me. You already do. Not the Council or the Pack, just y—" she gasped at the sudden sting in her neck, reaching up to swat what must be the mother of all mosquitos, and she felt what seemed to be a dart.

She yanked it out with a growl, and her hand came away bloody. She looked up at Ruby, who covered her mouth in horror.

"What—" Des started to say, dropping the bright yellow dart when her tongue went numb and her body began to tingle in a very unpleasant way. In seconds, it, too, was going numb and wobbly, unable to support her weight. She slumped forward in Ruby's arms, twitching and shaking. Ruby caught her easily and held her up.

"Des?!" she squeaked, her voice shrill with panic. Then she looked around frantically, squinting her eyes as her nostrils twitched.

Good idea, Des thought sluggishly, trying to crank up her sense of smell, sight, and hearing. But whatever was in that dart was already muddling her thinking and control. Her ears rang and the edges of her vision were quickly darkening. Every scent seemed to blur together in a disorienting cacophony. Alarms started shrilling in Des's body and mind, and she tried to shove Ruby away.

"*Run*," she croaked quietly, trying to impart with just her face, her numb, leaden face, how seriously *bad* this was. "Coming to get you. *Run*."

❖

Ruby shook her head grimly. "Not without you." And so saying, she scooped up Des and took the first shambling steps toward the safety of the trees.

But she felt the white-hot agony of a dart, herself, before she was halfway there. Unable to pull the dart out of her shoulder with Des in her arms, Ruby tried to keep running, but the trees seemed to get farther away with every step until darkness nibbled at the edges of her vision. Her knees wobbled, and she sank to the ground, Des slipping from her arms.

Then a blur of green rushed up toward her face, cool and wet, and she closed her eyes.

Just before she lost consciousness, the wind changed and she caught a familiar scent, like expensive wool and leather, astringent aftershave, and mulled wine.

Then everything went away for what seemed like a very long while.

❖

THE END OF BOOK ONE
CONTINUED IN
DYRE: A KNIGHT OF SPIRIT AND SHADOWS

About the Author

Rachel earned a bachelor's of fine arts in advertising, with a focus on copywriting and is in the process of earning a second bachelor's in English, with a minor in creative writing. She's been published in *Words 57, The Finger, The Stonesthrow Review*, on *Yahoo!Voices,* and *Amative Magazine, Writing.com 2014 Anthology*, the anthology *My Favorite Apocalypse*, and has had two short plays—*The Big Opening* and *Messenger*—performed for stage and screen, respectively.

Rachel currently lives in New York State's Hudson Valley, and has been a freelance everything, from copywriter to article writer. She's also worked in various retail and office jobs that have tried to, but haven't quite, sucked the soul out of her. Keep in the know about her future endeavors at RachelEBailey.Wix .com/TheWorks.

Books Available from Bold Strokes Books

Dyre: By Moon's Light by Rachel E. Bailey. A young werewolf, Des, guards the aging leader of all the Packs: the Dyre. Stable employment—nice work, if you can get it…at least until silver bullets start to fly. (978-1-62639-6-623)

Fragile Wings by Rebecca S. Buck. In Roaring Twenties London, can Evelyn Hopkins find love with Jos Singleton or will the scars of the Great War crush her dreams? (978-1-62639-5-466)

Live and Love Again by Jan Gayle. Jessica Whitney could be Sarah Jarret's second chance at love, but their differences and Sarah's grief continue to come between their budding relationship. (978-1-62639-5-176)

Starstruck by Lesley Davis. Actress Cassidy Hayes and writer Aiden Darrow find out the hard way not all life-threatening drama is confined to the TV screen or the pages of a manuscript. (978-1-62639-5-237)

Stealing Sunshine by Tina Michele. Under the Central Florida sun, two women struggle between fear and love as a dangerous plot of deception and revenge threatens to steal priceless art and lives. (978-1-62639-4-452)

The Fifth Gospel by Michelle Grubb. Hiding a Vatican secret is dangerous—sharing the secret suicidal—can Felicity survive a perilous book tour, and will her PR specialist, Anna, be there when it's all over? (978-1-62639-4-476)

Cold to the Touch by Cari Hunter. A drug addict's murder is the start of a dangerous investigation for Detective Sanne Jensen and Dr. Meg Fielding, as they try to stop a killer with no conscience. (978-1-62639-526-8)

Forsaken by Laydin Michaels. The hunt for a killer teaches one woman that she must overcome her fear in order to love, and another that success is meaningless without happiness. (978-1-62639-481-0)

Infiltration by Jackie D. When a CIA breach is imminent, a Marine instructor must stop the attack while protecting her heart from being disarmed by a recruit. (978-1-62639-521-3)

Midnight at the Orpheus by Alyssa Linn Palmer. Two women desperate to make their way in the world, a man hell-bent on revenge, and a cop risking his career: all in a day's work in Capone's Chicago. (978-1-62639-607-4)

Spirit of the Dance by Mardi Alexander. Major Sorla Reardon's return to her family farm to heal threatens Riley Johnson's safe life when small-town secrets are revealed, and love may not conquer all. (978-1-62639-583-1)

Sweet Hearts by Melissa Brayden, Rachel Spangler, and Karis Walsh. Do you ever wonder *Whatever happened to...*? Find out when you reconnect with your favorite characters from Melissa Brayden's *Heart Block*, Rachel Spangler's *LoveLife*, and Karis Walsh's *Worth the Risk*. (978-1-62639-475-9)

Totally Worth It by Maggie Cummings. Who knew there's an all-lesbian condo community in the NYC suburbs? Join twentysomething BFFs Meg and Lexi at Bay West as they navigate friendships, love, and everything in between. (978-1-62639-512-1)

Illicit Artifacts by Stevie Mikayne. Her foster mother's death cracked open a secret world Jil never wanted to see…and now she has to pick up the stolen pieces. (978-1-62639-472-8)

Pathfinder by Gun Brooke. Heading for their new homeworld, Exodus's chief engineer Adina Vantressa and nurse Briar Lindemay carry game-changing secrets that may well cause them to lose everything when disaster strikes. (978-1-62639-444-5)

Prescription for Love by Radclyffe. Dr. Flannery Rivers finds herself attracted to the new ER chief, city girl Abigail Remy, and the incendiary mix of city and country, fire and ice, tradition and change is combustible. (978-1-62639-570-1)

Ready or Not by Melissa Brayden. Uptight Mallory Spencer finds relinquishing control to bartender Hope Sanders too tall an order in fast-paced New York City. (978-1-62639-443-8)

Summer Passion by MJ Williamz. Women loving women is forbidden in 1946 Hollywood, yet Jean and Maggie strive to keep their love alive and away from prying eyes. (978-1-62639-540-4)

The Princess and the Prix by Nell Stark. "Ugly duckling" Princess Alix of Monaco was resigned to loneliness until she met racecar driver Thalia d'Angelis. (978-1-62639-474-2)

Winter's Harbor by Aurora Rey. Lia Brooks isn't looking for love in Provincetown, but when she discovers chocolate croissants and pastry chef Alex McKinnon, her winter retreat quickly starts heating up. (978-1-62639-498-8)

The Time Before Now by Missouri Vaun. Vivian flees a disastrous affair, embarking on an epic, transformative journey to escape her past, until destiny introduces her to Ida, who helps her rediscover trust, love, and hope. (978-1-62639-446-9)

Twisted Whispers by Sheri Lewis Wohl. Betrayal, lies, and secrets—whispers of a friend lost to darkness. Can a reluctant psychic set things right or will an evil soul destroy those she loves? (978-1-62639-439-1)

The Courage to Try by C.A. Popovich. Finding love is worth getting past the fear of trying. (978-1-62639-528-2)

Break Point by Yolanda Wallace. In a world readying for war, can love find a way? (978-1-62639-568-8)

Countdown by Julie Cannon. Can two strong-willed, powerful women overcome their differences to save the lives of seven others and begin a life they never imagined together? (978-1-62639-471-1)

Keep Hold by Michelle Grubb. Claire knew some things should be left alone and some rules should never be broken, but the most forbidden, well, they are the most tempting. (978-1-62639-502-2)

Deadly Medicine by Jaime Maddox. Dr. Ward Thrasher's life is in turmoil. Her partner Jess left her, and her job puts her in the path of a murderous physician who has Jess in his sights. (978-1-62639-424-7)

New Beginnings by KC Richardson. Can the connection and attraction between Jordan Roberts and Kirsten Murphy be enough for Jordan to trust Kirsten with her heart? (978-1-62639-450-6)

Officer Down by Erin Dutton. Can two women who've made careers out of being there for others in crisis find the strength to need each other? (978-1-62639-423-0)

Reasonable Doubt by Carsen Taite. Just when Sarah and Ellery think they've left dangerous careers behind, a new case sets them—and their hearts—on a collision course. (978-1-62639-442-1)

Tarnished Gold by Ann Aptaker. Cantor Gold must outsmart the Law, outrun New York's dockside gangsters, outplay a shady art dealer, his lover, and a beautiful curator, and stay out of a killer's gun sights. (978-1-62639-426-1)

White Horse in Winter by Franci McMahon. Love between two women collides with the inner poison of a closeted horse trainer in the green hills of Vermont. (978-1-62639-429-2)

Autumn Spring by Shelley Thrasher. Can Bree and Linda, two women in the autumn of their lives, put their hearts first and find the love they've never dared seize? (978-1-62639-365-3)

The Renegade by Amy Dunne. Post-apocalyptic survivors Alex and Evelyn secretly find love while held captive by a deranged cult, but when their relationship is discovered, they must fight for their freedom—or die trying. (978-1-62639-427-8)

Thrall by Barbara Ann Wright. Four women in a warrior society must work together to lift an insidious curse while caught between their own desires, the will of their peoples, and an ancient evil. (978-1-62639-437-7)

The Chameleon's Tale by Andrea Bramhall. Two old friends must work through a web of lies and deceit to find themselves again, but in the search they discover far more than they ever went looking for. (978-1-62639-363-9)

Side Effects by VK Powell. Detective Jordan Bishop and Dr. Neela Sahjani must decide if it's easier to trust someone with your heart or your life as they face threatening protestors, corrupt politicians, and their increasing attraction. (978-1-62639-364-6)

Warm November by Kathleen Knowles. What do you do if the one woman you want is the only one you can't have? (978-1-62639-366-0)

In Every Cloud by Tina Michele. When Bree finally leaves her shattered life behind, is she strong enough to salvage the remaining pieces of her heart and find the place where it truly fits? (978-1-62639-413-1)